Vanessa Gordon lives in Surrey and has spent many years working as a concert manager, musicians' agent and live music supplier. She has visited Greece as often as possible.

The Martin Day mystery series is set on Naxos, the largest island in the Cyclades, Greece. It is an island of contrasts. The modern port of Chora is crowned by a Venetian kastro surrounded by an interesting old town. You can find uninhabited central hills, the highest mountain in the Cyclades, attractive fishing villages, popular beaches, and archaeological sites. There are historic towers and welcoming tavernas, collectable art and ceramics. Naxos has produced some of the finest marble in Greece since ancient times. Now, Martin Day has moved in.

BY THE SAME AUTHOR

The Meaning of Friday

The Search for Artemis

Black Acorns

The Meaning of Friday

A Naxos mystery *with Martin Day*

Vanessa Gordon

Published by Pomeg Books 2021 www.pomeg.co.uk

Revised edition, December 2021

Cover Photograph and map © Alan Gordon

This is a work of fiction. The names, characters, business, events and incidents are the products of the author's imagination. Any resemblance to actual persons, living or dead, or actual events is purely coincidental.

ISBN 978-1-8384533-0-5

Pomeg Books is an imprint of
Dolman Scott Ltd
www.dolmanscott.co.uk

To our friends on Naxos and my family

Warm thanks to Christine Wilding and Cristine Mackie for their invaluable proofreading and encouragement.

I am grateful to Koula Crawley-Moore, Efthymios Stamos and Zois Kouris (Hellenic Centre), who have generously helped me with the Greek language.

Special thanks are due to Robert Pitt, who has shared with me his knowledge of the archaeology of Greece and enabled me to enjoy it myself in recent years.

For listening and contributing all along, Alan and Alastair, thank you.

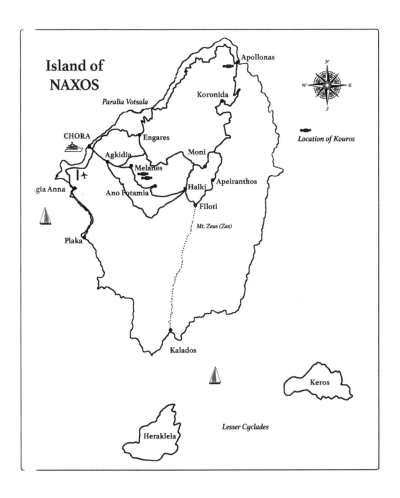

Island of NAXOS

Apollonas

Paralia Votsala

Koronida

CHORA

Engares

Location of Kouros

Agkidia

Moni

Melanes

gia Anna

Apeiranthos

Ano Potamia

Halki

Filoti

Mt. Zeus (Zas)

Plaka

Kalados

Keros

Herakleia

Lesser Cyclades

NOTE ABOUT GREEK WORDS

Readers without a knowledge of Greek might like to know about one or two things that they will find in the book.

'Mou' means 'my', often used with a name as a term of affection.

'Agapi mou' means 'my dear'.

Greek names sometimes have changed endings in the vocative, which is when the person is directly addressed. This is why you will see Nikos become Niko, Vasilios become Vasili, and other examples, when the characters are being spoken to directly.

Pater is the correct form of address to the papas or priest.

'Panagia mou!' is an exclamation which literally calls on the help of the Virgin Mary.

'Kali orexi' means 'Bon appétit!'

'Kalos irthatay!' means 'Welcome!'

'Kyrie' and 'Kyria' are forms of address like monsieur and madame.

Place names can be found in different spellings; spellings most likely to help with pronunciation are used in this book.

The main town of Naxos is called Chora or Naxos. You pronounce the ch in Chora as in the Scottish 'loch'.

'Kalispera sas' means 'Good evening'

1

The view hadn't changed since the age of Homer, but the killer paid it
no attention. The uncultivated centre of the Cycladic island of Naxos
was a playground only for goats and hikers. It was a beautiful but
lonely landscape, shaped by the weather. The summer sun scorched
the weather-enduring grass, and the tough scrub bent beneath the
winter winds. The higher peaks were grey with rockfalls, while on the
lower slopes the insects were now collecting the last nectar before
the summer drought. The spring air smelled of wild herbs, but in a
few weeks that rare softness would be overtaken by the dry scent of
dead leaves. Things like this had been constant for millennia.

Villages thrived in pockets of fertile land linked by serpentine country
roads. In the countryside near one of these, the hill village of Melanes,
where ancient peoples once quarried marble, a twentieth-century
farmer had built a stone hut to shelter him when he followed his
flock across the open land. No more than a square box, the hut was
made from rough rocks like those used for dry stone walls, and was
just big enough for a man to lie down in. It was far enough from the
road to go unnoticed, and even from the footpath nearby it looked
uninviting. Its flat concrete roof was littered with chunks of stone

as if to hold it down, but it wasn't going anywhere. By the entrance, a bit of rusty steel mesh lay discarded, grown through by weeds.

The stone hut had no windows, the entrance had no door, and for many years it had served no purpose. Its state of decrepitude was a guarantee of loneliness and eventual collapse. The little shelter had an air of having given up hope.

It was the perfect place to hide a body. The killer never expected anyone to venture inside.

2

Martin Day, archaeologist and television presenter, came laughing out of the office of the Curator of the Naxos Archaeological Museum, and took the steps two at a time to the ground floor. An English-speaking tour group filled the reception area of the museum, and they waited for them to disperse before trying to leave. He was quite keen, anyway, to hear what their tour guide was telling them. He had just recognised him as an old friend from England.

'Ladies and Gentlemen, welcome to the outstanding Archaeological Museum of Naxos. Inside you'll find a truly impressive collection of items, including the famous Roman mosaic floor. Naxos was an important centre of Cycladic culture through a range of periods, so the museum covers a great many fascinating eras. I know you're particularly excited to see the beautiful Cycladic figurines, like the ones which we saw in Athens when we visited the Museum of Cycladic Art. The figurines have a captivating beauty that appeals to us today and have inspired many of our great modern artists - think of the paintings of Picasso and Modigliani, and the sculptures of Barbara Hepworth and Henry Moore."

Day permitted himself a small smile. The tour guide paused for breath and glanced in Day's direction. Having been a Classics undergraduate at Cambridge alongside Day, Paul was a fellow escapee from a life of academia. Paul now led 'cultural tours' of Greek sites, while Day was freelance, writing successful books on Greek archaeology and presenting television history programmes on subjects that took his fancy. Neither of them found conventional careers appealing.

Paul grinned and nodded to Day, before continuing with his lecture without missing a beat.

"Cycladic figurines are often female in form, with arms crossed and marks on the belly that suggest pregnancy. Their original purpose is unknown, but they may have been fertility symbols or funerary items. Many are broken across the middle, and could even have been broken deliberately as part of some ceremonial event. Many of these lovely statuettes were found buried in one single, remote pit. Mysterious as well as beautiful objects."

Day squeezed round the group and out into the fresh air as the lecture continued. The spring morning was already very warm. He loitered outside and didn't have long to wait before Paul joined him. He laid a big hand on Day's arm.

"I've got ten minutes while they buy their tickets and guide books," he said. "So, how are you, Professor?"

Day had made a TV series recently in which the American director had insisted on giving him the title of Professor, which he had certainly not earned in any university. He grinned.

"And what are you doing here? I thought you were in Athens."

"I've just bought myself a place here on Naxos," Day replied. "Finally got round to it. I'll be spending the summers here."

' ucky bastard!"

' 'orking, of course. Never any rest from the job. You know me.
1)w about you?"

' m good, thanks. I bought a boat this year and went independent as
a)ur operator. Now I have the boat I can arrange my own itineraries
a 1 be my own master. Tourists never change, but the down-time
1 et now is much better. And I take them to places that I want to
g to, rather than having somebody else write the script. Look, how
a)ut a drink one evening?"

' ire. Whenever you like. I'll be living here till something else comes
ι ."

' reat, I'll text you. I'll be showing this group around here for a few
c s, and I get free time whenever they do. It'll be good to catch up,
i been months."

' ears more like."

' eally? OK, got to go, they're looking for their leader! Good to see
y 1, Martin."

1 1l hurried back to his group and Day's thoughts turned, as they
(en did, to coffee. He fancied a quiet table with a view of the sea.
1 walked towards the sea and found a café on the road near the
p rt. It was a favourite of his, because it had seating right on the edge
(the water. He ordered a frappé and sat back feeling great. He was
1 :k on Naxos, with the whole summer ahead of him, and now he
(ned his own place. Day intended that summers in his new house, for
v ich he had only received the deeds of ownership at the beginning
(the year, would be a simple regime of research and writing in the
g rious peace of the island's hilly centre. He had just informed his
(l friend Aristos Iraklidis, otherwise known as The Curator, that

he planned to pick the Greek's knowledgeable brain over a bottle or two of local wine from time to time, and now he realised he might occasionally see other friends and colleagues as they passed through the islands, as Paul was doing.

To add icing to the cake, his old friend Helen Aitchison was about to arrive for a long visit. Helen was the kind of person Day liked best: independent, undemanding, intelligent and, like himself, a lover of peace and quiet. She wrote novels now, quite successfully, and was planning on spending most of the summer in Day's new home up in Filoti village. His relationship with Helen was blissfully platonic, their friendship rooted securely in a shared past where they worked together, and they had proved that they could successfully spend long periods under the same roof without driving each other mad. She would be on Tuesday's ferry from Rafina.

Day's mood, as he drank his frappé, checked Facebook on his phone and gazed from time to time at the shining Aegean, was entirely in harmony with the serene May morning.

3

Xenia Iraklidis, Aristos's wife, had laid the table for Sunday lunch under the vine-covered pergola behind the Iraklidis's house in the rural suburb of Agkidia. The busy port of Chora, the main town and harbour of Naxos, was only a few kilometres away, but could have been on the other side of the island. The Iraklidis's house was quiet and idyllic.

Day had the same thought that always struck him when he saw Xenia, that having a historian for a husband clearly suited her. Their life seemed peaceful, their conversation was of history, food and the Aegean. The food was homemade and the wine local. They had no children of their own, but many friends, and in their early sixties they seemed to have arranged their lives exactly how they wanted them. This was Day's idea of married bliss. As a confirmed bachelor of nearly forty, he felt he was an expert judge of these things.

Day was really looking forward to Sunday lunch with his old friends. He politely declined an ouzo and allowed Aristos Iraklidis to press him to try a rather good white wine. The Curator, as he was commonly called on the island, was in the best of moods.

"We should begin with a toast to our good friend, Martin," he announced, his eyes twinkling above his straight, Greek nose. "To 'Professor' Day, TV celebrity and most private man. And now owner of a Naxian house, which makes him also a discerning man. To your good health, Martin!"

"And to yours! It's wonderful to be with you both again, in this haven of peace in your garden. Lunch smells delicious, too."

"We're looking forward to seeing a lot of you over the summer, Martin. Aristos has ordered more wine from his favourite vineyard especially."

Day soon felt decidedly light-headed. The wine was delicious, cool and scented as with an aroma of mountain herbs, and Aristos was generous with it. He and Aristos shared a love of wine, just as they shared a love of Greece, of archaeology, of beauty, and of peacefulness.

They ate Rania's delicately seasoned stew of lamb and potatoes with satisfaction. The lamb fell off the bone, the sauce was subtly flavoured with local oregano, and the chunks of local potatoes were rich with the flavour of the meat. Day thought Rania's cooking exemplified the best of Greek cuisine and never turned down an invitation to eat her food. There were the usual extras too: an olive-rich Greek salad boasting large chunks of tasty tomato and juicy onion, and extra homemade fried potatoes especially for Day, who had a rather soft spot for chips.

There was fresh fruit to follow. Day politely declined the fruit, as usual. Dessert wasn't his thing, he would say. Oddly, this applied to fruit, which he didn't object to but rarely ate. He helped himself to seconds of chips when he thought nobody would notice.

"Unbelievable!" he said, finally finishing. "That meal was truly something else. You two must visit me soon in my new house in Filoti and let me cook for you. As soon as I get more settled. Of course, I couldn't match this standard, Rania!"

' 'e'd love to, Martin, and I'm sure you cook beautifully. Tell us all a out your house."

' 's just outside Filoti, walking distance from a particularly good t erna where I shall eat whenever I can't be bothered to cook. The h use is a recent conversion, quite well done and very spacious. It c esn't need any more doing to it, and it has a spectacular view over t e valley. It's so quiet there … I can work either on the balcony or i loors, and there's decent internet connection. Lots of bookcases, a ooker, a fridge, and a currently empty wine rack the size of half a v ll. I'm expecting you to help me with that, Aristo."

' ounds like it might have been quite expensive?" grinned Aristos.

' wasn't cheap, but as you know I sold my father's house in London l t year. He would have approved of what I've done with my i heritance, I think."

' le certainly would. It sounds ideal for you. And when does your f end arrive? Her name is Helen, isn't it?"

' es, Helen. Tuesday, on the boat from Rafina. She can stay for weeks a d weeks, it'll be brilliant. The house is easy to divide between us. / I said, it's quite big. She'll have her own room and balcony. We'll g t lots of work done, and meet for coffee, lunch and dinner. And a eritifs, naturally. She'll be doing a project of her own. I think she's a out to start a new novel. She sketches and paints too. She's never l oked back since she took early retirement from the College. Thank (od she earns enough to afford trips to Greece to see me. Her novels l ng in good money now."

' ou must bring her to visit us soon - mustn't he, Aristo mou?" said I nia, and Aristos shrugged as if to say it went without saying.

"With pleasure, of course I will. I love to introduce my best friends to each other."

"I've heard of her novels," said Rania, rather to Day's surprise. "Maybe you'll be in one of them soon, Martin! Or perhaps you live too quiet a life."

4

The ferry 'Blue Star Naxos' from Rafina brought Helen Aitchison to the island on time. The ship did a cumbersome pirouette in the bay and reversed into port, where it lowered its huge steel ramp to release lorries, cars and pedestrians onto the crowded jetty. Helen concentrated on negotiating the ramp without being pulled down by her heavy suitcases or staggering in front of a car. She felt sweaty and dishevelled, but knew Martin would never notice. She saw him waiting for her just beyond the crowd. He was easy to pick out, taller by a head than most people and fair haired. He saw her and waved. He was one of the few people not holding a sign bearing someone's surname, and, typically of him, was standing on his own.

Helen joined the people and vehicles which jostled down the road towards the car park and the town, moving as one intolerant jumble. There were trucks laden with everything from bottled water to iron girders. There were taxis, minibuses, and the cars of hoteliers parked in the way with boot lids raised to receive their guests' luggage. Somehow everyone began to disperse. The fumes from the ferry were black as the boat turned up the power to leave the dock, having relieved itself of every passenger requiring Naxos and taken more on board.

Day's hug was stiff but his smile was sincere. He lifted Helen's cases into the boot of his second-hand Fiat 500 and said triumphantly, "Welcome to Naxos, Madame! Welcome to our Cycladic summer!"

Day had remarkably few airs and graces for a relatively successful TV figure, she thought. He ring-fenced his private life, refusing to be at the beck and call of publishers and programme-makers. Luckily these people wanted what he produced, acknowledged his need for 'research time,' and so far had indulged his idiosyncrasies. These included long periods in Greece. He was therefore a particularly contented man as people of forty go. If a dark mood overtook him, it was short-lived. He had a great many friends, and she had always understood why.

It took them twenty minutes to escape the congested port. Once on the road out of town the traffic dwindled and Helen began to relax. She knew Naxos and liked its combination of Cycladic culture and modernity. It had a busy summer season, but away from the beaches and towns its people still led fairly traditional lives. Goats, cheese and olives co-existed with car rental, pizzerias and souvenirs. There were beaches and mountains, fast food and outstanding cuisine. Naxos also had a reputation for seriously good art, including ceramics, marble work, textiles and photography. There were two good museums, several ancient archaeological sites, and in the centre of the island and round its rocky coasts there were villages which retained the feel of traditional Greece.

Day began to tell her about his new Greek house in the village of Filoti. She already knew Filoti, with its central road climbing languidly beneath overhanging plane trees, its tavernas and cafés with tables outside, its small market space and its ancient tower. Helen had not even seen a photograph of Day's house, however, the place where she was to stay for the next few months.

They reached Filoti and Day pulled up by an old house with an unimposing frontage in keeping with the other properties on the tskirts of Filoti. Day unlocked the main door and led the way inside. The cool of the main room enveloped her, her eyes struggling with dimness until he opened the shutters. He opened more and more them as they explored the house. The improvements made by the ent conversion became clear. The back of the house had not one t three balconies, all facing away from the road and overlooking valley at the back. The main room was large, consisting of a living a dominated by a large wooden table, a sofa, and a galley kitchen ked at the far end. Off this room was the largest balcony, where len thought she would spend most of her time, enjoying the light d the view of the valley.

y showed her round proudly. Her room had its own small balcony th a table and chair where she could also work. Day's room, sperately untidy but filled with light, was on a lower level cleverly into the hillside, and had a balcony which overlooked a garden of getables and fruit trees belonging to the people next door. Day's m, in the modern part of the house, had the complete seclusion cherished, while Helen's room had the better view. It was an angement that would suit them both.

n't it perfect, Helen? Our summer will be superb. We shall meet the main balcony for lunch, and again after siesta for aperitifs. We ll then wander into the village for a delicious meal at the excellent verna O Thanasis, I can't wait to take you there, it has the most nderful food. Thus we shall eke out our days throughout the nmer in a civilised manner. And some excellent work will be done!"

love it, Martin," she said. "It even smells wonderful."

e was right, he thought, having not noticed it before. The fresh untain breeze wafted through the open balcony doors carrying h it a green smell of cut grass and perhaps even a scent of the tant sea. The smell of wood old and new, lavender polish and fresh nish, books and coffee, floated round the house.

Day showed her round the main room pointing out his prize possession, his library, and important items such as the fridge and the cafetière. The floorboards in this older part of the house squeaked in a very pleasant, somehow Greek way. Helen nodded in approval.

"How much of this furniture did you have to bring out from the mainland, Martin? I presume transport to the islands is very expensive."

"I hired a guy with a van to bring my things over from Athens, including my books. The house came furnished, which is usual in the islands. The mattresses are new, I assure you - IKEA. All the bedding is brand new from a wonderful shop in Kolonaki. I bought things like the cafetière and the microwave on the island. I had some help from a friend of mine, Aristos, who's the museum curator, and his wife. We're invited to dinner with them, by the way, they want to meet you, and we'll have to entertain them too. You can cook!"

She threw him a look, but he was clearly trying to be funny.

"I could fix a cleaner to come in once a month. If you think so?" he continued.

"No need. It won't take you long."

"Right. So all we have to do now is go to the supermarket in Chora and buy vital supplies. Do you want to unpack first?"

"If I just get my cases in …"

"No problem," he said, and strode off towards the car.

Helen walked to the main balcony and stared out across the valley. It was going to be the best, quietest, most productive summer she had had for years, and it sounded like there would be some social occasions too. Here, surely, she would get the inspiration for her next book.

***

They bought what Day called their vital supplies in a reasonably large supermarket on the outskirts of Chora. Day, who was masterminding the expedition, filled the trolley with wine, gin, tonic, lemons, and toilet paper. Helen added some peaches, grapes and fruit juice. They began to get inspired and added tomatoes, rocket, two jars of Greek capers, Italian ham, feta cheese, oregano, good olive oil, and cheap grinders of salt and black pepper. Day found some nice-looking local flatbread which could be quickly grilled and drizzled with olive oil. Two six-packs of water in plastic litre bottles were essential. Nibbles for aperitifs. That sorted out lunches for a while, and they decided that dinner, at least to begin with, would be provided by the much-admired Thanasis; it was almost as cheap.

Back at the house, they put the shopping away and retired to their separate rooms for the afternoon. Helen tested her mattress and found it pleasantly firm. The pillows looked all right, but only a night on them would reassure her. Everything, thankfully, looked new. She unpacked and took her book to the balcony.

After a couple of hours, Day emerged from his room in fresh clothes to find Helen with her feet on the railings, contemplating the view.

'Gin and tonic?"

"Yes, please. Let's start as we mean to go on."

Day brought the drinks to the balcony and they watched as the sun began to sink and the coolness of evening creep over the valley.

"So, what do you plan to work on while you're here?" Day asked.

"I have an idea for the next book, but it's not coming together. I've brought some paints with me, and there are a couple of art supplies shops on the island if I need more. I'm just going to settle in gently, be a visitor for a while. There's plenty of time, the summer is long."

"Here's to that!"

"And you?"

"I'm going to take a look at the work of a Naxian archaeologist called Nikos Elias," he said enthusiastically. "He lived on Naxos most of his life and died a few years ago, and he was a mysterious and secretive figure. His house has been turned into a small museum, but I can't find anything written about him yet. Even here on Naxos he isn't well known, so it occurred to me I might do a short biography. Maurice, my agent in London, thinks he might have a publisher interested in it. Elias's former partner looks after the small museum and I've been in touch with him. I thought you and I could drive over there one day. I'd like to get going on the work as soon as I can. Rumour has it that Elias made one or two discoveries which he didn't publish, maybe something exciting, who knows? We'll see."

5

I y's favourite restaurant, Taverna O Thanasis, was on the main road
a the end of Filoti nearest Day's new house. As he and Helen walked
p st the outdoor tables to the door of the taverna, Thanasis greeted
t :m hospitably. The tables inside were laid with blue cloths topped
v h white cotton squares, neatly fastened with elastic beneath the table
r 1. Traditional wooden chairs with woven seats, and sepia photos
c the walls, completed the traditional feel of the taverna. There
v s a delicious smell from the kitchen. They chose a table, accepted
n :nus, and Thanasis brought a bottle of cold water and two glasses.

" hanasi, may I introduce my friend, Helen?"

" m delighted to meet you, Kyria. Martin has been looking forward
t your arrival, and so have we. Did you have a good journey?"

' ery good, thank you. Martin tells me the food here is the best on
] xos!"

" hen I shall bring you some excellent small plates to start. And for
r in course this evening we have some goat cooked slowly in a red

sauce, some cockerel with pasta, or, if you prefer fish, I have some fresh sardines."

Day asked for some local red wine while they chose their food, and watched as Thanasis walked purposefully towards the kitchen. He handed a menu to Helen and opened one himself. He sighed happily.

"Chicken for me, I think," he said. "Lots of chips. And we'd better have a salad. What would you like?"

"Not sure. Definitely a salad with plenty of beautiful Greek tomatoes. I've missed them!"

Thanasis returned with a large jug of red wine, followed by his daughter carrying a tray of small dishes to tempt their appetites. Thanasis introduced the food with pride.

"Something to begin! This is village sausage, this fried aubergine, and here a small fava. I hope you enjoy. Kali orexi, Martin, Kyria."

"I'd be happy if you'd call me Helen," she suggested.

"Ah, yes," the Greek beamed. "Helen, the most beautiful woman who ever lived! It suits you, Kyria. Helen."

Gratified, Thanasis returned to the kitchen. Day reached across to the bread basket in which serviette-wrapped pairs of cutlery nestled among pieces of fresh crusty bread. Placing cutlery at both their places, he then passed the basket so she could reach the bread. These odd little gallantries were customary with him, she remembered.

"You've made your first conquest, Helen!" he murmured.

"Don't be silly, Martin!"

They started on the food with enthusiasm. The small plates of appetisers were delicate, and the bread fresh. The thin slices of aubergine had been lightly dusted with fine batter which had crisped in the frying. The village sausage was served in dainty pieces and wallowed in a sauce rich with tomato. Best of all was the fava, yellow split-pea dip, slightly warm and topped with a splash of green olive oil and crunchy bits of finely chopped onion.

They ordered a portion of cockerel, a Greek salad and some fries. Thanasis persuaded them that instead of fries they should try his wife's home-style fried potatoes, which were slices of the waxy local potatoes perfectly crisped in the oven and topped with oregano and olive oil.

They shared all the dishes between them and Day admitted that the home-fried potato slices were superb, even for a lover of chips such as himself. The potatoes on Naxos had a well-deserved reputation for excellence. He raised his glass to her with a sense of theatre. "Here's to a wonderful, productive summer in the Cyclades. A great new novel for you, the biography of a generation for me, and a great deal of down-time and good food!"

"To the summer!"

Day waved the empty wine jug in Thanasis's direction and caught his eye. "Thanasi, another jug please, just a small one."

6

Day was washing up their morning coffee cups. "We need to get petrol today. Shall we go on to the Elias house afterwards and take a quick look?" he called from the kitchen. "I haven't managed to get hold of the custodian yet, but we can arrive like tourists and take a look around. The museum opened to the public on the first of May, apparently. Maybe we could get a coffee somewhere before heading back."

Day didn't eat breakfast, nor did he usually bother with lunch when he was on his own. Helen, who quite liked meals, sometimes pretended not to want breakfast when she was in Greece with Day. It soon became her normal routine. When she heard the plan for the morning, she resigned herself to the thought that a second coffee would have to do, and she might even order a pastry.

They drove to Chora to fill the Fiat's tank at a small garage on the outskirts of town, then headed north on the coast road in the direction of Engares. Traffic was light. Small roads led occasionally towards the sea on their left, roads serving only a small group of houses, a single hotel or an isolated beach. After half an hour they saw a sign saying

Italia Votsala, or Stony Beach, and another that advertised the Nikos Elias Museum. The road was unsurfaced but in good condition, and soon descended sharply. At the bottom of the road was the beach, a narrow strip of shingle which stretched two hundred yards in each direction. At the extreme left of the road was a sprawling white house against the cliffs. To the right, the road stopped at a headland, beneath which the tables of a taverna overflowed onto the shingle. It looked very inviting. Day, however, was focussed on the white house of the late Nikos Elias.

"That's the place, I think," he said, pointing left. "Let's take a closer look, shall we?"

He drove with care towards the archaeologist's old house, avoiding the occasional ruts in the road. Another sign in tourist office colours announced the Nikos Elias Museum. Day parked in front of the building and peered over the steering wheel. The place seemed closed. They got out and walked to the main door. A handwritten notice was pinned there, framed by a small bougainvillea, the roots of which were wedged in a rusted barrel. The notice said, 'Temporarily Closed to Public' in Greek, English and German.

There was only one thing to do, which was to get a coffee at the little taverna. Day parked the Fiat next to two hire cars which closely resembled his own. Day had, after all, bought an ex-hire car himself.

The taverna owner waved from the shingle beach where he was wiping sand from the tables.

"Kalos irthatay! Welcome!" he called.

"Kalimera. Are you serving coffee?"

"Of course! Please, take a seat!"

They chose a table in the shade of a tamarisk tree at the edge of the beach. The owner, a Greek of about Day's age, returned with menus that offered a selection of drinks, sweet snacks and toasted sandwiches. His wife appeared with a tray bearing two chilled glasses and a bottle of cold water with the condensation dripping from it. Day and Helen did not need the menus to make their coffee order.

"A frappé for me, please," said Day.

"Cappuccino, please, a double."

"Cold?"

Helen felt very English when she insisted on hot coffee. Day loved the tall, iced coffee preferred in Greece during the summer, but Helen held to her English tastes. She was rewarded with a large, hot coffee with a homemade biscuit on the teaspoon. Day stirred his frappé thoughtfully with the straw, and gave Helen his biscuit.

"Well, interesting that the house is closed," he said. "I'll have to ask around and see when it will open. I'm sure it will. This is Greece, everything happens at the right time."

"I hope so, because you're going to have a problem if it doesn't."

"Oh, I'm sure it will open soon. Elias's companion still lives there. It's his home, and anyway he wrote to me to confirm my visit. By the way, did I tell you Elias wrote some quite decent poetry? And he has an amazing library of Greek literature, I've heard. He seems quite a character."

"A library, in that house? They must have a problem with the damp in winter. It's really close to the sea."

' mm, maybe. I'm looking forward to seeing Elias's books, anyway;
might have collected some interesting bits and pieces."

' o you know much about the contents of the museum?"

' here are local finds, his papers, his personal writings, maps, drawings.
on't know exactly till I get inside."

' the poetry published?"

' on't think so, not sure. I've never come across it, but it's not my
t ng really."

' know! And his companion, who's he?"

' o my shame, I don't know the first thing about him. Not in the
f ld, I think, not an archaeologist. His name's Petros Tsifas. He's
l n the registered curator of the museum since Elias's death, but
l aven't read anything about him. It's an interesting set-up. There's
r funding for the upkeep of the place from the Greek State, but
l as seems to have been wealthy and I think the local tourist board
l Tsifas something to open for visitors."

' he tourist board won't be pleased that the museum's closed, will
t y?"

' deed. I wonder what's happened."

ey drank their coffee and Day looked at his phone. Helen looked
t to sea. There was nothing to look at except the water and the
rizon. So few gulls here, so few boats today. This was the rocky,
osed side of the island, facing the north-westerly winds. Lovers
solitude lived on this coast. So why was there a taverna here?
ere did their customers come from? Despite the other cars, there
eared to be nobody here apart from themselves.

After ten minutes she got up to visit the bathroom, mostly an excuse to look around. The inside of the taverna was spacious, with a bar against one wall and a chill cabinet against another in which desserts, beers and cold drinks were on display. Photographs of Naxian fishermen from long ago, mending nets or standing proudly by small boats, hung behind the bar. An old Greek flag was propped proudly in a corner of the room.

At a table by the bar sat the owner and his wife. He was reading a newspaper with one eye alert for customers, and she had a bowl of vegetables on her lap which she was preparing with a sharp knife. When Helen returned from the toilets she paused near them to exchange courtesies. Remembering that a cool day is regarded as excellent weather by the Greeks, she opted for a safe conversational gambit.

"Very good weather today, isn't it?"

"Very good! Are you holidaying on the island?"

"My friend has a house near Filoti, but I'm staying here on holiday, yes. I arrived yesterday for the summer."

"Oh, Kyria, you will have a very good summer on Naxos. I'm Vasilios, this is my wife Maroula. I hope you'll visit us often. And if your friends come to see you, we have rooms here, good rooms. As you can see, it's very beautiful in Paralia Votsala."

"It certainly is! You say you have rooms here? Do you get many visitors?"

"We do well enough, in June and August particularly. We are quite inexpensive, and we find that many archaeologists and their students stay with us while they explore the island. We also have some visitors who come with metal detectors, who hope they will have a lucky find ng our beach. There's nothing there to find, of course, but they enjoy mselves. And my wife cooks them an excellent dinner afterwards."

s wife lifted her head from her vegetables and spoke in a sad tone. 'e have two rooms, Kyria. When my husband says that *many* people y here, he means *a few*."

suppose the Elias Museum attracts them," said Helen, diplomatically. 'e notice it's closed today. Do you know when it might open again?"

f course!" answered Vasilios. "Petros lives there, it's his home. He l to go to the mainland on family business, but he'll be back soon. eep an eye on the house when he's away."

len thanked them and returned to Day, who had closed his phone l was staring at the sea.

love it here," he said, not turning to look at her. "I did the right ng buying the house."

ou did indeed."

ow were the facilities?"

ery clean. You go past the right-hand side of the taverna and turn t. I just had a little chat with the owners, actually. They're a nice ple, called Vasilios and Maroula. Keen to tell me they have two ms which they hire out to visitors, students and archaeologists stly, and people with metal detectors looking for things on the ch."

ekers after antiquities?"

st the usual hopefuls, I imagine. Vasilios said there was nothing und here to find."

"There certainly can't be anything of great age still undiscovered on Naxos, at least not lying about on the surface. But it explains how the taverna can possibly survive out here."

"They said the Elias Museum will open soon. They seem friendly with the owner, Petros. It seems he's visiting the mainland on a family matter."

"Excellent." Day slapped at an invisible insect on his neck and put his phone in his jacket pocket. "Well, shall we go home for lunch? I must just inspect the facilities first."

7

Several peaceful days passed for Helen. She would sit in her favourite place, on the main balcony with her feet up on the rungs of another chair, notebook and biro unused on the table. It was so easy to drift off into a dream here, and not usually one which inspired her to write or draw. She had fallen into a habit of quiet observation.

She would watch the man who strode across the uneven ground mid-morning to fetch his mule from the field and take it away for the day's work. She often saw in the distance a shepherd and his dogs as they walked from a house to the high sheep fields, sometimes disappearing from sight when the path wound behind buildings or stumpy trees. Yellow broom was starting to flower in the valley, and in the long grass were thistles, sprawling figs, untended olive trees and patches of wild geranium. Small birds sped about and twittered, butterflies floated in the breeze. Pigeons which believed the balcony belonged to them landed heavily on the woven cane canopy above where she sat.

Roy had gone for a walk to Filoti while the morning was still cool. She expected him back with a newspaper and fresh bread for lunch.

He would take his time. He planned to make small talk along the way, hoping to get to know his neighbours. The weekend had been rather quiet. Neither of them felt like starting work. They planned to phone the Elias Museum in a day or two and make a proper appointment for Day to visit. Meanwhile, Day slept most afternoons, and Thanasis was filling their evenings with entertainment of the best sort: home-cooked local food and Naxian wine.

Helen was just watching a distant figure moving towards some blue-painted bee-hives on the hillside when she heard the front door open and Day appeared with a bag of bread and a newspaper. He slammed the paper on the table next to her.

"Just when you think you're on a peaceful island in the Aegean where nothing ever happens, look at this!"

It was the local paper, The Naxian. Across the front was a sombre headline.

A MURDER ON NAXOS

An American visitor has been found dead in his room at the Hotel Philippos in Chora. The police are treating his death as murder, but have not released further details. The victim appeared to have been visiting the island alone, but the reason for his visit is unknown.

The police have named the victim as Dr Michael K. Moralis from New York. Inspector Cristopoulos of Naxos Police is in charge of the case, and a team from the Helladic Police in Athens is expected to arrive soon to assist with the investigation.

' know Michael Moralis, Helen!" said Day, interrupting her reading.
" /e met a couple of years ago in New York. I was covering an
c ibition of Mycenaean pottery at The Met Museum for the History
(annel, and Michael was hosting me. I think he was working for
s ne Classics department or other in New York. I wonder why he
v s on Naxos?"

I y stared in disbelief at the article, hands on hips. He walked into
t house, then back out to the balcony carrying a glass of water. He
l ned on the balcony rail and stared at the valley without seeing it.

' ll go and speak to this Inspector Cristopoulos, I think. There could
l a tremendous fuss about this. They might need a bit of help, and
a east I can tell them a bit more about their victim. Who would want
t kill an American academic, for goodness sake? The poor guy."

' m sorry about your friend, Martin."

' 's terrible. Really not what you expect as a classicist! They get pretty
v rked up about their research, of course, but hardly a murdering
n tter."

' o."

' think I'll go right away, in fact. I'll just check something on the
c mputer first. Coming?"

' don't have anything to tell the police!"

')K. I'll fill you in when I get back ."

***

] e Naxos Police Station was several streets from the main square.
] o marked police cars were parked outside, a Greek flag drooped on

the roof, and grilles were fixed over the windows. If it hadn't become a police station it might have served well as a small supermarket. Day's arrival forced the policeman on the desk to raise his head.

"Good morning. May I speak to Inspector Cristopoulos, please? My name's Martin Day. It's in connection with the death of Dr Moralis. I knew him."

"One moment, Kyrie," said the young officer.

A part-glazed door behind the reception desk stood slightly ajar. As the young policeman reached for his phone, a short figure with a significant moustache opened the door and came out. Unlike the policeman at the counter, this older man looked intelligent, authoritative and weary. He wore civilian clothes and looked a little like an academic. Day was rather pleasantly surprised at this first impression.

"Good morning. I'm Inspector Cristopoulos. And you're Professor Martin Day?"

"Hello, Inspector. You know who I am?"

"I know of your work in Greece, and that you have a house on Naxos, Kyrie. It's my business to know our new residents, especially those in your field."

The Inspector shook hands and continued to study Day carefully. As yet he had not felt the need to smile. The man on the desk avoided looking at them. Day decided to be direct.

"I've read in the newspaper of the death of my American colleague, Michael Moralis. I've come to offer any information I can, and to be of any possible assistance. If I may, Inspector?"

' he Greek Police welcome information and assistance from the
blic, Professor Day. Especially when the matter is as serious as
t s, when there are international ramifications on top of everything.
ay I suggest we talk in my office?"

ere was a certain lack of conviction in the Inspector's voice, but
l y decided it was best ignored.

e office into which the Inspector led him was clean and air-
nditioned. The station had recently been repainted, but it remained
old building and its windows were nailed shut on the inside. It
s, however, better equipped than Day had expected. Rumour was
t kind to the provincial Greek police, but in this case it seemed to
unfounded. Cristopoulos sat down behind a desk which seemed
her large for him and invited Day to sit opposite him. The Inspector
arded his visitor shrewdly from between his two computer screens.

ell me, Professor Day, how do you know our victim?"

met Michael Moralis in New York when we were working on an
ibition of Mycenaean pottery at the Metropolitan Museum. This
s two years ago, in March. I was preparing a television programme,
rhaps you saw it? Michael Moralis was showing me round and
king sure everything went smoothly; he introduced me to people,
t it kind of thing. He had a wide circle of professional contacts in
t city. At the time he was a lecturer at CUNY, the City University
New York. As far as I know he still is, or was. He specialised in
eek ceramics and was an expert on the Mycenaean period. He was
married, at least when I knew him. He had some kind of advisory
e at the Museum. We got to know each other reasonably well."

istopoulos regarded him meditatively, as if unimpressed.

hat was the nature of your relationship with Dr Moralis, Professor?
actly?"

Day felt a small surge of irritation but responded calmly.

"Just professional, Inspector. Can I ask how poor Michael was killed?"

"That information hasn't been released to the public," frowned the inspector. "However, I'm going to answer your question, Professor Day, because frankly I think you might be able to help me. You're part of the world in which the victim moved, you may be able to open up channels of information not readily accessible to me. Contacts, and so on. So, I need to ask for your absolute professional discretion?"

Day reassured him of his professional discretion.

"Very well." Cristopoulos leaned back from the desk and crossed his arms, regarding Day carefully. "Your colleague was stabbed to death in his hotel room. The assailant was not seen either arriving or leaving. Now, you can tell me something. I'd like to know why Dr Moralis was here on Naxos. Could it have been in connection with his work? Any information you could give me, or discover for me, would be extremely helpful at this stage."

"I didn't know he was on the island. Would you like me to make some enquiries?"

The inspector nodded and continued. "So you wouldn't know if he was here with a colleague or friend?"

"No, not at all."

"Did the victim's academic interests relate to Naxos?"

"Michael specialised in the Mycenaean period and wrote a superb book on the Mycenaeans in the Cyclades, so he did have an interest in this area, but I don't know of any specific or recent connection with Naxos."

The Inspector sighed, an expression not of disapproval but of despair. Day said nothing. He felt that a corner had been turned and Kostopoulos now regarded him somewhat more benignly. Indeed, Day sensed that the policeman needed his help. The inspector shifted his position and leaned his elbows on the desk, steepling his fingers, never taking his eyes off his visitor. He gave a small sniff and nodded.

"As you may know, Professor, my colleagues from Athens will be arriving soon to take over the case, by which time I should like to have made some positive progress …"

"I understand."

"So, the attack on Dr Moralis took place in his hotel room, as I said. Dr Moralis seems to have opened the door to his killer and not put up any resistance. He therefore may have known the killer, and there was no sign of a struggle. The hotel has informed us that Dr Moralis arrived a week ago, has apparently not received any visitors since checking in, and nobody saw anyone on the night of the murder who may have been the attacker. It looks as if the killer may have known the victim's room number and so was able to avoid reception staff."

"Is the reception desk constantly attended?"

"Usually it is, but Saturday night was busy. We did however receive an interesting piece of information from a member of staff. One evening, Dr Moralis chose to enjoy a glass of ouzo in the hotel reception lounge. During that time he spoke to someone on his mobile phone, which we know because the Duty Receptionist is a young woman with excellent English. She heard Dr Moralis referring to an unknown archaeological site on Naxos, and he seemed very excited. He spoke as if to a colleague or person of similar interests. Apparently he didn't mention the location of the place, or any details except the word sanctuary."

Day frowned and stretched his fingers, which had been resting on his knees.

"Now that's interesting," he said. "Did the receptionist hear anything more? No matter how unimportant?"

"I'm afraid not. Could you give this question your consideration for me, Professor Day? Might the victim have been here in search of an ancient sanctuary? And if so, perhaps he was in touch with somebody locally?"

"My first thought is that it seems unlikely that Michael would be here for that reason. Michael was an academic rather than a field archaeologist, but I'll look into his recent research interests, maybe explore a few avenues with colleagues, discretely of course ..."

Cristopoulos gave a small smile, his first of the interview.

"Good, that would be extremely helpful, Professor. We have a wonderful resource in our local Museum, of course, but you, I believe, have international contacts as well as a familiarity with Dr Moralis himself. Now, please don't leave the island without speaking to me first, and please leave my officer your contact details on the way out."

"Of course."

"And if I may repeat myself, all that I have told you must remain absolutely confidential. Oh, by the way, can you tell me your own whereabouts on the night of Saturday 18th May?"

"I was at home, Inspector, in my house in Filoti, with my friend Helen Aitchison, who's staying with me at the moment."

"Thank you. I'll be in touch."

Cristopoulos rose to signal the end of the interview and extended his short arm. The smile had subsided but the expression remained coolly benign.

8

Day drove back to Filoti for a late lunch with Helen and gave her an account of the interview with Cristopoulos. After lunch he picked up his laptop and headed to his room, saying he was going for a nap, though Helen thought he meant to delve into Michael Moralis and his possible connection with Naxos.

She moved to the balcony and looked out. The mule was back from its work and was now tethered by a long rope to graze in the shade of a solitary tree. The breeze had dropped, and subdued voices from houses on the far side of the valley could occasionally be heard. The locals had put up their shutters in every sense and retired for their afternoon rest. At this time of day in Greece everyone knew not to telephone, visit or otherwise disturb their neighbours and friends. Everyone, except possibly some keen construction workers and those in the tourist trade, respected the rest period. The May heat was nothing compared to what was to come, but the siesta was an enduring tradition.

Helen considered a rest too, but thought she wouldn't be able to sleep. She settled with a book on the sun lounger, and was rudely awoken from a light slumber when Day strode in from his part of the house. He seemed more lively now.

"Did you get a sleep? I did. I didn't expect to, but I got a good two hours. Wonderfully restorative."

"It seems I slept a little. At any rate, I just woke up," said Helen drily.

"I think a little work on the laptop for me now. Let's see what I can find out for the poor Inspector. Would you like a glass of water?"

I fetched two glasses of water from the kitchen. As they sat together with their laptops at the table, Helen saw that Day was sending many emails. She herself had to be content with making a few notes for the novel, observations on the sights and sounds from the balcony, the smell of the breeze, the quality of the heat. Her thoughts were interrupted when Day announced he was going to make a call.

"Aristo? Martin here. Can I have a word? Great. Look, I'm calling about the American who's been killed in Chora. He and I worked together a year or so ago in New York, so when I read about his death in the paper I went to talk to the police. They need to know why Michael was on Naxos, and anybody he might have met here. I thought I'd start with you, because there's some idea he might have been looking for antiquities. Any thoughts?"

"I'm sorry, Martin," said Aristos after a short pause, "all I know of Michael Moralis is his brilliant book on the Mycenaean sites in the Cyclades. If I'd known he was here, I would probably have invited him to the museum and laid on a glass of wine. However, I didn't. The first I knew was the bad news in the paper."

"It's a terrible loss. There's one piece of hearsay you might find interesting: an overheard phone conversation in which Michael spoke of an undiscovered sanctuary here on Naxos. That took me by surprise, of course, because Michael wasn't a field archaeologist. Have you heard of any rumour about any unexcavated sites here?"

"No, nothing credible. I suppose there's always a chance of some major discovery still to be made, but I'm not aware of any big excitement, rumour, anything. It's almost impossible to keep these things completely quiet. If you get any more information, come over and we'll talk it through together, OK?"

***

Not until that evening, when Day and Helen were sitting at their usual table at Thanasis's taverna, was Day ready to talk about Michael Moralis. He gave her the details of his interview with the police, before sharing his frustration.

"I haven't come up with anything useful about Michael, or his supposed sanctuary. I spoke to my friend Aristos, the museum curator, but he couldn't help. Michael doesn't seem to have published anything, or been mentioned in journals, for over a year. He spent most of his professional life - he was under fifty - studying other people's discoveries from Mycenaean excavations around Greece, and he published a superb book on Mycenaean settlements in the Cyclades a couple of years ago. Even though that's a link with this area, there's no obvious reason why he should be on Naxos now."

"Couldn't he simply have been on vacation?" asked Helen.

"Maybe. But don't forget that conversation overheard by the hotel receptionist. If she heard what she thinks she heard, Michael was interested in some 'sanctuary' here."

"Wasn't Michael a specialist on the Mycenaean period? I thought Naxos is famous for the Cycladic figurines."

'ycladic is just the name for the Aegean Bronze Age in the Cyclades. The period is divided into sections, so Early Cycladic 1 is the early Bronze Age in the Cyclades, when the Cycladic figurines were made. In fact, Naxos was inhabited from pre-history onwards. It was occupied throughout all the Bronze Age eras, including the later time when the Mycenaean peoples came and settled here. That's Michael's period, the Middle Bronze Age. But Michael would be more likely to stay in the library and do research than come and look for some sanctuary. That period on Naxos is very well excavated and documented, and there aren't any plans to excavate further that I can discover. I don't understand why he came in person."

'So how do you explain what the receptionist heard?"

'I can't, but I have one idea. Have you heard of a tholos tomb? They're huge, beehive-shaped things, absolutely stunning. There's one on Naxos, in the hills near the village of Koronida, or Komiaki as some people call it. It's very remote. It was looted way back, so we don't know much about it, but Michael did a lot of work on the tholos tombs of mainland Greece. The tholos tomb at Komiaki might have brought him here, I suppose."

'You don't sound convinced, Martin. Anyway, that tomb couldn't be called undiscovered, and it isn't a sanctuary. It doesn't match what Michael was overheard to say."

'Right, it's just the only thing I can think of, but it doesn't fit the facts. I've written to some of Michael's colleagues in the States to see if they have any ideas. Actually, it won't do me any harm to re-establish contact with them."

***

A waiter they didn't recognise brought their red wine and told them that the specials were lamb chops on the grill, stuffed tomatoes, or pastitsio. Helen's gesture told Day she had no preference.

"One portion of lamb chops, please," he said, cheering up at the prospect. "Some fried zucchini. And what's that dish on the table over there?"

"That's pantzaria," said the waiter, not knowing the English word. "It's fresh today from the local grower."

Day grinned and supplied the translation for Helen. "It's beetroot. That's quite unusual, at least I haven't had it in Greece yet. Shall we try some? A portion of pantzaria too, please, and what else do we need, Helen?"

They decided they had ordered enough and the waiter moved off to the kitchen, where the voices of Thanasis's wife and daughter were raised in an enthusiastic culinary dispute. Day poured two glasses from the jug of wine, lifted his with some relief, and raised his eyes to her.

"Well, here's to poor Michael Moralis," he said.

"To Michael."

9

There was a new smell in the room, the smell of heavy rain having fallen in the night. Helen had slept with her window ajar and shutters open, and when she first opened her eyes she saw a cloudy sky. The smell of wet grass was strong when she opened up the window, and her little balcony was damp. It looked like the rolls of thunder that she had taken for a dream had been real.

She lay thinking for a while. This time last week she had arrived on a ferry for a quiet working holiday. Since then, someone Martin knew had been murdered and he seemed to be working with the police.

Moreover, she still hadn't the faintest clue about her new novel. Her most recent one, the fifth in the series, had met with real success and the launch process had been exhausting. She was now financially secure for the moment. She felt, in fact, far more interested in the puzzle of Dr Moralis. What had he been doing on Naxos? And why had he been killed?

She threw on some clothes and sat with a blanket round her on the main balcony. Day appeared a short while later and poured them each a glass of water from the bottle in the fridge. He was not a morning person. He sat down at the balcony table and stared moodily across at the valley.

"Well, I think I'll spend the morning on my computer looking into Michael's work. I'll trace his professional life over the last year or so, see if he published anything at all, what courses he taught, anything he was involved in that might give me an insight into why he came here. It'll be like doing research for a programme. I used to have a special interest in Mycenae myself when I was at Cambridge, and Greek ceramics are close to my heart, as you know. I want to try to trace his steps from New York to the Hotel Philippos."

"Martin, I have a question. Do you think there really is a Mycenaean sanctuary on Naxos which no-one knows about? You said the island was already well excavated. Could there be an unknown site here?"

"It's unlikely, even extremely unlikely, but not impossible. It would be a major discovery to find one. Michael could have stumbled across some information which gave him the idea, I suppose, but he was an academic, and I just can't imagine him on some pointless search on Naxos or anywhere else."

"On the other hand, all the great archaeologists of the past who found major sites, like Howard Carter, Arthur Evans, Schliemann and so on, got just such an idea and it became an obsession," mused Helen. "And sometimes they were right."

"Indeed. Perhaps that was what happened to Michael. I need to find out more about him."

"If there was such a place, wouldn't it be for the Greek Archaeological Service to excavate it?"

es, or one of the foreign schools of archaeology like the American,
the British or the French Schools. There would still be immense
prestige for whoever first discovered it, though. Well, we'll see."

"ou don't think someone killed Michael over the sanctuary, do you?
There would have been big stakes involved."

"What an appalling thought. Murder in the field of ancient history."

"Hmm," said Helen. "I suspect there's ample precedent."

Day nodded ruefully, but his thoughts had taken a different direction.
"By the way, we should invite Aristos and Rania Iraklidis to dinner, the
Curator and his wife. Would you be up for that? Tomorrow maybe?"

"Of course, good idea. What suddenly put that in your mind? It was
quite a change of subject."

"I spoke to Aristos yesterday. I thought he might have heard about a
famous American scholar on the island looking for antiquities. When
it comes to the ancient history of Naxos, not much gets past Aristos.
He couldn't help, though."

***

Day worked for several hours, then abruptly closed his laptop and
declared it was time for lunch. This came as a welcome surprise to
Helen. "Have you found anything interesting?" she asked.

"Nothing much. I've had one or two replies from contacts in the US.
People haven't seen much of Michael recently because he's been on
sabbatical leave from the university."

Day's explanation, like his plans for lunch, were interrupted by the
unexpected arrival of a visitor. Day was for once at a loss for words

when Inspector Cristopoulos rapped on the front door, nudged it open, and inserted his waving hand closely followed by his voice.

"May I come in? Your door didn't seem to be quite closed. Good morning, Professor, please forgive me for not having telephoned. I'd like to ask you a few questions, if I may."

"Of course, Inspector. Come in. Take a seat. This is my friend, Helen Aitchison. Would you like a coffee?"

The Inspector hesitated. He was fussy about his coffee but put great store on good manners, so he claimed to have recently had one. He accepted a chair at the dining table, placing a folder in front of him. He wriggled discreetly in the old chair to find a comfortable position.

"I'll get straight to the point, if I may. On discovering the victim's body we did, of course, make a careful search of the hotel room. We found Dr Moralis's computer, which had apparently been wiped almost clean at some stage. It contained nothing about Naxos or any sanctuary site. Rather surprising, don't you think? No social media, no browsing history, no saved documents.

"However, there were three names on his calendar for April. Just names, no explanation. Two of the names appear to be connected to your line of work."

The inspector added some reading glasses to his face and opened his folder.

"The first name is Emil Gautier. He lives in Paris, and he's an antiquities dealer. Have you heard of him, Professor?"

"Please, Inspector, call me Martin. The 'Professor' thing is just for the television, I'm afraid. A series I made for the History Channel some time ago…"

istopoulos smiled and made no comment. Day suspected that the liceman had known all along and been making some kind of joke Day's expense. Day cursed his agent for ever agreeing to the use the title.

" lartin, then," said Cristopoulos. "So, what do you know about this il Gautier?"

" lot a thing. Sorry."

' erhaps the next name may mean something to you. Jim Grogan. seems to be an American who collects antique art."

" iteresting. But again, not a name I've come across. Did Michael ite anything about these men? Meeting places? Times?"

' lo, as I said, just the names. What a pity you can't tell me anything ut them. Perhaps you could ask your contacts, Martin? I would preciate it."

I y sighed, nodded and sat back in his chair. The Inspector bent er his folder again as if to study the third name.

' he final name is Alexander Harding-Jones."

I y stiffened. "Yes, I know him. He's attached to the British Museum."

' deed he is, Martin, and it would seem reasonable for Dr Moralis t have a note of his name, wouldn't it, as they work in a similar f ld? Frankly I'm more interested in Gautier and Grogan, and what c nnects them, apart from both their names being in Moralis's laptop. \ 've checked with the hotels, the airport and the ferry companies, t t there's no trace of these men arriving on the island. I just have a trong feeling they must be here, or why would Moralis have put t ir names on his April calendar? We're actively looking for them."

The policeman looked directly at Day. "Your job, Martin, is to find out what the connection is between them and our victim. Will you do that?"

"OK, if you think it will help. If the connection's in my field, there's a chance I might find something, and I want to find out who killed Michael as much as you."

The Inspector closed his folder and took off his reading glasses, but remained leaning on the table as if appreciating its support.

"Thank you. Now, you told me, Martin, that Dr Moralis was unmarried. You will be surprised to learn that he has a wife."

"He must have married within the last couple of years. We didn't keep in touch after New York."

"They lived at an address in Rockport, Massachusetts. We're trying to get hold of her to inform her of his death."

"Poor woman. She may be able to tell you why he came to Naxos."

"I hope so. However, there is a difficulty. It's possible that your colleague Michael was here with another woman."

"Wow! That's hard to believe. The impression I had of Michael was that he was married to the job. In fact, I thought he wasn't interested in women. Now I have to add a wife and possibly a mistress."

"Mmm. Well, the woman who may have been with Dr Moralis was booked into a different room of the same hotel. The name she gave was Katherine Russell."

"Sorry, I've not heard of her either."

" Well, there it is, Martin. There's one more thing. Katherine Russell seems to have disappeared."

10

When the policeman had left and they had eaten a little lunch, Helen spent the afternoon reading. Day had failed to sleep during the siesta hours and was not in a good mood when he appeared on the balcony at the hour of aperitifs.

"Gin?" he muttered.

"Looks like you need one, Martin."

"I didn't sleep. I've been on the laptop for the last hour, and you might be interested in what I've found. However, we also have a problem."

"Oh? Let's move indoors, I've got chilly sitting out here. Then you can tell me what the problem is."

Martin prepared the drinks with generous quantities of gin and ice, placed them on a small table, and lowered himself into an arm chair.

"First, I looked into this Frenchman, Emil Gautier. Nothing on the Internet, but then I wouldn't really expect anything, given the

i ormation I subsequently turned up about him. I contacted an old
(mbridge pal who works at the Sorbonne. He's got a prestigious
t e but a deadly dull appointment, so he dabbles in certain circles
i Paris, circles in which art is bought and sold. I'm not saying he's
s dy, but he undoubtedly knows people who are. Very nice objects
c inge hands, I believe. He told me that Emil Gautier is one of the
t) people in Paris if you want to buy something rather old and
r her special which won't appear in any auction house. So far, like
r Sorbonne friend, Gautier seems to have stayed just on the right
s e of the law, but he's very, very pivotal in the world of extremely
v althy private collectors."

" ood work, Martin. But does that mean Michael too was involved
i something murky?"

" ve thought of lots of scenarios. Michael could have been a customer
(Gautier's. Worse still, he could have supplied Gautier with antiquities.
} ither option seems in character to me. Another idea is that Michael
(ild have discovered Gautier's involvement in illegal trade and was
t eatening to report him to the police. If that was the case, I can
i agine that Gautier would be desperate to silence Michael.

" here's another possibility, one connected to the sanctuary puzzle. If
} chael was right about a new site, Gautier might see an opportunity
t get his hands on some valuables, items that could disappear onto
t collectors' market without even being catalogued."

" m getting confused now, Martin! And you're making Gautier out to
} a man of action, rather than an intermediary. What about Michael,
(you think he was corrupt?"

" nything's possible, I suppose. If Michael was here with a woman
(ier than his wife, that would have given Gautier leverage over
} n. Whatever the truth is, I hope Michael stayed well away from
} il Gautier."

Day took a sip of his drink and looked a lot happier.

"Now, here's what I discovered about Jim Grogan. He's a very different kettle of fish. An extremely wealthy American, his name appears all over the Internet. He travels a lot, and even wrote a book about taking some long journey on foot round Greece and Turkey with a backpack."

"Very Paddy Leigh Fermor," Helen murmured.

"This character isn't remotely in the same class as Fermor, Helen!" Day said sternly.

"That would be hard to imagine," she conceded.

"This Jim Grogan is now in his early forties. He's known to collect rare antiquities and has a special interest in ancient Greek artefacts. He reportedly collects a wide range of objects, but all of them are rare, expensive, sought-after and not necessarily catalogued in the public domain."

"How do you know all this if his collection is so private?"

"People like him have ways of spreading the word when they're in the market for a certain item. It wasn't too hard to find out that he's currently after a large black-figure hydria vessel with a particular octopus design, and the word is that he wants perfection. If such a thing could be obtained under the counter, it would be worth a fortune to a private collector. In reality it's priceless. It's also illegal to export such a thing from Greece, or have any part in such a trade. Emil Gautier, however, would be the perfect middle man."

"Right. So we're dealing with some really shady people."

' deed. Even though I haven't found a specific connection with Naxos, I think those pieces of information do get us a bit further, don't you? It's up to the police to find these people now, if they're on the island at all. But my real problem is Alex Harding-Jones. I need another gin before I explain. Want one?"

" wouldn't say no."

I y returned with the drinks and a bowl of savoury Greek biscuits.

' ow, this is my problem. When Inspector Cristopoulos mentioned Alex Harding-Jones, I didn't tell him that he's a particularly good friend of mine. We've known each other for years. Alex is the foremost Mycenaean ceramics expert at the British Museum, and it won't have taken Cristopoulos ten minutes on Google to find out about him. He's written an array of papers and several excellent books, and he's known for his lectures at the BM. A wonderful man, too. I've got a lot of time for him. I hope to God he's not mixed up with these other two, but his name is alongside theirs on that computer."

' s you know Alex so well, couldn't you just call him? Just ask him if he knows Michael Moralis."

' need to think about it some more. God, I'm suddenly really hungry. Are you ready for dinner? If I have any more gin without proper food I shall be very drunk."

***

They walked as usual to the taverna. It was dark, the cool breeze had appeared, and it was warmer than a few hours earlier. Helen loved this about Greece, the dark warmth of the night, eating late.

Thanasis's son, Vangelis, was on duty in the restaurant and introduced himself. Thanasis then arrived at their table with a half litre of white wine in a chilled metal jug, before Day and Helen had even ordered.

"This is on the house," said Thanasis. "It's a white wine made by my family in their own small vineyard. I'd like you to try it, and I'll bring you some small dishes to have with it."

The small dishes were more generous than Helen and Day expected. There was aubergine dip, vinegary 'politiki' salad and delicate pieces of boiled octopus in lemon juice. All talk of the Moralis question was postponed as they ate and drank. The wine was dry but quite tasty, and the sharp little salad and fresh fishy bites complimented it well.

Day used a piece of bread to finish the aubergine dip. "Very kind of Thanasis. To be honest, though, I could murder a plate of chips and a glass of red," said Day in a low voice.

"Since we're being honest, Martin, I've eaten enough already to last me till morning. Not to mention the wine."

All the same, Day ordered a plate of lamb chops and a portion of fried potatoes to share, and some red wine 'from the barrel'.

"Before I forget to tell you, Aristos and Rania can't come to dinner because they have Rania's niece and her family staying with them for a while. I said we'd see them another time."

"That's a shame. But maybe we wouldn't have been very good company. All we can talk about is murder."

"Good point, Helen. I can't stop worrying about Alex, you know. I don't think I'll call him just yet. He's a good friend, but we see each other rarely. I don't like to think he's involved in anything illegal, but he and Michael are linked by an obsession with the Mycenaean era,

a l there's an apparent connection between Michael and those two
c reputable characters. I don't know what to make of it."

') you're going to do nothing?" asked Helen, sounding surprised.

' 'f course not, just nothing about Alex for the moment. I think I
s)uld go to the Sanctuary of Flerio tomorrow. Of the sanctuaries on
] .xos, the one at Flerio has the most scope for further discoveries,
i a big sprawling site. I'll just ask around, see if anyone remembers
] chael. I don't hold out much hope, but I don't know how else to
f d where he was looking for an undiscovered sanctuary on an island
t s size. Want to come?"

' es, of course," she said. "But you could just leave it to the police,
) 1 know, Martin."

' [mm. I can't do that. I owe it to Michael to do something."

' et's go tomorrow then. But on one condition. We visit the Flerio
] 1ros at the same time."

11

Never known as an early riser, Day was later than usual to appear in the kitchen the next morning. Helen was washing up their glasses from the night before, having already spent a couple of hours working on the outline of her new book. It was tempting to involve a Greek policeman and a handsome waiter called Vangelis.

Before setting off for Flerio, they drove into Filoti for coffee at the café almost opposite O Thanasis. Helen liked the cheerfulness of this place, Café Ta Xromata was its name, meaning Colours. Customers sat on brightly coloured sofas with turquoise cushions, and were given bright cups and plates. Day checked his emails on his phone, but no significant replies had come in. They drank their coffee in contented silence, watching the village street going about its normal business. After half an hour, leaving payment on the table, they got back in the Fiat and set off to Flerio.

The lush sanctuary area of Flerio, near the village of Melanes, had been fertile even in ancient times, and was one of the oldest settled areas on the island. To get there from Filoti they first drove towards Halki, the village in the central hills which had once been regarded the capital of the island. Day drove sedately, as always. After passing the cement works, incongruously ugly buildings that quickly appeared after a bend in the road, they turned a sharp corner into Halki. Under the bulk of the white Barossi Tower several older men were sitting and talking in the shade by the roadside. Tourists sat outside cafés or wandered towards shops which sold woven goods, ceramics and souvenirs.

Leaving Halki again the road passed grassy fields of olive trees to the village of Ano Potamia. As far as Helen was concerned, Ano Potamia was famous for one thing: a favourite restaurant remembered from the distant time when she visited Naxos with her young Greek husband. It was clear, however, that Day had no thought of lunch. The countryside changed after Ano Potamia and the road climbed. Sometimes the landscape became almost moon-like in its rockiness, and a stunningly clear light filled the high hills. Day carefully negotiated the steep bends to circumvent the village of Melanes, and the road turned back on itself towards their destination.

Day parked the Fiat on the roadside by the entrance to the Sanctuary of Flerio. A crowd of tourists from a parked coach was heading towards the shadeless sanctuary site. Fallen columns and lintels could be seen across the fields. Day locked the car and placed his sunglasses on his face. Now he looked more like his TV presenter alter ego, and began to sound like him.

"That's the Flerio Sanctuary over there. It was dedicated to the deities of the underground – not the underworld as in Hades, but the deities of the veins of marble and underground springs that provided such benefit to the ancient Naxians. There are signs that the workers at the local marble quarry worshipped here, you can see interesting chisel marks, dedications, that kind of thing. We think there's a lot more of this sanctuary still buried beneath these fields awaiting some future excavation."

"I wonder if this is where Michael thought he could make some great new discovery," mused Helen. "Was he here a week ago?"

"Come on, let's go and ask a few people," said Day, and led the way.

***

The ticket office at the entrance to the sanctuary site was a wooden hut in which a young woman was issuing passes to the tourists from the coach. When the last of them had moved passed her, she greeted Day and Helen politely. Day showed his professional identity card and the woman seemed happy to answer his questions.

"Good morning, Kyria," he began. "I wonder if you can help me, please? A friend of mine was here recently, asking about an area of the sanctuary which is still to be excavated. He spoke to one of your colleagues, I believe. I was hoping to talk to him."

"I'm sorry, Kyrie Day, I don't think I can help you. I can't think which colleague you mean. I've been in charge here for the last two weeks, and nobody else from the Archaeological Service has been here. Nobody has mentioned a new excavation. Perhaps you could ring our head office?"

Day thanked her and said he would.

"If she's been the only attendant on this site since Michael arrived on the island, there isn't anyone else we can really ask, is there?" said Day crossly. "Oh yes, there is, let's try the visitor centre! Come on!"

He strode off down a path which disappeared down a slope towards a low building which served as the visitor centre. Its purpose was to explain the sanctuary, display copies of the more important discoveries, and provide visitors with bathroom facilities. Most people would pass

...ough it during a visit. Day asked his question again at the reception ...sk, and this time had his phone ready to show the receptionist a ...ture of Michael Moralis.

"...yrie, with respect, we have hundreds of visitors here every day. ...might have been here, but I really couldn't say. And nobody has ...ed me about a new excavation."

...y thanked the receptionist and rejoined Helen, who was waiting ...the sun outside.

"...othing," he said. "OK, at least we tried. Come on, let's go and pay ...mage to the old kouros!"

***

...ey left the Flerio sanctuary, rejoined the road where they had ...rked the Fiat and followed the sign to the famous Kouros of ...rio. Day strode off ahead, suddenly carried away with enthusiasm. ...len followed at her own pace, relieved to leave the crowds behind. ...e old tarmac road came to an end and became a shady lane with ...erarching trees. These were not the thirsty figs and unkempt olives ...und all over Naxos, but alder, plane and willow trees whose roots ...nk from the springs guarded by the deities of the underground. ...e reputed lushness of the ancient valley was still in evidence.

...smaller path led up a few steps to a cool glade off the lane. This was ...resting place of the Flerio kouros, an ancient marble statue of a male ...ure, one of three on the island. The floor of the glade, formerly part ...the ancient quarry, was nothing but well-swept earth lit by dappled ...light. It was a cool and silent place with a smell of dampness, or ...Day preferred to think, of antiquity. The huge marble statue lay ...inst a modern dry-stone wall, and a cordon of fine rope protected ...o some extent on the side closest to visitors. The recumbent statue ...s perhaps eighteen feet long, the roughly shaped figure of a naked man, lying on its back. It was made from a single piece of marble but resembled a chunk of old granite, being dark, rough and weatherworn. Disconcertingly, its head was at a lower level than its body, as if the man had fallen backwards. The right leg was broken through at the knee. Some shaping had been done to the chest and arms, and the marks of the quarrymen's tools were still visible, but at some point all work on the marble had been abandoned. This anonymous kouros had been left to lie where it fell for many hundreds of years, unwanted.

"He's quite a boy," reflected Day quietly. "The sheer size of him. Every time I see him, I'm amazed. It's the isolation of this place, the marks left by the original carving tools. And he's two and a half thousand years old."

"It's funny to think that he might have ended up somewhere like the Acropolis, if something hadn't gone wrong."

"Yes. He could have stood proudly inside a temple anywhere in Greece. I wonder what happened. Did the workers find flaws in the marble that made them stop work? Or perhaps they broke the block."

"Perhaps the customer changed their mind, or a war broke out, because it wasn't only this kouros that they abandoned."

"No, three in all. Worth seeing again, isn't he?"

They stood for many minutes looking at the fallen marble giant. On her first visit here, with her husband Zissis soon after they were married, Helen had found this place an oasis of peace. Now she found it rather unsettling. Here, in this silent place, was a piece of antiquity which had lain on the spot since about 570 BC, and normally she would have shared the awe that Martin was describing. Instead, she was thinking about the body of Michael Michaelis, whom she had never known, but who should still be alive.

' m so pleased to have seen the old kouros again," said Day, "but
t : whole trip was a bit of a waste of time, really, wasn't it? If only
\ knew what Michael did with his time between arriving on Naxos
a l his death."

'l ey left the glade, Day offering his hand to Helen at the steep step
c wn to the path. Looking up they noticed a small sign across the
l e which read 'GARDEN TAVERNA - DRINKS'. Day, curious
a usual, walked across and peered over the gate. An elderly woman
i ide the garden saw him and came over, indicating with a sweep
c her arm an old table set with jars of local honey, plastic pots of
l me-prepared olives, and unlabelled bottles of olive oil, each marked
\ ch a modest price. Her smile revealed missing teeth and her face
\ s darkened by the sun. She beckoned to him insistently.

l y politely went inside, wondering if perhaps Michael had been
l re. The old woman said something in a heavy local accent. When
l y replied in his carefully learned and excessively polite Greek, the
v man laughed in delight. He asked for two bottles of water, which
s : went to fetch from her fridge. He gave her the money and she
\ lked back to the gate with him.

' ou have a wonderful garden, Kyria," said Day, thinking of his next
c estion. "Are you busy with tourists this year?"

' o, Kyrie. Who wants to come to a place like this? They get back
c the coach and drive away to their hotels. I need a bigger sign, and
a riend among the coach drivers!"

I y laughed with her. He brought out his mobile phone, opened it
a the photograph of Michael, and showed it to the woman.

' yria, can you help me? Please could you tell me if you've seen this
r n?" he asked. Perhaps Michael had been here, spoken to this very
\ man, there was no reason why not.

She looked at the picture but shook her head. Disappointed but not surprised, Day went on to asked whether she had seen some friends of his, a Frenchman and an American, in the last week or so. The woman gave a small jump as if he had pulled a rabbit from a hat.

"There was a Frenchman here a few days ago, but he won't be any friend of yours, Kyrie!"

Lying with alarming ease, Day claimed that he had met the men on the ferry and was trying to find them again to return an item of value.

"You want to find *him*? He was a rude man and up to no good. You should keep the money, Kyrie, that's what I suggest."

"Oh? What happened, Kyria?"

The woman looked astonished, as if Day should already have known.

"He insulted me," she muttered.

"How, Kyria?"

"He offered me money for what he called my 'old rubbish'. You understand? He was trying to buy ancient pots and jewellery, Kyrie. In the old days people used to sell the things they found, it was one way to get the money to feed your family. But we don't do that any more. We respect our antiquities, and the law. He's a bad man, that one, you listen to me, Kyrie."

They had reached the gate to the lane. Day asked if the old woman knew anything else about the Frenchman. She raised her chin to indicate no in the Greek way, and shrugged. Day wasn't sure if her contempt was directed at the Frenchman or himself.

"ou could ask for him in Apollonas," she muttered as she turned
t ck into her garden.

12

As they walked back to the car, Day told Helen what the old woman had said. He was despondent again. They had not achieved anything useful, and this Frenchman was unlikely to be Emil Gautier. Day resigned himself to the facts. Looking for Michael's supposed sanctuary was a waste of time without more information. However, Day badly wanted to find the antiquities dealer from Paris, and he couldn't sit on his hands, he needed to do something.

Day spoke as if he had already been talking to Helen aloud. "So, although I was going to suggest a bit of lunch round here, why don't we head north to Apollonas, grab a bite to eat by the sea, and make a few enquiries there about this Frenchman? We could visit the other kouros while we're there."

"OK," she said, quite hungry now. "I don't mind that. Although without knowing what Emil Gautier looks like, I don't think we're going to find him."

They had a choice of two routes to Apollonas, neither of which were particularly easy. They chose the coast road, a high one with some tuous bends, but it would be easier than going back through the mountainous central part of the island.

The contrast between the coast road and the tourist hub of Chora couldn't have been more stark. It also looked nothing like the green valley of Flerio. It took them an hour just to cover thirty kilometres. Helen liked the fact that Day was a slow driver so she didn't have to worry about the road. It was narrow in parts and the barriers on the side which dropped away were broken or old. It was a high landscape with beautiful sea glimpses to the left, she would have liked to photograph it. Every few miles, though, there seemed to be a little altar signifying a fatal accident.

They reached the town of Apollonas on the northern tip of Naxos and decided to start by visiting their second kouros of the day, the Kouros of Apollo. A coach-load of visitors was climbing the steps to where the huge fallen statue lay on the open hillside. Blocks of black, grainy stone, now unrecognisable as ancient marble, lay scattered across the whole area. The giant figure of Naxos's largest kouros was about twice the size of its counterpart in Flerio, but Helen found it less impressive. For one thing, this statue had no face, only a roughly shaped head. Also, there were too many people around for her liking. They heard German, American and British accents. They admired the kouros briefly, then walked back down to the town.

The little town huddled round the small bay that formed its heart. Day's priority now was to find a café table within six feet of the sea. Three fishing-boats bobbed on the water near the beach, their hulls and cabins painted blue. Only gentle waves tickled the sand, as the bay and its little beach were protected from the sea beyond. They parked the Fiat in an empty parking area by the sea wall and walked back to the beach. The entire water's edge had been adopted by various tavernas, and their painted tables and chairs, their coloured awnings and bright tablecloths, all in combinations of blue and white, left

63

nobody in any doubt that this was Greece. It was as if the azure and white Greek flag was artfully wrapped around everything.

Waiters and waitresses invited them to their tables as they walked along. Day and Helen sat down at a blue table near the water and ordered a lemon juice with ginger for Day, a freshly squeezed orange juice for Helen, and two toasted sandwiches. Helen looked round with satisfaction, grateful that it was relatively quiet.

"This place will be packed in a few weeks," she said. "We're so lucky today."

"Let's hope our luck continues," he replied. "So what are our chances of finding this Frenchman, do you think?"

"Nil. Call me a pessimist, but I'm with Inspector Cristopoulos on that. How were you thinking of finding him, Martin?"

"I thought we'd just talk to people. That's all the police would do. I think the locals will be noticing strangers at this time of year. Everyone's on the alert for new customers. I'm a great believer in luck, did I tell you? I believe it's my affinity with the Ancient Greeks."

"Oh really, Martin!"

***

Day began his investigation at once by chatting to the man who brought their toasted sandwiches, and then to the girl who cleared the plates away, claiming to be looking for a French acquaintance. Neither of the staff knew anything. Day paid the bill and they started to amble along the beach road, pausing at shops where Day asked more questions. It seemed a pointless exercise to Helen, although Day's efforts made her laugh and it was quite fun to chat to so many locals. It was good to have a chance to practice her Greek.

Finally they had some luck. At a small shop selling pretty pottery they attracted the attention of the lady in charge, who turned out to be the wife of the potter. They admired her husband's ceramics and the woman was happy to talk.

"Yes, the visitors are starting to arrive now," she said. "I have a good feeling about this year. Already there are groups of Germans and Americans here, and the cruise ships will be arriving soon."

"I wish you a successful season, Kyria. Can you tell me, are there still any good rooms to rent here in Apollonas?" asked Day.

"Of course. My son has a small guesthouse just as you come into town. I can recommend it."

"Ah, thank you. We already have a place to stay, but I have a French colleague who's looking for accommodation."

"I'll bring you my son's card in a moment," the woman offered. "French, did you say? We don't have many French visitors so far. Funnily enough, one of them has a bit of a reputation. Everyone has noticed him! His Greek is really terrible. Yours is excellent, Kyrie, so I wouldn't say that to you! Although your Greek is actually quite funny, if you don't mind me saying so. It's like listening to Homer when I'm talking to you."

Day grimaced and Helen laughed. The woman, meanwhile, squinted into the sun as if looking for something and began pointing towards the beach. Walking towards the cafés that Day and Helen had just left were two men, deep in conversation.

"There, that's him, the shorter man," said the potter's wife. "I thought I saw him a minute ago! Isn't that funny! He isn't a typical tourist, that one. People think he must be here on business, but what business a

Frenchman does in Apollonas, the Lord only knows! We don't like him very much, although I shouldn't say it, I suppose."

Day thanked her and took her son's business card. He and Helen crossed the road and followed the two men, who had ducked into one of the tavernas near the beach. Day and Helen took a table as close to them as they dared. They tried to eavesdrop but the men spoke too quietly. What they could make out was that the shorter man had a French accent, and the other seemed to be American.

Helen had the best view of the men. The American's physique suggested he worked out, but his belly spoke of over-indulgence. His clothes looked expensive. The Frenchman was a little younger, short and thin, black-haired with a bald patch on top. They wore sunglasses so she couldn't see their faces. Helen pushed back her chair and took out her phone. Pretending to take a picture of Day, she managed to get a picture of the men. Day gave a tight smile. He hated having his photo taken. The two men took no notice.

Within five minutes of Helen sitting down again, the American got up and held out his hand to the Frenchman.

"Keep in touch. I'll expect to hear from you in a few days. You have my number."

"OK, and I'll send Panos over."

The American nodded and walked away. The Frenchman signalled to the waiter and asked for a menu.

13

There was no point in staying to watch the Frenchman eat his lunch. Day and Helen left some money on the table and walked back to the sea wall. Spray had splattered the Fiat with salt water, which had dried crisp and blotchy in the sun. It now looked like a real island car.

The drive back to Filoti seemed long, and the cool of the house was welcome. Day voiced his frustration.

"Such a pity we couldn't hear what they were saying. No names, no place names, nothing useful."

"Well, we have my photos."

"The sunglasses made the men pretty unrecognisable, I'm afraid. It was a good idea of yours, though."

Helen nodded. "They were probably just innocent visitors, you know, Martin."

"Probably. We had a good outing, though, and I'm pleased with the bowl. I think I'll go for a nap. I'll look at my emails afterwards, but if nothing fresh turns up, I think we've reached a dead end."

Day splashed cold water from a bottle into a glass, spilled some on the counter, and crossly left it there to evaporate. Picking up his glass and laptop, he went to his room.

Helen settled herself on the balcony with her notebook, binoculars and sunhat. After watching the mule and the beehives through the binoculars, and pondering the plot for the novel that was failing to take shape in her imagination, she gave up trying to stay awake. It was now very hot, the dazzling sun fell full on the balcony. The sun lounger beckoned from the shade and Helen gave in, pulling her sunhat over her eyes.

***

A different Day emerged from his room at six o'clock exactly, newly showered and wearing fresh clothes, announcing that he had slept well. He fetched two small glasses of red wine from the kitchen, sat next to Helen, and opened his laptop.

"I had a bit of success," he said. "I just found this recent picture of Jim Grogan, taken a couple of years ago. I think it could be the man we saw today; what do you think? There's something about the physique and posture that reminds me of our American in Apollonas. I still can't find anything on the net about Emil Gautier, and none of my enquiries have turned up anything about him. Oh, and there's been a new development. The police have released more details of Katherine Russell. It's in The Naxian. You remember, Katherine Russell was the woman Cristopoulos linked with Michael. She's still missing."

"What? Still?"

' he article say she works at a British university. I'm going to look
h r up now. I really want to know if she was here with Michael."

I set to work on his laptop accordingly. Helen took her wineglass to
h r room, showered and changed. Day looked up as she came back
a d grinned. He read triumphantly from the screen.

' r Katherine Russell, 32, junior lecturer at the University of Warwick.
A varded her doctorate at the University of California, Berkeley.
T at explains her research subject, which was the Mycenaean tomb
a Nemea in the Peloponnese. It was discovered in 2018 by an
i ernational team of archaeologists, including some from Berkeley.
I a possible connection with Michael."

T ey finished their drinks, locked the house and began to walk into
t village. There was still no food in the house as they hadn't been
s opping, but it didn't cost any more to eat at the taverna and it tasted
a ot better. The barrel wine was cheap too.

' /hat else we can do to find out why Michael was on Naxos?" asked
H len after a while.

' irst we need to find the connection between Michael and Katherine
R ssell. If they came here together to work on something there
v uld be no need for secrecy. They would have been supported by
b th their institutions, and might even have obtained funding. So it
c ldn't have been a professional visit. I suppose they could have been
i a relationship. Did they meet when she was at Berkeley, perhaps?"

' ave you thought that maybe Katherine Russell killed Michael? The
p lice said he probably opened the door to his killer. It could have
b en her, and it would explain her disappearance."

' mm. In that case, the murder has nothing to do with a sanctuary."

There were just too many unknowns for Day's liking. Historical research was much less difficult, he thought crossly.

"Did that article in the newspaper say if the police from Athens have arrived?" asked Helen.

"It didn't say. That's Cristopoulos's problem! Are you hungry? I'm looking forward to something tasty."

They found their favourite table occupied when they arrived at O Thanasis. From their new table, Helen had a view into the kitchen, where large pans were steaming on the hob. It was a shame, she reflected, that she wasn't very hungry.

"I don't need a big meal tonight, Martin," she warned him as he scanned the menu.

"Me neither. Let's have a few bits and pieces between us. What do you fancy? Maybe some aubergine? There's an aubergine dip, or fried aubergine slices?"

"Either."

"And what about the little meatballs? They're light."

"OK. And some gigantes, the giant beans. I fancy comfort food."

"Fine. Oh, and chips."

Vangelis came to the table confidently with no notebook, bringing their bread and bottled water. Helen did the ordering and Vangelis asked if they would like red wine from the barrel as usual. He had guessed correctly and soon returned with the jug and two small glasses.

"Are you going to talk to the police tomorrow, Martin?"

' don't think so. They know where I am. I want to get on with my
I as work, but I checked again this afternoon and the house is still
c sed. So I might pop to Paros and check an inscription there. We
c ild take the ferry in the morning, unless you want to stay here and
v rk? We could see the museum and walk round the craft shops in
t old town, have some fun. I feel like being a carefree tourist for
a afternoon. And on the way home we can call at the supermarket
a d stock up. We need to replenish supplies."

14

The next morning, very early, Day was tired and moody. He declared an interest in eating breakfast, a meal he only enjoyed when he was hung over. Unfortunately there was no time because their ferry left early. Paros was the first port of call for the ferries leaving Naxos on their way to the mainland.

They drove to the port, parked the Fiat on the main road, and crossed the busy street to the Blue Star Ferries office. Having acquired tickets on the Blue Star Naxos to Paros departing at nine thirty, they settled for a coffee in one of the port-side cafés. Fortunately the sailing to Paros would take only forty-five minutes. Day was a reluctant sailor.

The ship was not full and they found comfortable seats. Before Day could become queasy, Paros appeared on the starboard side, its harbour one of the prettiest in the Cyclades, with a white windmill near the disembarkation point. There were a great many people at the port to meet the boat. Most of the other ferry passengers dragged suitcases and were hunting for taxis, or were being met by family or hoteliers. Day and Helen, no bags between them, left them behind and soon the pedestrian shopping lanes of Parikia, the island's main town, enfolded them.

Day had recovered his energy and enthusiasm, possibly because he was again on dry land.

"Too late for breakfast," he announced breezily, "especially if we want a nice fish lunch. How about a stroll through the shopping lanes? The museum will close at three, so we'd better go there before lunch."

"Is there something special you need to do at the museum?"

"No. The inscription I want to check is on a stone that's been incorporated into a house wall just beyond the museum, but we can have a browse inside while we're here. Have you been before?"

"Yes, years ago. I remember the open area at the front, with the mosaic and grave sculptures, and some things inside that I liked."

"We shall have a good look round. But first, the shops!"

***

The narrow lanes of old Parikia were already full of visitors. As it wasn't yet mid-day, the lanes were sunny on one side and shady on the other. A range of jewellery, shoes, handicrafts and clothes were displayed outside the shops. Some vendors hovered encouragingly, while others waited in the cool interior like spiders. Older women sat on wooden chairs on the shaded side of the lane, or under awnings, drinking coffee or chatting to a friend. A shop selling traditional woven goods caught Day's eye, and Helen found a shop selling hand-made, brightly-glazed pottery. They enjoyed being tourists under no pressure to buy.

Leaving the shops, they walked towards the largest church in the town, the one known as the Church of a Hundred Doors. A sign pointed past it to the Archaeological Museum of Paros. The heat was reflecting up from the glazed pavement and off the elaborately buttressed church. They passed the school playground and the museum entrance and, at a house wall further up the hill, Day pulled back the leaves of a jasmine and showed Helen the inscription he had come to revisit. He took a photo of it with his phone.

"Good, that's what I thought," he said mysteriously. "This inscription isn't written up, so don't tell anyone. Let's go to the museum now, shall we?"

The front courtyard of the Paros Museum had not changed since Helen's last visit. There were column drums, statue bases, urns and funerary statues round the walls, and a Roman floor mosaic occupied the central space. Inside, in the coolness of the museum's two spacious rooms, they wandered separately. Day had changed back into a historian, silently studying each object like a mildly interesting acquaintance who has just said something surprising.

Helen was looking at the decorated amphorae, contentedly choosing her favourite, when she heard voices at the ticket window. Day looked up in displeasure, but then he started to smile. He came over to Helen.

"That tour guide over there is my mad friend Paul. Come and meet him."

Once the tour group were inside, Day walked over to Paul and introduced Helen. She thought Paul looked like a student who had never quite grown up. He was probably Day's age, about forty, but lacked a sense of having arrived where he wanted to be. A cheerful man, his sleeves rolled up, full of enthusiasm and goodwill, he seemed to be adored by his tour group. His pale skin, which matched his curly red hair and beard, was turning pink in the early season sun.

' Martin, fancy seeing you twice in one week! What are you doing
on Paros?"

" The same as you, I suspect. Visiting the museum."

" Sorry I haven't been in touch to fix up that drink. This group's really
keen, they take up all my time, literally all of it. But I'll be back on
Naxos soon, so I'll call you."

" I'm up for it whenever. You're doing OK then?"

" Never busier, and it's only May. This will help pay the overdraft on
the boat!"

***

The taverna they chose for lunch was a psarotaverna, a fish restaurant,
but it looked quieter than the popular seafood restaurants along the
shoreline. This place was some way out of town and Greek families
were eating inside. Day and Helen also chose a table in the cool interior.
Immaculately scrubbed wood characterised the place, and a quiet
buzz arose from the diners. The waiter came to their table promptly.

" Good afternoon, what can I get you?"

" What do you have today?"

" We have squid, octopus, bream, small fish, whatever you want." The
waiter sounded rather bored.

" OK," said Day. "What would you choose for your mother?"

The waiter smiled as if this were the most normal question in the
world. "A plate of baby squid and then the barbounia. Freshly caught
this morning."

"That sounds good, we'll have a portion of each and a portion of fried potatoes. And a large bottle of water."

There was a considerable wait until the food arrived, during which time Day finished the bread. When the squid and fish arrived, with more bread, the curly baby squid, fried in a light batter, was crisp and succulent, and the small pink barbounia, attractively laid on an oval dish, were grilled, lightly salted and drizzled with oil, and needed nothing else to make them perfect.

Finally, a minute or two after they had finished the fish, the fried potatoes were brought to their table. This was Day's ideal hang-over remedy. He did them justice, sat back, and finally felt better.

Helen eased back her chair, wiped her fingers on the serviette, and crossed her legs comfortably.

"That was an excellent fish lunch. Now, why don't you tell me more about Paul."

"We were students together at Cambridge; we both did Classics. After graduation we went different ways. We didn't have that much in common really, and even within the subject our interests were different. Paul had no idea what he wanted to do with his life. I didn't hear from him for fifteen years or so, until I came across him doing the business he's doing now."

"Tour guiding?"

"Yes, well specifically he led cultural tours of Greece. He worked for several different companies. He'd work in the summer season mostly, as there was much less demand in the winter. I used to bump into him on sites around Greece, gamely lecturing to his wealthy clients. He has his own boat and his own tour company now. Maybe that will work out better for him."

'Does he have a partner?"

'Not that I know of. It's hardly a settled lifestyle."

'Does he live in Greece?"

'I don't actually know. Perhaps I'll find out when we meet up for a drink."

'His life sounds as if it could be ideal, or it could be a nightmare," remarked Helen.

15

"Utterly frustrating!"

Day closed his mobile with a snap.

"What did they say?"

"They can't tell me when the Elias house will be open again. Petros Tsifas is still away and they have no idea when he'll return. All the Tourist Information office can say is that they'll call me when they hear from him."

"Look, shall we get out of the house for a while?" said Helen. "I fancy taking the camera out, exploring a bit. Would you like to come with me?"

"Might as well. Do you have anywhere in mind? We could go and see the last kouros, perhaps. It's not far, just near Melanes, and the landscape around there is stunning. There are hills, dry stone walls, terracing, and some nice long views."

' ounds good. I can be ready in fifteen minutes."

***

The road to Melanes was the same as they had taken when they visited the Sanctuary at Flerio. They parked the Fiat next to the only other car, a rental Fiat 500, and took the track towards the last of Naxos's famous kouroi. The morning was warm and the air clear. The low sun still created shadows across a landscape usually bleached by sunshine, and clouds flowed languidly across the sky from the distant and invisible sea. The countryside here was a rolling, rock-strewn wildness of grass, spiky flowers and scrubby vegetation. Haphazard old stone walls in an advanced state of disrepair failed to provide any sense of order but bore witness to a vanished past.

The path rose steadily, overhung in places by wind-wizened trees that nobody tended. Day took the steps two at a time. He was looking forward to reaching this final kouros. He remembered it clearly from previous visits. It was isolated far from human habitation, abandoned near the place where it had been hewn from the hillside. It was now an attraction for visitors and historians, but it could have been so much more, had it not been deemed imperfect.

Helen, following slowly, felt she was in a forgotten part of the island, that the modern era was an irrelevance here. The huge rocks, stone walls, and thickets of scrub were somehow outside time. The hills were quiet, as if the birds had found easier places to live.

Ahead of her, Day had stopped to savour the solitude, the silence, the timelessness of the place. In the shade of an old, neglected tree that stretched over the pathway, he sat watching Helen taking photographs. He loved this island. This part of Naxos spoke to him as if from the heart of antiquity. To the west, the rolling hills climbed from level to level, scrubby denseness changing to open grass and then to rock. Sun fell on it all, as if to unite the past and the present. Day was content.

He had everything he needed for the moment: a good companion, the wild landscape, and a hint of antiquity.

A noise on the path above him interrupted his thoughts. There was a man coming down the path from the kouros, carefully minding his step. The man passed Day without a word or glance, and Day likewise offered the stranger no greeting and quickly forgot him.

Helen was looking intently towards the hills. After the man had gone past, small stones slipping with him down the path, she called to Day. She wore an expression so preoccupied that he remembered it afterwards.

"I'm going over there to take a photograph, Martin. Look!"

Turning away, she followed a track through the grass. She was walking towards a single-storey building with a primitive flat roof, abandoned and almost a ruin. It had been roughly built using large chunks of local stone, and only its perpendicular sides marked it out from the rock-strewn terrain. Day guessed it had been the refuge of a shepherd or goatherd. He imagined a solitary man following the traditions of his father and grandfather, following the flock across the hills and sheltering in such places as this. The contrast between this and his own twenty-first century life was sobering.

The stone hut had a narrow opening for a front entrance and no door. There were no windows either, which made it a better shelter during the windy season. Helen switched her camera to its monochrome setting, capturing the way the stones of the walls blended with the rocks of the hillside. Day watched her lazily, still deep in his own thoughts. She disappeared into the hut. After a few moments, Day decided to follow her. He found her inside, standing in silence and near darkness.

thing could have prepared Helen for this. She felt frozen, incapable
moving or even speaking. She heard Day enter the hut behind
but didn't turn round. He said nothing at first, and when he did
speak his voice sounded strange.

need to find a signal and call the police. Come outside with me,
Helen."

"One of us needs to stay with him," she managed to say.

Day left the hut quietly and the sound of his footsteps faded. The
body was only a few feet from Helen, lying on its back on the hard
earth floor of the hut. She tried to make it out more clearly as her eyes
became accustomed to the darkness, but she couldn't make herself
closer. It was a man, and he looked quite young. She knew he was
dead, but there was a peacefulness about him. She heard flies. She
began to realise there was a smell, faint but unpleasant. She knew she
must wait for Martin and the police, and stay with the body.

Panic and horror were beginning to overcome her when there was a
movement behind her. Day put his arm round her shoulders, a firm
and reassuring arm. "Police on their way," he said. "Come on."

He helped her outside. She leaned against Day feeling dizzy. It was
bizarre, she could only see in black and white, so the sky was white,
the hills were a palette of dark greys, and the rocks were monochrome,
etched and sinister. Even Martin was colourless. She sat on the
ground and put her head between her knees. The spinning in her
head seemed part of some strange spell that had drawn her towards
the hut and its silent occupant.

Time passed slowly. First one of them then the other spoke platitudes
that were comforting. There was nothing to do but be patient and
wait. It was nearly forty minutes before the police arrived. Inspector
Cristopoulos walked ahead of the group that approached from the

direction of the car park. Their arrival destroyed the peacefulness, the solemnity of the place.

Cristopoulos tried to be sensitive. The isolated location, the body in the dark building, the couple sitting silently waiting, impressed him.

"I'm sorry for your shock," he began. "May I speak to you, please? I'm afraid I must ask you a few questions right away. When did you find the body?"

"Just before I called you. Forty-five minutes ago. We came to see the kouros, but we stopped first by this little shelter, and Helen …"

"I was taking photographs. I was drawn to it," she said.

"Which of you entered the building first?"

"I did, then Martin followed."

"Have you touched the body? How far inside did you walk?"

"We only went just inside the entrance, and we didn't touch anything."

"Did you see anyone else nearby?"

"There was one man," Day recalled. "He was going downhill from the kouros towards the car park."

"I see. Could you describe him?"

Day ran his hand across his eyes. "Perhaps…"

"It would be better to talk at the station," said Cristopoulos. "I suggest you follow me in your car. Are you safe to drive? Good. Let's get Miss Aitchison away from here."

He turned away to give orders to his men, then beckoned Day and Helen to join him on the path away from the stone hut.

16

As they were driving towards Chora following the inspector's car, several police vehicles passed them heading out towards Melanes, probably the scene of crime team, if there was one on the island, or a doctor. For the first time Day parked the Fiat right outside the police station. Ordering a young policeman to fetch coffee from the nearby café, Cristopoulos led Day and Helen to his office and pointed them to the chairs facing his desk. They made small talk for a few minutes, waiting for a uniformed officer to take a seat at the back of the room to take notes. The Inspector then pursed his lips and looked at them frankly.

"I appreciate you're in a state of shock, but regrettably I need to ask you some more questions right away."

"Of course."

"Firstly, tell me how you came to be in the hut."

' 'e wanted to visit the Melanes kouros and for Helen to do some
ı otography. We never actually reached the kouros. Halfway up the
s ps Helen noticed the stone hut."

' /as there anything unusual about the building?"

' .o," answered Helen. "It was just interesting, I was curious. I went
iı ide and Martin followed me after a minute or two."

' nd what did you see, Miss Aitchison, when you entered? I'm sorry
t ask, but please try to recall every detail."

' was exactly as you saw it when you arrived. He was on his back,
a d his hands were folded on his chest. His head was furthest from
t ˸ door, away from me. He was clearly dead but I couldn't see any
c ıse of death. He looked quite young."

' /ere his eyes open or closed?"

' .. I'm sorry, I'm not sure. It was dark, but I think they were closed.
˥ ere was hardly any light inside that place."

' see. What else was in the hut, apart from the body?"

' .othing else. Nothing that I could see."

' fartin, you followed Miss Aitchison into the place?"

' es. When she didn't come back out I went to find her."

' low long was it between her entering the building and you joining
ł ˸?"

' wo or three minutes. Maybe five."

"And what did you see when you entered?"

"Well, when I stood in the doorway it blocked out any light from outside. There are no windows in the hut, so I just saw Helen at first. She was standing inside the door with her back to me. When I moved round a little I saw the body."

"Do you agree with Miss Aitchison's description of the appearance of the body? And there was nothing else in the place?"

"Yes. The hut was really empty, like it was swept clean. The man was just lying there on his back."

"You said you saw a man walking down the steps from the kouros. When was that?"

"Oh, that was before we went into the hut."

"I see. Can either of you describe him?"

Helen shook her head without looking up at the inspector. "By the time the man came round the bend in the steps, my mind was set on the hut. I assumed he was a tourist."

"Martin? What do you remember of him?"

"Just dark-coloured trousers and some kind of beige jacket, like a summer anorak. I took him for Greek. Middle aged. He didn't say anything to us. It must have been his car we saw in the car park, a rented Fiat 500, light blue. The logo of the hire company was green and red."

"And you're sure you touched nothing, and left nothing behind?"

"Absolutely. I left at once to call you. Helen?"

' stayed inside while Martin went to call you, but I touched nothing. Then we both went outside."

' hank you. Now, I've arranged for some coffee, so I suggest you go and sit in the front office while you drink it. I need you to remain in the station while my officer types up your statements, and sign them before you go. I'll need to speak to you again."

" Of course, Inspector," said Day, "and thank you for your kindness with the coffee. But perhaps later or tomorrow we could have a word? I have something else to tell you regarding the death of Dr Moralis."

As Cristopoulos had also arranged coffee for himself, the three of them stayed where they were and the young officer left to type up the statements. Cristopoulos sipped his coffee gratefully. He looked even more weary than usual, and leaned heavily on his desk.

" Mrs Moralis has arrived to make arrangements for her husband's body to be taken back to America," he said soberly. "They've only been married for a couple of years. She hasn't been able to tell us why her husband was here. I believe she didn't even know he meant to come to Naxos."

" Poor woman," Helen said, looking up from her lap for the first time. "I hope she's been spared the rumour about her husband and this Katherine Russell?"

" I'm afraid that's been in the newspapers, so she's probably heard about it. Katherine Russell is still missing and we need to find her. The investigation into the death of Dr Moralis is now out of my hands, of course. The Athens police are on Naxos and have taken charge. They believe the murder is linked to a group of antiquities smugglers they've been tracking for many months."

"You mean, the kind of thing that Emil Gautier is supposed to do?" Day asked.

"I believe so, Martin. Inspector Andreas Nomikos of Athens keeps his cards very close to his chest."

"Well, what I wanted to tell you concerns Gautier. On Wednesday Helen and I went to see the sanctuary at Flerio. We met an old local woman there, she sells refreshments and local produce. She told us about a certain Frenchman who had offended her by wanting to buy old artefacts. She was very keen to tell me that she knew it was illegal. She mentioned that the man was staying near Apollonas, so we decided to go there and ask around. We got lucky, a Frenchman matching the old woman's description was pointed out to us in Apollonas, and he was talking to a man with an American accent. We couldn't hear what they said, unfortunately. I know it might be a coincidence, but we thought they might be Emil Gautier and Jim Grogan."

Cristopoulos steepled his stubby fingers and pressed them on his eyes.

"But surely, Martin, there are many French and American men having coffee together on Naxos at any one time? What makes you think these men are connected to Dr Moralis?"

"It's a long shot," Day conceded.

"Even if it was the man described by the old woman, you must realise that half our tourists hope to pick up a Cycladic figurine while they're here. I'm afraid you'd better leave the police work to us, Martin, or rather to the men from Athens. I'll send one of my officers to Apollonas to make enquiries, but I'm afraid from now on I'll have my hands full with the body in the stone hut, which falls to me to investigate."

17

Το Ναξιακό

The Naxian Newspaper

A SECOND MURDER, AND A BRITISH WOMAN VANISHES

Another murder victim has been discovered near Melanes, and a British woman has disappeared. Inspector Cristopoulos of Naxos Police said:

'The body of a man was discovered yesterday in a traditional shepherd's hut a few kilometres from Melanes. We are trying to establish the victim's identity, the cause and time of his death, and his recent movements. The victim was in his thirties and may be a local man. His death probably occurred about a week ago. The police urgently want to hear from anyone with information that would assist them in their investigation.'

The police investigating the recent murder of American archaeologist, Dr Michael K. Moralis, have released more information and issued an appeal for information concerning a missing British woman connected to their enquiries.

Inspector Andreas Nomikos of the Athens Police said that Dr Moralis was stabbed to death in his hotel room at the Hotel Philippos, where there was no sign of a struggle. His widow, Mrs Nancy Moralis, has arrived on Naxos to make arrangements for the return of her husband's body to Massachusetts as soon as the authorities release it.

There is no suggestion that the victim was in a relationship with British university teacher Dr Katherine Russell, who was also staying at the Hotel Philippos, who has disappeared. The police are concerned for her safety, and are appealing to anyone with information concerning the lady to contact them.

The Athens police believe that the murder of Dr Moralis may be connected to a criminal network of international antiquities smugglers who are thought to be active in Greece, and whose activities Dr Moralis may have accidentally discovered.

18

Day and Helen sat at Café Ta Xromata reading the newspaper over coffee. It seemed hard to believe that only yesterday they had found the body in the stone hut. Day was aware that Helen had not said a word about it since they had left the police station. He had no idea whether to encourage her to talk or not. She didn't seem to want to, but not discussing it seemed unhealthy to Day.

They picked up a few groceries in the local shop and began the walk back to the house. Day's mobile rang. It was Petros Tsifas, the curator of the Nikos Elias Museum, who apologised for the inconvenience caused by his absence and invited Day over the following morning. A private visit on a Sunday, he said, would allow time for Kyrie Day to examine the material while the house was still closed to visitors. Day fixed an appointment for eleven o'clock, pocketed the phone and shifted a carrier bag of food back to his right hand.

"That was Petros Tsifas," he said to Helen. "You probably heard, I'm going to meet him tomorrow at the Elias place. Well, that's something. Maybe we can move on now. It'll be good to start work at last."

"Why don't I come with you in the car, and while you visit the museum I'll go to the taverna? I fancy doing a bit of sketching. I might even take my watercolours. Then we can have lunch and you can tell me all about the house."

"That's a good idea. You probably need some time to get over the shock of yesterday. Sketching sounds just the thing." Day glanced at her, but she was looking elsewhere. "Oh, work at last, something I can get my teeth into! No more about murders, the police can deal with it all."

Helen nodded, keeping her eyes on the pavement ahead. "Did you ever contact your friend from the British Museum? Alex?" she asked.

"No, I still need to do that. I'll give him a call when we get home. Ha, 'home'. I do like to say that about my Naxian house."

***

Day found Alex's mobile number and took the phone onto the balcony. It was eleven thirty in the morning Greek time, so half past nine in London. That would be OK on a Saturday. Alex was not a man to lie in bed.

"Alex? It's Martin Day. I'm absolutely fine thanks. Good. Yes, I'm calling from my new house on Naxos! Yes! I finally shelled out the money. You must come and stay, any time you like. I'll be here till September at least this year.

"What? You're *here*? Where? Well, grab a taxi and come for lunch. Seriously. So much to talk about. Ask the taxi to drive through Filoti village, I'm the last house on the road out towards Apeiranthos. Green shutters. You'll see my car, a white Fiat 500. Call me if you can't find it. Right, see you soon. Bye."

Helen, who had heard Day's side of the call, was staring in surprise.

"He's here on Naxos?"

"Yes. He's staying in Agia Anna. You heard, I think, he's coming over. "

"I better throw some lunch together. At least we just bought food."

"Don't worry, it must be my turn to fix the food. I reckon it'll take him forty-five minutes to get here anyway. My God, Helen, what's Alex doing on Naxos? What's going on? Surely Alex isn't involved in all this? There are far too many coincidences for my liking."

***

An hour later, a text alerted Day to Alex's arrival. He was on the road outside, keeping the taxi in case he was in the wrong place. Day strode through the house to the door and pulled it open. On seeing his old friend, Day's shoulders softened and he grinned.

"Really good to see you, Alex! This really is the most tremendous surprise. You must tell me all about it."

"You're not the only one to be surprised. When did you buy this house? You've managed all these years in a studio apartment in Athens, so what changed? It's great!"

"All in good time! Come in, and meet another good friend of mine from England. Alex, this is Helen; Helen, this is Alex."

They sat round the balcony table with cheese, olives, salad and bread, sharing a bottle of white wine from the neighbouring island of Syros. Pigeons often landed on the cane canopy but flew off again when anyone moved. A rich smell of cut grass was wafting up from the valley, and in the garden below them the neighbour was working among his vegetables. His dog ran from time to time to the end of its rope, barked for no reason and retired to its kennel in the shade.

"This is idyllic," Alex said.

"So, when was the last time we met, Alex?"

"Must have been over a year ago, when you came to the BM to look at that bequest. I remember an excellent and very boozy meal somewhere in King's Cross."

"Good times. So what brings you to Naxos now? When did you arrive?"

"I came via Athens, popped into the British School, mooched about there for a few days before coming here. We're trying to arrange an exhibition on Cycladic culture to take place at the BM the year after next. My boss thought it would be useful if I came in person to ease the way a bit. I came to Naxos because we're hoping to negotiate the loan of the Naxos Museum's collection of Cycladic figurines for a period of two months. Of course, the Museum of Naxos is likely to resist this, it would be tantamount to emptying their best display cabinets. So I'm here to discuss whether some exchange of artefacts would make the proposal more palatable."

"You could lend them the Parthenon Sculptures perhaps?" Day suggested mischievously.

"Ha! The Director had in mind some Mycenaean items I could sort out for them that would complement the good pieces they already have here. I'm not at all confident, as you can imagine, Martin. I don't suppose you know the curator, by any chance?"

"Actually, he's a good friend. I'll introduce you. His name's Aristos Iraklidis, he's a really nice man, extremely knowledgeable. You haven't arranged to meet him yet, then?"

' ot yet. I've been having a bit of a holiday. Perhaps when I go to
s Iraklidis you might be able to join us? I'd be very grateful."

' ll think about it. I'm going to be very busy with a project of my
c n. You might be interested, in fact…."

***

' e lunch period passed smoothly as they caught up with news. Then
t shutters in the houses of Filoti began to close as people retired
f the siesta, and Alex phoned for a taxi.

' ood luck with your Nikos Elias project, Martin, and I'll speak to
y 1 soon about fixing up to meet the Curator. Thanks for an excellent
l ch, good to see you again. It was a real pleasure to meet you, Helen.
l ope the island inspires a wonderful novel."

\ 1en the front door closed after Alex, Day and Helen returned to
t balcony. Helen was the first to speak, reservation in her voice.

' ovely man. I wish we'd met up under different circumstances."

' know what you mean."

' 'hat puzzles me is why Alex hasn't arranged to meet Aristos already.
I 's been on Naxos a week."

' wondered about that too, Helen, although he did say he was having
a oliday. And, nothing at all against Agia Anna, but why not stay in a
I tel in Chora? The BM must be paying. Why stay in a beach resort
f away from the Naxos Museum?"

' ossibly for the wonderful tavernas in Agia Anna and the great
I ach! It is a bit odd, though. Alex didn't seem in any rush, maybe
t it accounts for it."

"Mmm. I hope to God nothing sinister's going on. I like Alex. Did you notice he didn't make any reference to Michael's death? It's been in the papers. They must have known about each other, possibly they even met. They were really counterparts in the UK and the US. And let's not forget Alex's name on Michael's computer."

"To be fair, we didn't bring up Michael's death either, Martin."

"That was deliberate - I was waiting to see if Alex would."

19

They arrived at Paralia Votsala just in time for Day's appointment at the Elias house at eleven, so to his chagrin he had no time for a coffee at the taverna. Helen got out of the car at the T-junction and started to walk towards the taverna with her bag of art materials, and Day turned the Fiat in the other direction to negotiate the ruts in the road towards the white house.

Helen felt her spirits lift as she sat enjoying the quietness of the taverna and the steady blue water beyond. There was barely a breeze, only the smallest ripple tickled the stoney beach. She could hear the sound of distant goat bells, and so quiet was it that she heard Day turn off the car engine and close his door at the other end of the bay.

She was the only customer at the taverna. Cushions in bright colours had been placed on the chairs and wicker sofas since their last visit, their pink and lilac shades striking an unusual note in Greece but reflecting the move to modernisation that she was noticing across Naxos. On each table was a pink and lilac flowerpot containing a miniature olive tree six inches tall. She gave Vasilios her coffee order and opened her bag, laying out a sketch pad and pencils on the table.

When Vasilios brought her coffee, they started to chat until eventually he pulled out a chair from the adjacent table and sat with her. She was pleased enough to be distracted. In the week or more since her last visit, he told her, he had seen an improvement in the number of their visitors, and that evening he was expecting a large group of people who had booked for dinner. Already there was a new resident in their accommodation, an American who had taken a room for an unlimited period. It was a positive sign, perhaps the season would be a good one for the tourist industry after all.

They talked of recent lean years when Greece had been affected by everything from the world financial crisis to mass migration, both of which had led to a serious reduction in visitors to all the islands. Characteristically, Vasilios ended on a positive note.

"But here on Naxos we are fortunate. It's a lucky island and always has been. Our visitors have returned."

At this moment a man in a floral shirt and dark chinos walked across the far end of the terrace, stepped onto the beach, and headed towards the low headland to their right. He wore sunglasses and a white cap. Vasilios waved and called to him, but the man gave no sign of having heard.

"That's our American visitor. Every day he walks on the beach on his own. He seems to enjoy the sea and the quietness. He sometimes goes off in a taxi, but he's never gone for more than an hour. I think he's a man who seeks the true peacefulness of our island. He told us that he works in marine ecology, but he doesn't say a lot."

Helen stared after the American. She hadn't seen his face, but something about his build and his clothes made Helen think of the man in Apollonas who had been talking to the Frenchman. What should she do? Vasilios excused himself and returned to the taverna. The American was now out of sight beyond the headland. Helen made

ecision. Leaving her bag on the chair, she got up and followed in
direction the American had taken.

the headland she had a choice. She could either clamber over the
ks to get round the headland, which looked precarious, or scale the
pe to the top in the hope of seeing the American on the further
e. Neither option appealed to her. She turned back and retraced
steps along the beach to the taverna, occasionally looking over
shoulder. She reasoned that the man would return to his lodgings
some point. She would be waiting.

***

y arrived looking excited, despite having spent less than an hour
d a half with Petros Tsifas looking round the Elias house.

's really promising. Petros is very pleased that I'm taking an interest
Nikos and his work, and he's given me free rein of the house and
rary. I can visit whenever I want. The story is that he and Elias got
ether almost as soon as Petros arrived on Naxos. Elias was older
n him, and they always planned that Petros would look after Nikos's
acy eventually, but sadly Elias died quite young, in his early fifties. I
n't yet have a feel for how much material there is or how valuable
vill be, but there's more than enough to interest me for now, and
'll see where it leads. The library's amazing. Elias must have been
lecting it all his adult life. There are some rare things, some things
u would never otherwise find, long out of print. The books cover
as's interests in antiquity and the modern history of the Cyclades.
ere's also a folder of stories dictated to him by islanders from all
lks of life, all in his own handwriting."

there a collection of artefacts?"

its and pieces. I wouldn't say the things I saw this morning would
ticularly attract international antiquities smugglers. Of course, it's

possible Petros has more valuable things in safe keeping somewhere, and I wouldn't expect him to show me anything like that on our first meeting. There's some jewellery that looks a hundred years old or so, and some household and farming implements, nothing interesting, to me at least. I'll dig about a bit more over the next few weeks. How has your morning been?"

"I've got something to tell you. I think I saw Jim Grogan!"

"What?"

"I chatted to Vasilios, who said that business was picking up, and that he's just got his first house guest, an American who arrived since we were last here. He told Vasilios that he works in marine ecology. Just as Vasilios was telling me this, the man appeared and walked straight past us and off down the beach. Martin, he had the same build and wore the same type of clothes as our American in Apollonas, the one talking with the Frenchman. He even walked in the same way."

"It doesn't mean he's Grogan."

"I know, but he did look very similar. I actually followed him down the beach, but I never caught up with him."

"I think that's probably a good thing."

"So you agree he's a suspicious character?"

"Well, …"

"Also, this man sometimes gets a taxi to take him somewhere for an hour, according to Vasilios. That fits with our man in Apollonas, doesn't it?"

"You'll be telling me next that he wore sunglasses."

")K, point taken."

" hall we see what Maroula's lunch menu looks like?"

N iroula brought them her standard menu, typed on a piece of A4. A
c ick scan of it told Day there were toasted sandwiches, omelettes,
s ighetti and pizza. He stopped reading; by now he had lost interest.
N iroula gave him a smile of approval.

" ou should come into the kitchen and see what I'm cooking. I can
r ike you fish baked in tomato sauce, and I have fresh anchovies
c)ked on the grill, I have stuffed aubergines and peppers, and my
c 'n salads."

] is sounded much more promising. Day and Helen colluded in a
c ick glance and asked what the fish was. The woman gave a happy
l le shrug.

")me bream, a little grouper, I bought what I liked from today's
c ch."

" xcellent, we'll have a portion of fish, please, whatever you choose,
a l a few anchovies and a salad. And a large bottle of water. Thank
y l!"

***

I vas home-made food to savour: fresh fish and fresh vegetables, eaten
a :one's throw from the sea. Soon the handful of lunch guests had gone
a l Maroula and Vasilios were eating their own lunch inside. Just as
I y and Helen were thinking of leaving, Vasilios came over and asked
i they would care to join his wife and him for coffee as their guests.
\ ien they were settled together, Vasilios began polite conversation.

")id you find Kyrie Tsifas helpful this morning?"

"He's been extremely kind, and already I've seen much to interest me in the house. I'll need to visit many times, I think."

"I hope we have the pleasure of the Kyria's company while you're working. My wife and I hope to be characters in her next book!"

Day smiled. "I'm sure we'll see a lot of you this summer. I'm planning to work on Nikos Elias's papers, and I hope it may lead to a biography. Elias's work should be more widely known, and it's what Petros wants. Elias was an important twentieth-century Naxian, and I'd be happy if I can help make him better known."

A companionable silence fell. Legs were stretched, sighs heaved, and they smiled into the sun which was beginning to shimmer in the slight haze over the sea. It would soon be the quiet time of the afternoon when everyone took their rest. Vasilios broke the silence, this time in a sombre tone.

"It's terrible news about the poor man who was found dead near Melanes. People are talking in the villages. The police say he may have been local. Somebody must know who he was. Men don't just disappear for a week without someone noticing."

His wife disagreed. "That's not quite true, Vasili. What about the men who go off on the ferry to the mainland on some business or other, and nobody counts the time they're gone?"

"True enough, but if he was an island man, he'll soon be missed, you can be sure."

Day made a decision. "Let's hope so," he said. "Actually, it was we who found the body."

The Greek couple immediately exclaimed in sympathy and Maroula went to put on more coffee. A new bond had been formed, no nger hosts and guests but friends. Such a discovery must be one of the worst moments in a person's life, Maroula exclaimed when she returned. They all took comfort in the fresh coffee. Vasilios made an eloquent gesture of despair.

"As if one tragedy was not enough, there was that poor American who was murdered in the Philippos Hotel. What a terrible thing! Even the Athens Police have come to the island now. I read in the newspaper they suspect the murder was to do with antiquities smuggling, is that right? Some sort of Mafia group perhaps? Nothing like that has ever happened here, not in my lifetime. It's unbelievable."

Maroula touched her husband's arm to calm him. "The American who was killed in Chora has a Greek surname," she observed to Day. "I wondered if that was important in some way. What do you think, Vasili?"

"In America there are lots of people with Greek surnames, my dear. I don't think that will have anything to do with it. He was a professor from an American university, wasn't he, Martin?"

"That's right. In fact, I met him once in New York. It was the year before last. I went and talked to the police when we read about his death in the paper. We've been trying to understand what could have happened. It may even be possible that your American visitor is connected in some way."

"Panagia mou!" exclaimed Maroula.

"Don't worry, Maroula, we don't know for certain. What's the name of your visitor?"

Vasilios looked distressed and alarmed.

"He said his name was John Gregory and that he comes from Seattle. I didn't see his passport. Just between ourselves, Martin, I keep out of the way of the authorities. Not just for tax reasons. They want to examine all your facilities, force you to make changes, stick up ugly signs, tell you what to charge. I've never registered as offering accommodation, so I don't have to submit photocopies of our guests's passports. In fact, I don't often ask to see them. What would be the point?"

Day's eyebrows rose fractionally. "So, if he wanted to give you a false name, he could. Same initials too, Helen .... "

"Look, I'll keep an eye on the man, Martin, and let you know if anything funny happens. May I have your phone number?"

"Of course, I'll give it to you now, Vasili. And don't worry. He's probably just a simple tourist."

20

Το Ναξιακό

The Naxian Newspaper

WOMAN'S BODY DISCOVERED NEAR MELANES

The body of a young woman has been found by police in a shallow grave near Melanes. It is the third body to have been discovered in suspicious circumstances on Naxos this month.

The woman, who is said to have been in her early twenties at the time of her death, was found only days after a man's body was discovered by tourists in the same location last Friday. Both bodies were concealed inside a stone shepherd's hut in the hills near the famous 'Kouros of Melanes'.

A police spokesman said: 'The female skeleton, which has been buried for as long as 20 years, might never have been discovered if not for forensic examination of the scene in connection with the other victim to be found in this location.'

Police have not revealed further details of the bodies, other than to say that they are treating the deaths as suspicious, and are appealing for information regarding the identity of the two victims.

Naxos Police have recently been joined by a distinguished team of detectives from the Athenian police, who are leading the investigation into the murder of American academic, Dr Michael K. Moralis, two weeks ago in Chora.

The unprecedented series of tragedies which Naxos has witnessed in the last fortnight is truly a matter of the greatest concern. *The Naxian* has opened a telephone line for anyone with information, or in need of support.

21

Day and Helen had driven for coffee in Chora. They had parked the car near the port, taken a pleasant stroll through the town and sat down to relax for half an hour at the Café Kitron before going home. The Café Kitron belonged to the producers of the island's famous liqueur of the same name. The outdoor seating was pleasant and the coffee was excellent. Day sipped his frappé appreciatively, and Helen drank her cappuccino quickly to enjoy its warmth. She watched the passers-by while Day looked at his phone.

At the table to Day's left a man opened his newspaper and Day noticed the headline. He went and bought a copy from the local vendor and placed it in front of Helen theatrically, throwing himself back down into his chair.

"When will this end?" he said, trying to keep his voice down. She read the article.

"What next, Martin? Three deaths on an island where you would scarcely expect a broken window."

"Twenty years separates this dead woman from our man in the hut and Michael, but they have to be connected."

"What possible link could there be between Michael and the two bodies out near Melanes, which are presumably local anyway, when there's no connection between Michael and anybody on the island?"

"No idea. I even feel quite sorry for Inspector Cristopoulos."

With remarkable timing, Day's mobile rang.

"Inspector! How are you? Mmm, yes, of course. We're in Chora at the moment, in fact. Half an hour is fine. Goodbye."

He closed his phone and felt in his jacket pocket for change to pay for their coffee.

"You got that, I suppose? Cristopoulos wants to see me as soon as possible in his office. I've said we'll be there in about half an hour."

Day's phone beeped an alert and Day flipped it open.

"Text from Vasilios," he said. "Apparently there was a scene last night at the taverna. A Greek man and John Gregory had dinner together and it turned into a blazing row."

"So he does know someone on Naxos," she observed.

***

Cristopoulos rose from his chair to half standing, while politely removing his reading glasses. He gave a smile which Day hoped indicated that he wasn't on the shortlist of suspects. The Inspector passed one hand over his hair and extended the other to shake hands in a single, smooth gesture before retaking his seat.

" hank you for coming in. Do take a seat."

" /e've just seen this morning's 'Naxian'. Terrible news. Another
 (id body."

" 's appalling, Martin. In my seventeen years here I've never known
 a thing like it. I've asked you to come in, however, to talk about
 I Moralis. The Athens team is convinced his murder is linked to an
 a tiquities smuggling operation, as I told you. Thanks to you both,
 v have found Emil Gautier. They brought him in last night, he's
 t ng questioned about both the murder and the suspected smuggling.
 I wever, he'll be released soon for lack of evidence, that much seems
 c tain. I want to keep you involved, Martin. This business is all tied
 t with our ancient heritage: artefact thieves, hidden sanctuaries,
 a idemics. I'm out of my depth! And I don't see my colleagues
 t aking new ground either!"

I y concealed his surprise and glanced at Helen. Cristopoulos was
 a animated as Day had ever seen him.

" 's not a case of looking for the jealous husband, the angry lover,
 t : ruined business partner and so on. This is no domestic killing,"
 (istopoulos continued. "If the death of Dr Moralis is connected to
 a illegal trade in antiquities, or indeed to some venture to discover
 t ried treasure, it is you who have the knowledge and the connections
 t it could be extremely useful to us, Martin."

" hope I can live up to your expectations, Inspector. But go on."

(istopoulos sat back in his chair and drew himself up to his full
 t ght. This was not very high, but it suggested that he was settling
 i for a serious discussion.

" autier claims he's on Naxos purely for a vacation. He's staying
 i farmhouse accommodation near Apollonas. The owners didn't

register his booking and passport number as required by law, so without you we wouldn't have known he was here. Gautier claims to run a legitimate antiques business in Europe, buying and selling artefacts using private contacts. We knew this already, so he wasn't giving anything away. He claims he has always submitted a French tax return, which we're also checking. We know he arrived in Greece three weeks ago, but we have no way to investigate his movements since then. It's true, this man is an offensive individual and speaks very bad Greek. Unfortunately neither is a criminal offence. He claims not to know either Jim Grogan or Dr Moralis, and is indeed appalled that we're connecting him to a murder about which he has only read in the local newspaper."

"Mmm. Do you believe him?"

"The only thing we have that isn't pure conjecture is his name being in Dr Moralis's computer. It's clear that Moralis knew of Gautier, but impossible to prove the other way round."

"And the American, Grogan, have you traced him at all? We need to find some link between them if this is going to take us anywhere."

"There's no record of Grogan arriving here, but that doesn't mean he isn't on the island. All we have so far is his name next to Gautier's on Moralis's computer, and we know that he is a wealthy private collector, possibly one who is not deterred by scruples. So, Martin, please tell me your researches have turned up something useful."

"Actually, I have found out a few things," said Day.

The Inspector's small smile hinted at a sense of vindication. He nodded.

"Let me start with Emil Gautier. From a colleague in Paris I learned that he's a supplier of rare antiquities to wealthy private collectors, a

rative and probably illegal side to his business. A collector gives
utier a specific instruction and Gautier locates the desired artefact.
hile some of Gautier's business may be above board, some very
rative transactions are happening under the radar. Jim Grogan, by
ntrast, seems to be highly respectable. His family is very wealthy even
American standards. There's no mention of him having to earn a
ng. On the surface, he's a writer who published an account of his
periences in Turkey and Greece as a young man. I've been reliably
d that he owns a very valuable antiques collection. A contact of
ne told me that Grogan's been spreading the word that he wants to
quire a virtually unique Ancient Greek water vessel called a hydria.
e design he wants is very uncommon. Just the kind of thing that
ght connect him to someone like Gautier."

there anything to suggest they know each other?" interrupted
inspector.

ot that I'm aware, unless that was them in Apollonas last Sunday.
you know the Taverna Ta Votsala, Inspector? It's owned by friends
ours. They have an American staying there who calls himself John
egory from Seattle, but they didn't ask to see his passport. I'm
picious of this guy, it could be a false identity for Jim Grogan.
len saw him at a distance and thought it could be the same man
saw in Apollonas with the Frenchman. Just before you called me
s morning I heard from Vasilios Papathoma, the owner of the
verna Ta Votsala. Apparently a Greek joined the American for
ner at the taverna last night, and there was a heated argument."

he Taverna Ta Votsala, you say? I'll send a man over there."

e Inspector lifted the phone and gave instructions. Day wondered
w helpful the American was likely to be, before reflecting that the
eek police could be persuasive.

Cristopoulos turned back to Day. "Now, am I mistaken, or did my sergeant see you leaving the island on a ferry last Thursday, Martin?"

"Oh my God! You asked me not to leave the island. The thing is, I needed to re-visit the museum on Paros, and frankly we just wanted a change of scene ... Am I in a lot of trouble?"

"I can probably overlook it," conceded Cristopoulos sternly. "Who did you speak to on Paros? You do understand how completely confidential our conversations must remain?"

"Of course. We didn't speak to any ... oh yes, we met an old friend of mine in the museum, a tour guide by the name of Paul Metts. We just said hello, nothing confidential."

The phone rang on the desk and Cristopoulos answered it. He grunted and replaced the receiver.

"You did some interesting research there, Martin. I happen to agree with my colleague Nomikos that Dr Moralis's death will turn out to be connected to antiquities dealers in some way, and our Frenchman and American may be involved."

"With respect, Inspector, the bodies at Melanes must change everything. Three bodies in less than three weeks must be connected."

"I really don't see how they can be connected to Dr Moralis at all. Best leave everything to the police now, Martin. Your role was to help with information which you're in the best position to acquire for us, and I'm very grateful."

Day shrugged.

' discovered something new about Michael, too. I knew he was
a Mycenaean specialist, but I found out that his current sabbatical
research is the Mycenaean history of Naxos."

The Inspector's chin rose from his chest. He picked up his pen and
clicked the button on and off before slamming it back on the desk.

" That might explain his presence on the island. In fact, it adds
some weight to the possibility that he was linked with the antiquities
smugglers, I would say."

Before Day could protest, Helen interrupted.

' May I ask if the missing girl has been found, the history lecturer
from the UK?"

" I'm afraid not, Miss Aitchison. We know who she is, but not where
she is. Or why she's disappeared, or if she was here with Dr Moralis."

" So she could be a fourth victim?" Helen said. "And have you identified
the body we discovered?"

With an air of resignation Cristopoulos picked up his reading glasses,
only to fiddle with the arms as he spoke.

' The body in the stone hut belonged to a local man called Dimitris
Makris. He's thought to have been about thirty-five and lived alone
not far from the kouros in a very isolated spot. He'd lived there rather
like a hermit ever since his family emigrated without him, leaving the
island to find a better life. Nobody knows why young Dimitris didn't
go with them. We don't know very much about Dimitris Makris. People
rarely heard him talk. Local women would leave food for him on his
doorstep and the priest looked out for him. Nobody seems to have
seen him for a long time, and in fact the priest held a service several

weeks ago because there were rumours he must have drowned in the sea or be lying dead in a ditch somewhere."

"How did he die?"

"He had been stabbed in the back. Fortunately, as he was lying on his back when you found him, the wound was concealed from you."

"But his hands were folded over his chest…"

"Yes, that's very interesting. He had been turned onto his back and his arms folded. The killer could have done it, or someone who came later. We will find out in time, I trust."

Inspector Cristopoulos sighed. An air of despondency had come over him. He was talking to Helen particularly now.

"Then there's the other body. The scene of crime officers who examined the hut after Makris was taken to the morgue noticed that the earth floor beneath the body had been disturbed. We were given permission to conduct a police excavation, otherwise I don't think her body would ever have been found."

"It was the body of a woman, then? It said so in the local paper."

"Yes, a young woman buried many years ago. I haven't received all the reports yet. She had a broken skull, it's possible she was deliberately killed. We haven't made an identification. The clothes had rotted, there was no jewellery. I'm still waiting for dental records and DNA results."

With an air of finality Cristopoulos closed the file in front of him and gave them a grim but civil smile.

"Martin, I'd like you to come in tomorrow, please," he said. "My colleague, Inspector Nomikos, wants to talk to you as soon as possible.

S all we say ten o'clock? I'll be present, of course. For now I'm a aid I have a great deal to do. Tomorrow I should also like to know c rything you can find out about the other name on Dr Moralis's l top – Dr Alexander Harding-Jones."

22

With some relief Day and Helen emerged into the street. It was around noon and seemed appallingly hot after the cool of the station. There were still plenty of people around as they entered the square, mostly visitors in shorts and sandals carrying colourful bags who seemed to be seeking lunch. This was not lost on Helen; Day, however, was preoccupied.

"That was thought-provoking. I can't avoid talking about Alex for much longer. Shall we go home?"

"OK. Shall we pick up some food on the way?"

They drove to the supermarket just off the road to the villages, and bought fresh cheese, salad and bread, various things for supper, more bottled water and tonic. Back at the house they sat on the balcony enjoying a gentle breeze. The word 'zephyr' popped into Helen's mind, a Greek word suggested by the little movement of air that wafted up from the valley. As the perspiration on her face dried, she savoured the word and wondered if it was much used in these islands, which were better known for the huge winds that halted the ferries. On nearby

Santorini the wind could blow so hard that the grapevines had to be cultivated over low wicker baskets for protection.

They ate lunch watching the valley from the balcony. The mule barely moved in its comfortable patch of shade, the sheep only occasionally changed the pattern they created on the slope, and the workmen on the building site were preparing to leave for the siesta. Only the pigeons seemed to have any energy, as pigeons always do, but even their movements were few.

"I shall forego my siesta today, and spend an hour or two planning how I want to proceed on the Elias project," announced Day. "Then I'll go to the house this evening. It'll be quieter after the tourists have gone. I need to get on with work. How about you, any plans?"

"Yes, I'm going to look back over what I drafted yesterday while I digest lunch, and then I fancy a swim. OK if I take the car? I'll be back by six."

"Sure, I won't go to the Elias place till about then anyway. Could we eat here this evening, later than usual? I might work till about nine if I can get my teeth into something."

"Fine by me, I'll get some work done while you're out. Martin, do you think there might really be an undiscovered sanctuary somewhere around here?"

"Nothing's impossible, but I'm afraid it's very unlikely. I suggested to Cristopoulos that he should contact the Greek Archaeological Service and ask them officially, but if Aristos hasn't heard anything, I bet there's nothing to hear."

"How can we find out?"

"Ask me another one!"

"You could ask Alex. He's in the Mycenaean field, he was on Michael's computer and he's on Naxos."

Day let out a big sigh, whether of tiredness or irritation she wasn't sure, and pushed back his chair.

"I'll think about it. But right now I'm going to plan the Elias research. If you go out before I reappear, I may have fallen asleep. Car keys on the table. Enjoy yourself."

"See you later."

***

By half past three the sun was high and hot, but the breeze had strengthened. Helen was stalled on the novel and decided to go out. Agia Anna was her favourite swimming beach, but it was years since she was last there. Wearing her swimming costume beneath her dress, she grabbed a towel and the car keys.

She took Day's Fiat for the first time, grateful that he'd added her to the insurance. She enjoyed driving, although on the islands it had its challenges. It wasn't so much the roads, although they could be tricky, as the other road-users. Between the summer visitors driving hire cars, motorbikes and quad bikes, and the exasperated locals with mopeds or speedy little vans, driving on Naxos could be an exciting experience.

Agia Anna was a coastal village south of Chora. Helen parked in the dusty car park, crossed the road, walked between the hotels and houses and down to the sand, remembering the way easily. She walked for ten minutes till she reached the quietest end of the beach, where a young couple were throwing a ball flirtatiously to each other in the shallows. She plunged in and swam away strongly, soon leaving the beach behind. The sea was still not very warm in May, but it seemed

s cold as she swam. Beginning to enjoy herself, she swam further
t and looked back at the shore; the buildings looked like dolls'
uses. She found the one she remembered from years ago. It was in
ow of elegant, white-painted houses with attractive balconies and
tters painted in different shades of blue, but her favourite house
s a tall one with light grey woodwork. Once she had dreamed of
ng there.

rning in the water, she swam further out towards a thin strip of
ks that separated the end of the bay from the open sea. Various
tty vessels were moored there, small pleasure boats with imposing
nes like Agios Ioannis, Minerva and Poseidon. Their hulls tugged
tly at mooring ropes that disappeared beneath the water. They
re all unoccupied. Passing the last boat, she reached the rocky
omontory and got out of the water. A few people were paddling,
bathing, or sitting together to talk. Smiling at the two little children
o played under a beach umbrella near their dozing parents, she
lked across the promontory to look at the open sea on the other
e. It glittered serenely between her and the grey-blue bulk of
ros. She was facing the less inhabited side of Paros, where only a
ttering of white houses decorated the slopes.

e sat down to dry off and think. It was impossible not to be saddened
the story of Dimitris Makris, she felt a strong connection to him
w. What had finally made his family decide to leave without him?
d they argue with him, trying to convince him to go with them?
d they part in tears, or in anger? She wondered whether their
ving had been the cause of Dimitris's fragile state of mind and
lonely lifestyle, or whether he had always been a troubled child,
aid and stubborn.

en suddenly she was overwhelmed with the memory of finding the
dy, something she had chased from her mind since that moment.
dden beneath Dimitris there had been a knife wound, maybe the
ife itself. If the hut had not been so dark, she might have seen his

blood, or twisted features. She had entered a place of violence. Yet she remembered Dimitris Makris lying as still as a kouros, on his back, empty gaze towards the heavens, arms crossed over his chest. Like the kouros, Dimitris was broken and abandoned. It was a scene of horror, but also of peacefulness, and she couldn't account for that.

Another body had lain buried beneath Dimitris Makris. Not even Helen could find a story to explain that.

23

y arrived at the Elias house just after six thirty. The sea in front
it was glittering from the westerly wind that now blew towards
land, fluttering the Greek flag that waved from the end of the
f. A sign had appeared announcing opening hours for the coming
nmer season. Day saw that closing time was always four o'clock.

Day approached, the door was opened by Petros Tsifas. A tall
n, Tsifas wore casual trousers and shirt, and moved with natural
ce. He had the calm manner of a natural host, and spoke softly
h inherent gentleness. He and Day had got on well from the start.
y couldn't have wished for a better person to facilitate his research,
help him find a way to approach the life of the historian and get
el for the man and his work.

m sorry I'm a bit late, Petro," said Day. "My friend took the car to
for a swim. It was so beautiful at Agia Anna, she lost track of time."

ho's this?"

"My old friend from England, Helen. We've known each other for many years. She's a novelist, and she's staying with me for the summer to do some writing."

"I'd be happy to meet her one day, if she'd like to come and see the house. Now, I've set you up in a small office at the back. It's quite tiny but I thought it would be quiet there away from the visitors, and you can leave your papers out on the table between your visits."

"Excellent, that will be perfect. Thanks, Petro."

It was Day's second time inside the Elias house, and now he began to appreciate the size of it. It was a rambling old building, originally a pair of fisherman's cottages, but it had been extended many times over the years. Petros showed Day to his new study at the end of a little hallway, and opened the shutters. The low evening light shone in. Some papers had been laid out ready for him on a table, and piles of material in files and binders were ranged on the nearby bookcase, just as he had requested.

"Can I bring you a coffee, Martin?"

"No, thanks. I've brought some water with me. I have everything I need here, it's wonderful."

Petros smiled and left Day to start work.

The files covered the fifteen years until the year of Elias's death. They were mostly in foolscap ring binders of the old kind he remembered from his father's house, mottled black board marked with use and age. Inside the binders were hand-written sheets interspersed with hole-punched documents, cuttings, articles from journals, and photographs. These were professional papers, the collection of a local historian who wanted to note all his thoughts, observations, important reading, interesting snippets, and anything else that might one day be relevant.

ere seemed to be a lot of really good stuff, Day thought, leafing
ough. Had Elias intended to collate the work himself? Perhaps
early death had prevented him.

ere was no apparent order within each binder, no indexing or
isions, and a quick survey revealed very little dating. Day would
ve to trace the direction of Elias's thoughts using the dates of the
wspaper cuttings and articles. In different handwriting, probably
ros's, most binders had been dated with a year. Several binders
re required per year. It would be a long job, but Day relished it. It
s something to get his teeth into. At least, that's how he felt today.
ssibly after a few weeks of this, he might feel differently.

ros knocked at the door and put his head in. "Sorry, Martin, I just
nt to say that when you need to examine the artefacts room, go
ht ahead, you know where it is, and if you want me for anything
t call. I'll be in the kitchen, it's out of here and on your left."

"[any thanks, Petro."

y was finally on his own. He plugged in his laptop and opened it.
it booted up, he arranged the binders in date order and opened
one marked 1984.

***

the time he left that evening Day had made preliminary notes on
binders covering 1984 to 1996. In his laptop he had listed, with
es, the journals from which Elias had cut articles, the site maps
had sketched, and the major headings under which, as far as Day
ld judge, Elias's interests could be summarised. He felt pleased
h the start he had made. One or two things resonated in his
nd, the seeds perhaps of the eventual biography, and in a separate
cument on his laptop he typed these as headings. He logged off
l closed the computer.

"Petro?" he called down the hall. "Ah, Petro, I'm finished for today. I'll see you tomorrow, after you close to visitors. OK?"

"Fine, Martin. Goodnight!"

It was dark and Day drove with extra care along the unlit shore road and on across country towards Filoti. The front light of the house was on when he parked, and good smells of cooking greeted him from the kitchen. He realised he was hungry. There was no sign of Helen. He poured two glasses of red wine and took one with him to his room, leaving a glass for Helen on the dining room table. He showered and changed into a crisp, new Oxford shirt. Returning to the main balcony, he was in an excellent mood.

Helen had cooked one of her signature curries, having no intention of setting herself up against Thanasis by attempting Greek cuisine. She had brought some spices from London in her luggage, enough to see them through the summer. Day loved spicy food from time to time; in fact he could get bored of the wonderful Greek dishes, although he was ashamed to admit it.

Helen joined him wearing a dress he hadn't seen before, long and flowing, dark red. In the subdued light of the balcony she was almost a shadow. They drank their wine talking quietly, aware that in the evening silence their voices would carry to the neighbours and be an unwelcome rupture of the rural quiet. Day offered to serve the supper and bring it out. Two bowls of chicken jalfrezi and rice, with chopped fresh Naxian herbs on top, soon steamed on the dark balcony table under the inadequate solitary bulb.

"We must buy some candles," he murmured. "I think we'll be out here a lot this summer, don't you?"

"Absolutely. Do you want some of my insect repellent?"

"No thanks, I won't bother. Bon appétit! This looks wonderful!"

"Kali orexi!"

They ate contentedly until nothing but the aroma of spices remained.

"That was excellent. Thank you for cooking, Helen. Just what I needed. I didn't realise how much I wanted some Indian."

"We've only had a bit of salad and cheese today, so no wonder we were hungry. So, how did you get on at the Elias house?"

"I made a good start. Petros has given me a room where I can work in peace and leave my stuff out on the desk between visits. There's an enormous quantity of binders full of Elias's notes, articles and references to what he was working on. I made a start, just listing what was in there. His interests covered different areas of the island and different sites and periods. He records his own explorations and notes down his thoughts. He's quite good at cross-referencing with bits and pieces in his own collection, from ancient pottery sherds to nineteenth century pitchforks. It's intriguing. If ever there was a man who died before he'd completed his life's work, it was Elias."

"Has no interest been taken in his work by the Archaeological Service or foreign schools?"

"I don't think so. The collection doesn't contain anything of great value or interest. There's no major discovery. The papers seem to be the work-in-progress of a rather eccentric loner. I only heard of Elias by chance, from an elderly scholar in Athens who had met him long ago, before Petros arrived on the scene. I think Elias lived under the radar."

"And Elias died in 2000, is that right?"

"Yes. Judging by what I've seen, he was still working in the early part of that year. He died in the November."

"Well, I'm glad you've made a good start. Just what you needed."

"Oh god, yes, and I have to go back to the police station tomorrow morning. I'd almost managed to forget. I still have to decide what to tell them about Alex."

"The truth, surely?" said Helen with regal candour, an impression enhanced by the long red dress. "What else?"

"You know the problem. Of course, I'm sure that Alex isn't really involved in anything illegal. But I'm not confident the police will agree. The difficulty, apart from Alex being on Naxos at this exact time, is why his name was in Michael's computer. And the fact that Alex made no mention of Michael's death; he must have known about it, and his silence seems odd."

"Look. Since you said you'd set up a meeting for Alex with the Curator, why not do that now, and it will make Alex's presence on Naxos look a lot better. Then you could talk to Alex again and get the truth out of him. Sitting here worrying isn't getting you anywhere."

"You're right. I'll give Aristos a call now, then I'll get back to Alex."

Day opened his mobile and dialled Aristos's number. "Hi Aristo, Martin here. I'm sorry it's quite late…"

"Martin! No problem. What can I do for you?"

"A friend of mine from the British Museum is on the island, Alex Harding-Jones. He wants to talk to you about an idea for a collaboration between the two museums, and I rather hoped to set up the meeting

a d be there myself. Could you find a space in your diary? We could
c ne to the museum."

" /hat are you up to, Martin? But of course, I'd be happy to talk to
y a both. Tomorrow I'm busy, maybe on Wednesday? Eleven o'clock
v uld be good. You and I can then go for lunch, I know a good place,
a d if your friend has not upset me we can take him too."

l y smiled. Aristos was no fool. He said that all being well, he and
, ex would be there on Wednesday. Replacing his mobile on the
t le, Day reflected that Alex's name had not meant anything to his
c l friend. Clearly, Alex had not paved the way for his visit in any
v y at all.

24

Day woke up early the next morning and dressed with care. When he thought Alex would be awake, he texted to tell him of the meeting with Aristos Iraklidis and suggested a coffee first at a bar called Diogenes on the port road. From there they could easily stroll up to the Kastro and the Museum. He took the car and drove to Chora, leaving time for an espresso in the café nearest the police station to set him up for his grilling by the Inspector from Athens. He was not looking forward to it.

Cristopoulos came out to meet him and took him into a different room where several people were poring over screens. One, a lion of a man with a light-brown mane and pale blue eyes, introduced himself as Andreas Nomikos of Athens. It startled Day when Greeks had this light hair and blue eye colouring, even though it was not exceptionally rare, especially in the north of Greece. Nomikos resembled a blonde Greek god from Olympus. Day tried not to be overawed.

Andreas Nomikos was as charming as Cristopoulos was civil. Day suspected that the man from Athens used his charm to conceal some sort of ferocity, either of temperament or of intelligence.

Day was asked to repeat to Nomikos everything that he had told Christopoulos about Gautier, Grogan and the late Dr Moralis. Starting cautiously, Day soon gained in confidence and pace. He was not inexperienced in relating a gripping narrative. Nomikos was an attentive listener, barely interrupting except to clarify the occasional point. His English was excellent.

"Thank you, Mr Day," he said when Day had finished. "You've been extremely clear. I'd like to talk to you about your British colleague, Dr Harding-Jones, in a moment, but first let's talk about Emil Gautier. We're about to release him, for the moment at least. There isn't anything we can prove against him. However, in his early twenties Gautier and another man were arrested in Paris for disturbance of the peace. Both were later released without charge. The interesting thing is the name of the man who was arrested with Gautier."

Day jumped involuntarily.

"Petros?"

"This Mr Tsifas now lives on Naxos. In fact, he came here from Paris the year after the arrest."

"I've met him. He's the custodian of the Nikos Elias house, he was Elias's partner. I was talking to him only yesterday. Perhaps Inspector Christopoulos has told you that I'm researching into Nikos Elias at the moment? I've started visiting the house, with the cooperation of Petros Tsifas."

"Yes, yes, I know something of it. So many connections in this case, are there not, Mr Day?"

Day had an uneasy feeling this was a loaded question. He chose to ignore it. Nomikos continued.

"We know that Petros Tsifas and the late Nikos Elias began a relationship when Tsifas first came to Naxos from Paris. Tsifas came from a poor part of Athens and was trying to make his fortune in France, but when it went wrong he moved to Naxos. I imagine he was pleased to forget the whole Paris episode and make a fresh start. It may be unconnected to Tsifas that Gautier is currently on Naxos, but there may be a connection that we need to discover. I'd also like to know why Jim Grogan, a suspected associate of Gautier, has taken a room at a taverna not 500 metres from where Tsifas lives. What is your opinion, Mr Day?"

"I suppose we should look for a connection, as you say. On the one hand, Gautier may not have known that Petros had moved to Naxos, he may not even remember him from all that time ago. On the other hand, Petros was with Elias, Elias was an archaeologist who might be assumed to have a collection of antiquities, and this might have interested Gautier."

Nomikos lowered his chin and studied Day with interest. Day was encouraged to continue.

"Nikos Elias's papers, of which I've only made a quick survey so far, suggest he was more concerned with sites than with artefacts, Inspector. The collection in the house contains nothing of great originality and certainly nothing of value, which is more to the point here. That is, unless ..."

"Unless Tsifas has concealed the valuable items?"

"As you say."

"I've requested a warrant to search the Elias house, even though I suspect that any valuable artefacts would be hidden elsewhere. I don't think we'll find anything that connects directly with Gautier, but we

r ed to go through the motions. You, on the other hand, might well
c cover more during your research into Elias. Hm?"

' erhaps," said Day, recognising that he was being asked to find out.
" ave you released Gautier unconditionally? How will you know if
l meets Grogan?"

N mikos smiled. Day was embarrassed; the police were not about
t tell him if they had Gautier under surveillance. Nomikos ran his
l nd through his blonde mane.

" ll move on to Jim Grogan, the American who purported to be
J n Gregory of Seattle. He's admitted to the false ID. He explained
i aying he enjoys privacy when he's on holiday, as the fame of his
t vel writing can lead to his peace and quiet being disrupted by his
a niring readers."

I y snorted involuntarily.

' evertheless, that's his excuse. He asserts that marine ecology, which
l allows people to believe is his profession, is a hobby, and claims
r t to know Gautier, nor to have heard of Dr Moralis until he read
a out the murder in the newspaper."

' ou've released him too?"

' ot yet, but we will do shortly. However, I was interested to hear
f m the Greek Archaeological Service that they have long suspected
(ogan of owning some rare Greek antiquities which he came by
c honestly. Their suspicions date back to when Grogan made his
v lking tour of Greece and Turkey, the journey which he turned into
l travel book. They think he was illegally acquiring antiquities along
t way and sending them home to America. There's a close correlation
l tween the route of his journey and a trail of missing items. His

book, ironically, illustrates this neatly. He was, in fact, apprehended and questioned in Istanbul several years after its publication, but his family sent an excellent American lawyer ..."

"I heard from my contacts in the US that the majority of his collection is private. The word is that it's a considerable and impressive horde. Grogan presents himself as a great collector, but the precise nature of his collection is a well-kept secret."

"That describes the world of the illegal antiquities trade, my friend," Nomikos said. "I want to know what brings both these characters to Naxos at the same time, and why now? They each claim not to know the other, which I don't believe. I need to find a connection between them."

"I've just remembered something! My friend Helen took some pictures of the two men we thought were Gautier and Grogan in Apollonas. I'm sorry, I forgot to mention it. If it was them, it proves they know each other. Of course, they were wearing sunglasses, but it might be helpful."

Cristopoulos rose from his seat and took a business card from his wallet.

"Can you get Miss Aitchison to send me the pictures immediately by email? Here's the address..."

He handed Day his card, from which Day noted all the contact details. He messaged Helen while the two policemen were talking in low voices. When Day looked up, Nomikos prepared to speak.

"If I may interrupt, Andrea," said Cristopoulos, "Can I ask Martin about the couple who run the taverna where Grogan's staying? Taverna Ta Votsala, did you say, Martin? Their name is Papathoma, isn't it? I'll send someone to speak to them. Can you tell me more about the argument involving Grogan the night before last?"

" es, Vasilios texted me that a man dined with Grogan and there
v s a heated argument. He didn't give me any details, but he thought
t man was Greek."

' nd do we know anything at all about this Greek? Such as whether
l 's local?"

' asilios just said he was Greek."

" /e asked Grogan about it, and he said the man was a chance
a quaintance who was also interested in marine ecology, and he didn't
r nember his name."

' r where they met, I suppose? Vasilios says that Grogan hardly ever
l ves the taverna. Hardly conducive to striking up a friendship with
a tranger and discovering mutual interests."

' o, but it's not impossible. We can't hold Grogan or Gautier, but
t ist me, this doesn't end here."

I y decided to ask some of his own questions while he had the
c nce. He addressed himself to Nomikos.

' believe Michael Moralis was overheard speaking on the phone about
a undiscovered sanctuary. Did you ask the Greek Archaeological
S vice about it?"

N mikos sighed. "Apparently there are several locations of interest,
l t no excavation has been authorised nor will be in the foreseeable
f ure. One site is submerged off the coast, and another two are in
i ccessible locations beneath modern buildings. I was told that none
a thought to be sanctuaries."

' o we can assume Michael was not here looking for a sanctuary,
g ntlemen. Whatever brought him here, and whatever he meant on

the phone when he was overheard, he did not come to Naxos on a wild goose chase. That's my considered opinion at the moment."

Inspector Nomikos dragged his hand through his hair, grunting with reluctant agreement. He pushed back his chair and crossed his arms.

"The most likely explanation, in my opinion, is that Dr Moralis came across the smugglers going about their illegal business. He might have been involved in that business with them or he might simply have got in their way, but they decided to kill him. I intend to focus on the two men we suspect of being involved, and eventually the truth will come to light. I'll make sure of that. All these people are connected, I only need to find out how."

"That doesn't account for Michael coming to Naxos in the first place, or letting his killer into the room," said Day.

"It accounts for both if he was working with them, Mr Day. Now, talking of people being here without good reason, tell me about your friend Alexander Harding-Jones. I understand he too is on the island, but we don't yet know why. I believe that's still the case, Cristopoulo?"

Day noted that the Athenian knew about his friendship with Alex, and he was pretty sure he had not already disclosed that. It was Day's moment to decide how protective of Alex he was going to be, versus how honest. Helen was right, he decided. The time for prevarication was over and he must simply tell the truth.

Then, with all the assurance of a professional, he lied.

"Alex Harding-Jones is here on official business to negotiate on behalf of the British Museum regarding an exhibition in London in 2022. The exhibition will feature the Cycladic objects in the Naxos museum, if permission is granted. This is absolutely normal procedure between museums, I can assure you. As Alex had some leave to take, has been enjoying the resort of Agia Anna for a week or so before speaking to the Curator. However, there's a meeting between Alex, the Curator Aristos Iraklidis and myself tomorrow. There's no cause for concern."

Cristopoulos looked thoughtful, Nomikos impassive.

"Do you have any suggestions concerning why his name was on Dr Moralis's computer, Martin?"

"They have a common field of scholarship," said Day, sounding as authoritative as he could.

He was interrupted by an officer who had risen from his desk on the far side of the room and stood waiting to speak to Cristopoulos.

"A message from Forensics, sir."

The officer handed a sheet of paper to Cristopoulos, who glanced at it and passed it to Nomikos.

"Well, that makes things more difficult, Andrea." He turned to Day. "Forensics confirm that both Dr Moralis and Dimitris Makris were stabbed with the same knife."

25

Day left the police station in a sweat which had little to do with the midday heat. He was on a real high, he had to admit. The reason was the heady mixture of the amazing Nomikos, his own strange but flattering relationship with the police, going out on a limb for Alex, and finally the revelation about the murder weapon. The deaths were linked after all. It was nothing short of an adrenalin bath. Or maybe he shouldn't have had that espresso before he went in. Either way, it was time to calm down and think clearly.

A text from Helen told him she was walking into Filoti for a break from work, and he could join her in the Café Ta Xromata. At the café Helen was already sitting at a kerbside table. He joined her and ordered a lemon juice with ginger. No more coffee for him.

"You look exhausted, Martin. What happened at the police station?" she asked.

"It was amazing. The man from Athens is an astonishing character, a tall, blonde Greek with an intellect that positively cowed me."

" Don't exaggerate, Martin. You don't cower."

" Well, Cristopoulos and this Athens man, Nomikos, made me repeat everything I've said so far about Gautier and Grogan, then amazingly they updated me on the investigation. Mind you, they want more work out of me! Gautier and Grogan have been found and questioned, but will have to be released for lack of evidence. The story is that Grogan illegally acquired antiquities in the past, and Gautier was once arrested for affray in Paris, along with Petros Tsifas. That's a pair we hadn't put together.

" Inspector Nomikos firmly believes Michael's murder is tied up with an antiquities racket, possibly run by Gautier, and hasn't discounted the possibility that Michael was part of it. They asked me about Alex and I managed to cover for him. Sorry, it's no good, my head's spinning. I'll tell you the rest later, in as much details as you like. Are you ready to go back to the house? I think I need to get my head down for an hour. And then, well, I'm keen to get back over to the Elias house. I might go abut four o'clock and stay for a few hours."

Day fell asleep almost as soon as he lay on the bed. Waking two and a half hours later, he felt refreshed and energetic. Day was never so happy as when his brain was working well. His ideal life would be filled with mental gymnastics and challenges, food, drink and, of course, precious sleep. The Elias research was beckoning him, and not only for the work itself. The thought of Petros Tsifas's brush with the Paris police and youthful association with Emil Gautier had added spice to the mix.

***

It was after four o'clock when Day reached the Elias house. Helen had asked to be dropped off at the taverna to chat with Maroula, and as soon as she had got out of the car Day kicked himself for not asking about her work. He was getting very self-absorbed, he thought, and vowed to ask her later.

Petros opened the door quickly to his knock. Day realised immediately that his liking for Petros had not been tarnished by what he had been told about his past. Petros at sixty was likeable and seemed trustworthy. He disapproved of condemning people for the mistakes of their youth.

Petros looked tired. He said he had been looking after a German tour group who were knowledgeable and had asked many clever questions. Though he appreciated anyone who showed an interest in Nikos, he said, he really struggled to answer some of the questions people asked. He smiled sadly, and disappeared to the kitchen to leave Day to his work.

Day began by finishing his initial overview of the binders, bringing himself up to date in a general way with the aim and scope of Nikos Elias's activities since the early 1980s. Elias seemed to have focused on two areas of the island. One of these was in the rolling inland uplands, the other on the coast some kilometres north of the Paralia Votsala. He had repeatedly surveyed both places, trawled old newspapers for any mention of the areas, and noted any references in professional publications which might possibly pertain to them. As far as Day could see, Elias had not communicated even once with any scholars who might have helped him. Moreover, unless he had missed something, Day saw nothing that confirmed exactly what Elias had been looking for.

Joining Petros in the kitchen, Day asked him what he knew about Elias's research.

"I had some idea what Nikos was looking for," said Petros, "but because I'm not an archaeologist and not even particularly well-educated, it didn't mean a lot to me."

" air enough. Can you tell me what you can remember?"

" just know that Niko thought there was something really important
t be found on this island. He said he was determined to find it before
l died. Even though the place might have been robbed or spoiled
y irs ago, Niko wanted to be the one who discovered it. That was
s like him."

")o you remember what it was he was looking for, or where?"

I tros shook his head.

" low old was Nikos when he died, if you don't mind me asking?"

" ifty two. It was cancer, it spread incredibly quickly. Within a few
n onths he was an invalid. We thought he'd have more time, and he
t :d to keep working, but it beat him."

" hat must have been very hard, for both of you. And he never
f ind what he was searching for?"

I tros shook his head again. "I'm sorry I can't help you, Martin…"
I s eyes were suddenly sorrowful and he seemed to be gazing inward
t the events of the past.

")on't worry. Can you remember anything else that I won't find in
l papers?"

I tros hesitated, then appeared to remember something. "There was
s ne problem about a girl wearing a bracelet," he muttered, then
s :med to regret starting the subject. Day felt embarrassment creep
i o Petros's voice.

" real girl? Or a historical one?" he prompted.

Petros shrugged. "I've no idea, Martin. Nikos didn't want to talk about it. I don't know why I told you."

Day agreed with him on that, but filed the snippet away in case he needed it later.

***

After less than two hours, Day gave up work and joined Helen at the taverna. He certainly didn't want any more coffee, and seriously needed a gin, but not here. They said goodbye to Maroula, who had been sitting with Helen when Day arrived, and drove back to Filoti, where they left the Fiat outside the house and walked straight into Filoti village for something to eat.

The serene evening, which felt like a warm June night, began to quieten Day's brain in a very satisfactory way. His adrenalin high had turned to stress when he had realised the sheer amount of work involved in the Elias project, the mass of material to be examined. It was overwhelming. He knew that with time he would get through it, and that with luck he would sift the gold from the sand. At the moment he was still just starting to pan, with no certainly that there was any gold in the stream. He needed a relaxing evening before trying to get a good night's sleep.

A persistent irritant, an unformulated idea, had begun to flutter in his head like a moth near a candle. Elias's reluctance to confide in anyone, even in his partner, suggested some kind of exciting secret. Day wanted to believe it, to believe that he himself might unveil it.

They sat outside Thanasis's taverna in the warm night and ordered gin and tonic, knowing they were under no time pressure to order the food. This was Greece, people ate late. As the alcohol gradually relaxed him, the way ahead with the Elias project began to look more promising. He said as much to Helen, hoping to convince himself.

that moment, Vangelis placed in front of them two saucers of
bles to have with their drinks. Day dived into the cubes of cheese
d tiny parcels of spinach pie. As he chewed a piece of pie he made
ronouncement.

have a feeling we'll be here a long time tonight. I have so much
tell you."

xcellent. And I have some news too."

h?" This possibility had not occurred to Day.

want to hear yours first. Start with the police station this morning."

insisted that Alex was a man of good character and honesty, and
d them about the meeting with Aristos tomorrow. I think they
re satisfied."

, are the police going to question him?"

hey didn't say. I suggested that perhaps Alex's name was in Michael's
mputer simply because they were in the same field. I hope that's
ough."

this point Vangelis arrived take their order. He had not brought
nus, prompting Day to ask what he recommended.

would advise my mother's chicken souvlaki …"

y's expression stopped him. Day was not a great lover of souvlaki.
ngelis resumed enthusiastically.

ou see, this is prepared in a way unique to our family. My mother
oks the chicken pieces first in olive oil, wine, mountain herbs,
namon, lemon and garlic, …"

"Of course we will have the souvlaki, Vangeli," said Day hungrily. "And can we also have some fries, and a salad, please? Thank you very much."

Delighted, Vangelis beamed and returned to the kitchen. Day called after him to add a jug of local red wine. He poured for Helen and himself from the bottle of cold water on the table, and picked up a piece of bread from the basket.

"I hope you agree about the food, Helen? Sorry, I didn't think we could turn down Kyria Thanasis's best souvlaki."

"Absolutely, to order anything else would have been rude. Now, what else did the police say?"

"Something shocking. Both Michael and Makris were killed with the same knife."

"My God! So the killings really are linked? The knife hasn't been found, has it?"

"I don't think so," said Day. "So now it looks like the same person killed both of them, first Makris then Michael."

"What possible link could there be between an American academic and a Naxos recluse?" she asked, almost to herself. "I have more to tell you about Makris, actually."

She was interrupted by a smiling Thanasis, apologising for not coming to welcome them before. He put two clean plates in front of them, asked to know if they were well, commented on the weather, and expressed his pleasure that they had ordered his wife's souvlaki. He was followed by Vangelis, carrying a dish in each hand and one balanced on his forearm. He placed the chips before Day with a rather knowing smile. A local salad that shone with freshness and olive oil

s set down by Helen, and next to it a homemade tsatziki, the tasty
yogurt and mint dip traditionally served with souvlaki.

Finally, Thanasis's wife brought out her speciality. It gave off an
aroma that made their tastebuds tingle. There was much thanking and
smiling and nodding before she returned to her domain to produce
another miracle.

Day and Helen ate for a while without talking. They knew each
other well enough not to ruin a meal by distracting attention from
it. Day ordered another small jug of wine, and Helen reflected for
the hundredth time that she was pleased Greek barrel wine did not
appear to have the alcoholic strength of bottled wine at home.

"So, I was going to tell you what I heard today," she began, forking
the last olive from the salad. "When we were talking with Vasilios
and Maroula about your work at the Elias house, I sensed Maroula
was keeping something back, so I went today to see what I could
find out. It turns out that she was very close to the Makris family as
a child, and in particular Dimitris's sister.

"The sister's name was Maria Eleni, and she and Maroula were very
close. Even after Maroula's marriage they went to the same church
and Maroula would visit Maria Eleni weekly.

"One day Maroula heard a rumour that Maria Eleni had left Naxos
and wasn't coming back. Maroula was really hurt because Maria
Eleni had not told her anything about it, and they'd always shared
everything important. Maroula never heard from Maria Eleni again,
not even a letter. The Makris family wouldn't speak about it and soon
they had left too.

"Of course, the younger brother, Dimitris, stayed behind. He'd
never been very bright, Maroula said, but now he became sullen and
withdrawn. She didn't see him speak to anybody in the village except

the priest. He lived alone in the old family cottage in the hills, seemingly living on what he could catch and find. He got a reputation for being mentally disturbed, and so the traditional recipient of charity. Some of the village women would take him food."

"Perhaps in her excitement Maria Eleni simply forgot to tell Maroula?"

"You don't know what young girls are like, Martin, let's face it. That excitement would have taken her straight to tell her best friend. Also, I think it's strange that she left before her parents."

"How old were the Makris children at the time?"

"Maria Eleni was nineteen or twenty, Dimitris mid-teens."

"Maria Eleni was at an age when she might prefer to set off alone."

"Well, it doesn't sound very likely to me, Martin."

"Whatever the truth of it, I don't think it gets us any further with who killed Dimitris and Michael."

Helen smiled as she picked up her glass. "Actually, Martin, I've thought of something that might," she said.

26

the Chora Police Station the combined teams from Naxos and
hens, in total seven men, met at nine in the morning for briefing.
was to be a busy day. A warrant had been granted with unusual
omptitude for a search of the premises of Petros Tsifas. They were
ooking for two things: valuable ancient artefacts, and anything that
might have a bearing on the recent murders, particularly a knife that
might be the murder weapon.

Inspector Cristopoulos was planning a separate trip to question the
owners of the Taverna Ta Votsala, Vasilios and Maroula Papathoma.
Of special interest was information about their current visitor, Jim
Logan, who called himself John Gregory, currently about to be
released from custody without charge. They would also question the
Papathomas about the Makris family, and about any persons recently
asking about items of a valuable or antique nature.

Inspector Nomikos would remain at the station during the morning
and all parties would report their findings to him. During the

afternoon, Nomikos and his sergeant planned to visit and question Dr Alex Harding-Jones.

***

Day had spent several hours worrying about his meeting with Alex. He was the first to arrive at Diogenes bar and took a table at the back of the terrace. The other customers, mostly tourists, were seated at the sunnier tables on the pavement, or in the canopied area towards the sea. Providing they were discreet, Day thought he could have a confidential chat with Alex without being overheard.

Alex arrived on time carrying a canvas laptop bag which he placed on the ground next to him. He seemed excited.

"This is really very good of you, Martin," he said. "I'd probably have procrastinated still longer if you hadn't arranged this meeting with the Curator. How long have you known Aristos Iraklidis?"

"Oh, eight or ten years I suppose. I liked him from the first time we met, and used to look him up whenever I passed through Naxos. Now that I have a home here, I'm going to see a lot more of him."

"What's he like? Has he been Curator here long?"

"Yes, many years. I don't know how many, but he's a respected figure locally now. People seem to call him 'Curator' unless they know him personally. I think you'll like him."

"Good. I doubt it will change anything, though. I don't think he's going to go for the proposal of the exhibit exchange. My Director doesn't think so either. The whole thing will be clouded by the Parthenon Sculptures issue. The only chance is if Iraklidis and I hit the right note. Then he would have to convince his superiors. That's probably impossible too. It's a shame because I have some top students who

…uld do some tremendous work on such an important exhibition …t happened. It would be extremely valuable in many respects."

"…see why you decided to come in person, Alex. But it's unusual, …'t it?"

"…ertainly. The Curator will find it so too."

"…hy didn't you get in touch with him before you left the UK, or …ntact him when you first arrived? Too busy building up your tan?"

"…a! With my complexion? Hardly."

…eir coffees arrived. Day stirred his frappé with the straw, laid it on …e saucer, and started to sip his drink. He was waiting for Alex to …ntinue, letting the silence draw out. Alex drank half his espresso …fore putting it down.

"…may as well tell you, Martin."

…at was more like it, Day thought. "Tell me what?"

"…came here with a woman. She used to be one of my students, …e's now an aspiring young lecturer. We planned a holiday together …fore I started work."

"…atherine Russell?"

…ex looked at Day sharply. Day enjoyed a brief moment of satisfaction …fore remembering that Katherine Russell could currently be in …nsiderable danger.

"…ook, you're not married, Alex, and you're not, as far as I know, in …other relationship, so why the secrecy?"

"Kate wanted it that way. But how did you know her name?"

"I know more than that, Alex. I know she's missing."

Alex heaved a sigh and his excitement vanished. His expression confirmed the anxiety that Day had sensed behind the facade since they had sat down.

"Why the hell haven't you told the police, Alex?"

"The Greek police? To report a missing woman, when I was 'the last to see her alive'? Anyway, I know she's fine. We've been texting. It's complicated."

"I'm sure it is," Day said wryly. "But you need to tell me the truth, then pull yourself together and talk to the police. Where is Kate?"

"She's in Athens. She's in a hotel there. She overheard something that frightened her to death. I've told her she must go to the police, and I think she'll agree soon. Look, Martin, we need to get going to see Iraklidis, but I promise I'll come and talk to you tomorrow. There's more I want to tell you anyway. And I'll definitely go to the police straight after this morning's meeting. I give you my word."

Day nodded and took out some coins to leave on the table for the coffee. They prepared to leave, and when Alex stood after lifting his briefcase from the ground he found himself looking straight into Day's face, and the face was resolute.

"Look, Alex," he said, "after the meeting I'm going for some lunch with Aristos. I'll do what I can to support you. But you really must go directly to the police station. It's just off the square behind the port. Ask for Inspector Nomikos. OK? And come to see me tomorrow at the house. Any time."

' ill do. If I haven't been arrested …"

***

istos Iraklidis and Day sat at the back of a taverna near the square, eiving the personal attention of the proprietor, a lady called terina. She spoke to Aristos with respect bordering on reverence. e real benefit of this was that she knew Aristos's preference for ice and quiet, and seated the other customers as far as possible m their table.

' m not inclined to accept your friend's proposal, I'm afraid, Martin," ʒan Aristos.

" understand that. It would be very difficult to get the authorisation, s it would represent a huge amount of work, and worst of all you uld be without your prize exhibits for some months."

istos looked puzzled. "I thought you'd try and convince me."

' wouldn't insult you, Aristo."

' did briefly consider it, actually. There would be a certain kudos an association with any of the world's top museums, generally aking. But, the British Museum? With the way the Greek public l about the so-called 'Elgin Marbles'?"

' ideed. Unless it was seen as part of a *détente* which might, just ght, nudge the issue in Greece's favour."

' ood try, Martin, but I truly believe the British Museum has absolutely intention of ever giving the Parthenon Sculptures back to Greece. r one thing, it would cause a precedent worldwide. Every nation ild demand its antiquities back from all the major museums of the world. But you know all this. I couldn't see my superiors agreeing to Alex's idea."

"I completely appreciate that. Let me just say that, in spite of everything, I believe Alex is a good man, a good scholar, and is genuinely trying to act for the good of the field. That's not to say he's showing much common sense at the moment."

Aristos looked at Day thoughtfully before turning to the waiting Katerina. He placed his order as if he ate the same dish every time he ate at her taverna.

"Moussaka for me, please, Katerina. And a salad."

"I'll take a stuffed tomato and pepper, thank you," said Day, realising he was hungry.

"Good choice, Martin. The food's very good here. So, when are we going to see you and your friend Helen at our house?"

"Soon, I hope, although it should be you and Rania who come to Filoti. Are your family still with you?"

"They've gone back to Syros now, but as it happens it's Rania's birthday on Saturday. The family are coming back for the celebration, which will be just a quiet meal with them and my mother. Rania and I are hoping that you and Helen can join us. About 7pm?"

"Absolutely, we'd love to. I'll send you a message to confirm, but I'm sure we have nothing planned. Thank you very much."

Their food arrived, well-cooked and restorative, and they chatted about museum business. Then Day took the chance to talk about Elias.

' want to pick your brains, Aristo. You've been on Naxos for a long
t 1e, and you know everybody and everything about the place …"

/ 1stos laughed and poured water into their glasses with a slight shake
(the head. Day continued undeterred.

' ɔ, here's a little puzzle. It's about Nikos Elias. I've only just started
\ ɪrk on his biography, but already there's something very odd.
\ ɔuldn't you think it unusual for an archaeologist not to mention
a ɪwhere in his own papers what it is that he's searching for?"

' , that the case with Elias?"

' es."

' ` you're satisfied the man was genuinely on the track of something
(ɪcrete, perhaps the item he sought was so valuable, or vulnerable,
t ɪt he wanted to protect it."

'· hat's what I concluded too. But I don't think it's an item, I think
i a place. So, here's what I want to ask you. Is there anywhere on
t ɪ island where local people have been talking about anything being
l ried? An ancient site still to be unearthed?"

'· ou already asked me this, some sanctuary connected to your friend
\ ɪo was killed. Martin, local rumours abound. We would dig up half
(Naxos on the strength of the word of farmers. But we don't."

' ɔK, I get your point. But I'm starting to think that whatever Elias
\ s looking for has attracted the attention of some people beyond
ʔ xos, even beyond Greece. Other people on the island today are
l ɔking for the same place."

'· ou mean, Elias and your American friend weren't the only ones?"

"That's what I'm beginning to think. These other people seem to be serious, and not the scholarly type."

"In that case – thank you, Katerina, excellent as always! – I'll ask around discreetly. Keep me up to date, eh?"

27

When Aristos left to return to the museum, having insisted on paying for their lunch, Day decided to call Nomikos. First he needed to call Helen and tell her that he was going straight to the Elias house for the afternoon. While they were on the phone, he told her of Aristos's invitation to Rania's birthday celebration, and that he had some news of Alex. Thus having aroused her curiosity and left it dangling in the air, he rang off.

Damn, he thought. I've done it again. I didn't ask if her morning had gone well. I must apologise later. He also forgot to call Nomikos, and set off right away to Paralia Votsala. His lunch lay lightly in his stomach and he felt energised. He felt better about Alex. He trusted Alex to be talking to the police by now, and tomorrow he would hear all about Kate Russell. He was fired up for a few hours of productive research.

Day was somewhat taken aback, as his car descended towards the sea at Paralia Votsala, to see police vehicles at both ends of the bay. To his right, a police car was just leaving Vasilios's taverna, dust rising from its tyres. To the left, uniformed police were standing by a police van in front of the Elias house. Day turned the wheel and headed there.

He parked the Fiat carefully so as not to block in the police van. Petros Tsifas was standing with a senior officer in front of the house, while from inside there was the sound of voices. Day introduced himself to the policeman, who gave him a nod of recognition.

"They're searching the house, Martin," said Petros quietly. "They've been here for hours."

He looked stressed and his voice was tight. He had lost his usual self-assurance. His perfect poise, too, was gone. Day tried to reassure him, and was thinking of leaving when two policemen emerged from the house. The man standing with Petros talked to them briefly, then came back to Petros, thanked him for his cooperation and left. Day and Petros watched as the police van reversed down the drive and drove back towards the main road.

"What reason did they give for the search, Petro?"

"They showed me a warrant, but they didn't tell me what they were looking for. I dread to think what mess they've made inside. Excuse me, I must go and check. Do go in and get started, Martin, there's no need for you to change your plans."

"I'll be in soon, Petro. I'll just go and see if they're OK over at the taverna. They had a visit from the police too."

Petros, however, had already gone. Day drove down to the taverna, where Vasilios came over to him. He could see Maroula, her face flushed, sitting with a man wearing the black robes of the Greek Orthodox church. Martin asked Vasilios in a low voice what the police had wanted.

"They asked about the American, and the argument the other night. Then they asked about Dimitris Makris. Maroula was close to the family, especially before we were married. She's quite upset now, any

ntion of that family upsets her. That's Pater Giannis, our priest.
was fortunately here with us when the police arrived."

y swallowed his deep-seated dislike of organised religion. "Do you
nk you could introduce me to the Pater?" he asked.

'f course. Come this way."

***

ter Giannis was nursing a Greek coffee and smoking; he had the
k of a man with the entire day to sit and talk. Day and Vasilios
ned the table, and Day explained his interest in the Makris family.
was mostly the priest who answered.

e family had always been poor, he explained. The father was a
erman, and the mother sometimes looked after the children of
althy families. They had three children, a boy, a girl, and a little
erthought, what they call a luck child, little Dimitris. Happy enough
ldren, and a devout family.

en one day people said that Maria Eleni had left Naxos without
vord to anyone, and the priest found it strange that she had not
n asked for his blessing before she left. Shortly afterwards the rest
the family went too. All except the youngest boy, Dimitris, who
yed behind in the cottage. He was a teenager and young for his
, so it was strange that his family left without him.

ere were rumours, of course. Some people said that Kyrie Makris
d used treasure from a smugglers' cave to pay for their journey.
her people said that a saint had come to rescue the family from
verty, but for some reason the younger boy was excluded from their
od fortune. A few people whispered that the money came from a
althy man who wanted to get Dimitris's mother out of his life; this
came quite a scandal for a while, but there was never any truth to it.

Not surprisingly, the boy Dimitris became increasingly incommunicative. He lived like a hermit, hiding from people. Giannis tried to speak to him, but rarely seemed to make himself understood. People would take Dimitris food and old clothes, until quite recently when they realised that nobody had seen him for a while. More rumours began. He had fallen into an old quarry and died, some said. He had thrown himself off a cliff and his body was lost in the sea. One Sunday, at his weekly sermon, Giannis had given a blessing for Dimitris, and asked everyone to stop spreading the stories.

"Now," said the priest, "the mystery of Dimitris's disappearance is resolved, at least partially. It seems that Dimitris was alive all the time, only to be killed in a cruel and wicked way at the hands of a stranger."

Day thanked him and agreed that it was a very sad story. He excused himself, leaving Maroula with the priest. Vasilios accompanied Day to his car.

"You going home now, Martin?"

"I'm going up to the Elias place to do a bit of work. Call me if you need me, Vasili. I'll pop in soon, I expect Helen will come with me. Give my best wishes to Maroula."

"I will. What was the fuss up there this morning? We saw the police were there too."

"They were searching the house. Nothing was found. Kalispera."

A while later, seated at his desk with his laptop open and Elias's papers round about him, Day remembered what he had meant to do earlier, and as he no longer felt like making a telephone call, he sent an email to Inspector Nomikos.

28

Inspector Andreas Nomikos had found himself a private office to indulge in an hour of reflection. The station was practically empty: the search of the Elias house was in progress and Cristopoulos was conducting interviews at Taverna Ta Votsala. Nomikos had taken the precaution before starting work of standing at the counter of a nearby café to fortify himself with a Greek coffee, just how he liked it, medium sweet. Nobody in the café had tried to engage him in small talk.

In contrast to the assertiveness he had shown during the team briefing earlier, Nomikos felt the investigation had stalled. There were many problems. There was only so much he could do with the available manpower, for one thing. With men already deployed in the surveillance of Gautier and Grogan, he had only a skeleton force. Another problem was that he couldn't find any decent information on the three victims, certainly not enough to understand them. Without that, the motivation for any of the murders was impossible to establish, and his way forward very hard to see.

Nomikos opened his computer with a sigh, and brought up his investigation files in an attempt to establish order in his mind. He was an unconventional policeman, he knew that, but he did like method. He needed to find a way forward that had so far evaded him.

His work was soon interrupted. Cristopoulos phoned to report that he had learned nothing helpful from the owners of the taverna, and was heading to the Hotel Philippos, where he wanted to question the receptionist again. He would therefore be back in the office some time in the afternoon. Nomikos interpreted this as his colleague requiring a decent lunch and maybe a siesta. The team who had conducted the search of the Elias property then returned to the station saying they had found nothing. Nomikos ordered them to write up their reports anyway and added that he should not be disturbed.

He filled the first page of a new spread sheet with what he knew of the first death to have taken place: the girl buried beneath the floor of the stone hut. There was little enough to write. Identity still unknown, pathology report still awaited. He didn't expect much from the report when he finally received it, the corpse being so decomposed. Buried some twenty years ago, discovered by accident, and the grave recently disturbed (but Nomikos frankly had no clue about why or by whom). Murder? He couldn't prove how she died, but if not murder, why was she buried in a shallow grave without the usual rites?

Next, Dimitris Makris. More or less a missing person before he turned up dead, Makris had no relations, no known enemies, and there was absolutely no reason why anyone should have stabbed him in the back. Why kill a recluse? Had he perhaps witnessed something he shouldn't? In the empty hills? How did he end up in the stone hut in the middle of nowhere? Most confusing of all to the inspector's mind was the forensic report stating that Makris had been killed with the same knife that killed the American historian. Both had been stabbed from behind. The same killer must have killed both men, but Nomikos remained as confused as ever.

Finally, the most difficult of the three investigations was the murder of the American, Dr Moralis. Nomikos was under pressure: his superiors were being hassled already by their US counterparts, and his immediate boss was demanding results. Had Moralis just been here on holiday? Had he been alone, or with the missing British woman? Did Moralis have any connection with the illegal traffic in antiquities? Was there indeed any such activity around the island, or was Nomikos wrong about Gautier and Grogan? It was essential to establish whether Moralis was an innocent victim, or was somehow involved in the illegal trade. Why were the names of Grogan and Gautier on his computer? Was Moralis really searching for some ancient sanctuary that nobody knew about?

Nomikos stood up and paced round the room. He didn't know on which spreadsheet to put Alexander Harding-Jones, so he had started a new page for him. Harding-Jones's name was on Moralis's computer, and Nomikos thought it impossible that Moralis would need to make a note of it if he already knew the man. Also, Harding-Jones was on Naxos at the time Moralis was killed, a massive coincidence, if coincidence it was.

On the positive side, the name of Alex Harding-Jones appeared quite separately from the names Gautier and Grogan, and Martin Day vouched for him. Nomikos sighed again, stabbing the exit key on his machine. Could he even trust Day himself?

As if the hand of Fate had chosen to intervene, an officer entered the room apologetically to tell Nomikos of the arrival at the station of Dr Alexander Harding-Jones.

29

Day worked until late afternoon, when his mind lost its sharpness and he yearned for an hour of refreshing sleep. The heat was really powerful, and the Elias house, though its thick walls kept out the heat, was not air-conditioned. He yawned, closed down his laptop and sneaked out of the little study. Circumventing the last visitors being shown into the main room, he waved goodbye to Petros and got to his car. It had been almost blocked in by the visitors, and it took five minutes to manoeuvre his way out.

As he drove eastwards towards Filoti, the sun flooded through the car from behind. The route wound in and out of patches of shade as he followed the bends in the road. Day thought about the only good idea he had come up with that afternoon, and decided it might be worth a try. He would see what Helen thought, and ask for her help.

He found her absorbed in her work, typing thoughtfully. Deciding not to disturb her yet, Day went to his bedroom for a short nap, pausing only to drink a large glass of cold water from the fridge. He slept deeply and woke forty minutes later with no recollection of even lying down. The sun had dropped lower in the sky and the heat was a ttle less intense. He showered, put on a completely fresh set of c thes and went to look for Helen.

I r laptop was closed on the dining table, and she was sitting with a c p of tea on the balcony. He thought she looked particularly English, s ing there with her feet up on the low strut of another chair, teacup i hand. She had changed into a light blue dress and looked cool. S e lifted her sunglasses and laid them on the table as he sat down.

" ood morning, Martin," she teased. "Nice nap?"

" es, thanks, much needed. You OK?"

" ve had a very good day, thank you. I had lunch at a little place in I oti that we haven't tried yet, good coffee and a salad, it was lovely. I w, tell me what's been happening to you. There's an aura of s ppressed excitement about you. Did you meet Alex? And Aristos?"

I y edged his chair a little way along the balcony to move out of a haft of light that found its way through a gap in opposite hills s aight into his eyes.

" es, and the bombshell from Alex is that he and Kate Russell are a ouple. Kate wasn't here with Michael after all. She and Alex were I ving a discreet vacation before Alex began work on the exhibition p oposal."

" e must be out of his mind with worry now, not knowing where s e is."

" e does know where she is. She's in Athens. He didn't go to the p lice for fear of being suspected of something."

" That's this all about?" she said, shaking her head. "He should still h ve reported it."

"Kate apparently had a bad fright and left the island in a panic. Alex promised me he would go straight to the police station after our meeting with Aristos, and I think that will start the process of getting the girl to safety. I told him to come here tomorrow and clear everything up with us."

"Good. You must get to the bottom of this, Martin. He has to explain why his girlfriend was staying in a different hotel, coincidentally the one where a murder was committed."

"Don't worry, we'll get the truth out of him, whatever it is." Day decided to change the subject and told Helen about the police search at the Elias house and his meeting with the priest.

"The priest told me there were unpleasant rumours about the Makris family after they left the island. They hadn't told anybody how they'd funded their departure, so people started making up stories. One particularly unkind rumour suggested that young Dimitris, still in his teens, had offended a saint and was punished by being left behind."

"That sounds harsh."

"All the same, local people kept an eye out for young Makris for many years, until he recently disappeared. We knew that already. He'd been missing for some time before he was killed. The priest gave a blessing for him, in case he was lying dead somewhere, but Makris must still have been alive then."

Helen shook her head sadly. She felt the tears prickle in her eyes and fought to control them. They both watched the steady progress of the shepherd and his dog wending their way up the slopes to the flock, to move it to safety before nightfall.

"Is your book going to include a shepherd and his dog?" murmured Day. Helen laughed and rubbed the back of her index finger over her eye.

"Would you like a walk into the village? It might be good to get out for a while," Day suggested.

He thought this was the first time he had seen Helen nearly in tears. She was very far from having recovered from discovering Dimitris Ikris's body, he realised, she was trying to bury the memory. Day wondered whether he should avoid mentioning the subject again. Or perhaps he should get her extremely drunk and encourage her to let it all out. He had no idea.

They decided on a walk in the mellow evening. They took a footpath leading away from the village, the ground became steep and they found themselves on a narrow path overhung with Mediterranean oak trees and littered with empty cartridge cases. Somebody had been out shooting their dinner.

Helen was delighted to hear of the invitation to Rania Iraklidis's birthday celebration and Day sent a quick text of confirmation to Aristos while he remembered. Then he told her about his recent work on Elias's papers, which had amounted to examining the handwritten comments in the margins. The idea was to get closer to Elias's thought processes. It was of central importance to any biography to understand the subject's intentions, and up to this point Day had no clear idea what they were.

"I've also started to make a note of every location mentioned in the papers. It's deeply frustrating, because the places are often described very vaguely, so many metres from unnamed footpaths and so on. But I keep at it. I have a feeling it's the only way to find what I need."

"Do you have a good map you can use to trace these places?"

"Yes, I brought one from Athens. It shows the topography of the island in detail. Actually, I had good idea today and it involves you."

"Me?"

"Do you remember I said that Elias had written some poetry? I asked Petros if he would allow you to look at it, as you're a writer and a literature teacher, much better qualified than me in that respect."

"Isn't it in Greek?"

"Of course, but your Greek is better than you think, and I'll help where I can. Petros agreed, as long as the poetry stays in the house. You could come with me tomorrow and look at it, maybe?"

"If you want. What do you want me to find, Martin?"

"Imagine you're Elias. You're obsessed with finding something, but don't want to write anything down that might lead other people to find it first. You're determined to claim sole credit for the discovery. All the same, you still need to write your findings down."

"So you think he hid his ideas in his poetry? I think they call that a long shot, but I'll give it a try if you like."

Their footpath led to an abandoned church at the top of a rugged hill, from which they could look down at the village. The KTEL bus was just leaving, carrying the tourists back to their hotels in Chora, and the village seemed once again a quiet, local place. Day and Helen followed the path back to the main village road and chose a table for an aperitif at one of the traditional kafenions. Another black-robed Orthodox priest was reading at a table with a Greek coffee in front of him, and an old man sat on a chair by the kitchen door, smoking and slowly fingering his komboloi beads. Day ordered ouzo, and they diluted their drinks with a little cold water before lifting the small glasses in a melancholy toast. Day wondered whether getting her drunk on ouzo was really the action of a friend. He gave an involuntary smile.

" asked Aristos today about what Elias could have been looking for
t it was so important it had to be kept secret. He didn't have any
i as," Day mused. "Maybe Elias was a bit dotty."

ey almost fell into Thanasis's taverna, not drunk on ouzo but to
e ape from murders and intrigues, secrets and muddles, and the
f strations of plotting a novel. They weren't even very hungry. The
t erna was not busy, and Thanasis was sitting at a table by the kitchen.

" ly friends!" he called, getting up. "Kalispera sas! You can sit
a where you like. You want a table outside?"

" hanasi, how are the family? Yes, outside please. That table there
l ks perfect."

" ll well, thank you, Martin," said the taverna owner, pulling out a
c ir for Helen. "Now, I have something important to tell you. On
S urday we are completely booked up for dinner. It's a large group
f m the first of the cruise ships. I will reserve you a table if …"

")on't worry, Thanasi. On Saturday we're invited to a birthday
c ebration in Agkidia."

" ery good, Martin, you will have a good time. Now, what can I
t ng you?"

I len took her opportunity to get a word in. "I'd like a lovely cold
v ite wine, please."

" h," said Day, "half a litre of white and the same of red, please,
l anasi. And we'd better have a large bottle of water too. And just
s nething small to eat tonight. We're not very hungry."

I y felt his mobile vibrate in his pocket. He read the message.

"Paul. You remember, my old university friend, the tour guide? He's inviting me for a drink on Friday evening."

"You should take a break from Elias. At least Paul has nothing to do with all this mystery."

"Yes. If you don't mind, I think I'll accept." Day texted back and confirmed seven o'clock on Friday evening at Diogenes bar.

They settled back in their traditional wooden chairs to watch the world go by along Filoti's quiet main street. Vangelis brought their wine, placing the little jug of icy white wine by Helen, and some traditional meze plates. He left them to enjoy the gentle atmosphere of the evening. Local people were slowly walking home. One carried a bag of food from the local store, another was pushing an ancient bicycle. A couple stood in the road to chat to friends who occupied a café table under the trees in the growing darkness. An elderly man wearing an old cap and comfortable blue trousers held up by braces, gently propelling himself with a walking stick, stopped to acknowledge Day and Helen with a slight raising of his stick and a gap-toothed smile.

"Do you know him, Martin?"

"No. Do you?"

"Don't be silly!" And with that, tears escaped down her cheeks. Day saw, and topped up her glass.

30

Morning light flooded the balcony at the house in Filoti. Alex was seated between Day and Helen at the table, wearing a short-sleeved shirt and sandals, his body relaxed as it had not been on his previous visit.

They helped themselves to coffee and the cakes which Alex had brought from a bakery as he drove over in a hire car. Waving away a fly, Alex began to speak. He was clearly embarrassed.

"First of all, Martin, I'm sorry for not being frank with you from the start. I can only say that I was in a bit of a panic, and I didn't know who to trust or what to think. I even wondered if you were involved somehow in this business. It was such a massive coincidence that you should be here on Naxos."

"That's pretty much how I felt too, when I discovered you were in Agia Anna. I found it difficult not to find it very odd, I admit. It all seemed a bit cloak and dagger, you know."

"That's exactly how it felt, and it still does in many ways, though not regarding you, of course. I went to see Nomikos yesterday afternoon. It wasn't easy, but I told him everything and I think he believed me. After the initial shock. He seems a decent man."

"I think so too. How did you explain not telling them about Kate?"

"The truth. She begged me to tell nobody, she didn't want any contact with the island, she was afraid someone would follow her to Athens. She was very emotional. She was hiding in a small hotel in Plaka and not going out."

"What did Nomikos say to that?"

"I think he understood. On his advice I've told Kate that I've spoken to the police, and she agrees that we should tell them everything we know. Nomikos has arranged for her to see a colleague of his in Athens, and she feels OK about that now. The police will bring her back here soon."

Helen laid her hand on Alex's arm. "So Alex, please tell us everything from the beginning. I'm suffering from a painful case of natural curiosity!"

Alex spoke with a speed that suggested the pleasure he felt at finally speaking openly. He and Kate had met while she was a postgraduate student at University College, London. Despite the age gap between them, Alex and Kate had been strongly attracted to each other, having a lot in common both professionally and personally. Kate had gone to the USA to finish her doctoral research, and their relationship had lasted throughout the year she was away. Once Kate had returned and accepted her appointment at Warwick University, she and Alex could meet regularly. Kate shared Alex's passion for Greece, and alongside their romantic relationship they began a collaboration as joint editors of an edition of articles on the Mycenaean burial sites of the Cyclades. This, Alex added unnecessarily, was where the current story began.

One of the authors who submitted an article was Michael Moralis, whom Kate had met in New York. The article proposed the existence of an unexplored Mycenaean burial site on Naxos. Moralis sent Kate a friendly covering letter. He had never visited Naxos himself, he said, but through comparing references in ancient writers and the accounts of modern travellers, he had become convinced that his conjecture was on the mark.

The article was thrilling, a wonderful piece of scholarly deduction. Kate emailed the American and they set up a video call for the following week to discuss details. When the call took place, much to her surprise, Moralis told her he was withdrawing the article. The reason, he said, was that he did not want the information in the public domain because he believed disreputable people had become aware of his research. He was worried that their intention was to break into the site and remove whatever they found. He even had names.

Furthermore, Michael Moralis told Kate that he had resolved to go to Naxos himself and find the site. Kate told Michael about Alex at this point, and the three of them decided to go to Naxos together. It would be easier to find the place if they worked as a team. They would keep a low profile and not share their plans with anyone; not even Michael's wife was to know. They agreed that Alex and Michael would book separate accommodation and pretend not to know each other, because their professional association might alert the wrong people that something was afoot.

Day interrupted. "Did you say Michael knew the names of the people he was afraid of, Alex?"

"Yes. He had two names."

"Emil Gautier? Jim Grogan?"

"Yes. How on earth did you know that? Micha was part of a collaboration between the American museums an Interpol which aimed to stop the illegal trade in antiquities. Mich l had been the Metropolitan Museum's representative for several ars. These two particular men were suspected, but there was no ev ience regarding their activities. Michael found out that a group f people were supposedly using the Cyclades to store and forwar heir shipments and thought it might involve those two men. He   ln't tell me any more than that."

"How far did you get with trying to find Michael's   before he was killed?" asked Helen.

"Nowhere. Michael had said we would hire a car d the three of us would go out together every day. The plan w to explore the places where Michael thought the burial site might e, and with our combined experience we might find something. hen we would approach the Greek Archaeological Service and ar nge for the site to be protected. Michael was afraid of illegal di ing. The place sounded fairly remote, and casual looting is always possibility, not to mention more sinister interests."

"Illegal antiquities traders don't usually dig for the iff themselves, though, do they, Alex?" Day pointed out.

"That didn't stop Michael being afraid of it! This   s like a baby to him. At least, that's what we thought at first."

Alex paused and sighed.

"Kate and I couldn't be quite certain of Michael. W wanted to trust him, but the fact is we had reservations. That's w y Kate had the idea of staying at the same hotel as Michael, to kee an eye on him.

By the time Michael found out, she was established in her room in the Philippos Hotel. She and Michael pretended not to know each other, as I said. One day she overheard him on his mobile talking about 'an undiscovered sanctuary'. We weren't looking for a *sanctuary*, of course, so our suspicions were even further aroused. Why had he said that? And to whom? Another thing that worried us was that Michael came up with pretext after pretext to delay our search. We never once went to look for the site together."

"And what do you believe now? About Michael?" asked Helen.

"Well, now poor Michael's dead."

"But my question is the same. Do you think he was concealing something from you?"

"Yes, I do. I don't know what. I don't think he wanted to keep us from finding the site, and I don't believe he was a criminal. Whatever he was hiding, I don't believe that."

Day did not share Alex's certainty, and could think of nothing to say. Alex appeared to have run out of steam. There was clearly a great deal about this that he had simply not managed to understand.

"How did you find out Michael was dead?" Day asked eventually.

"The first we knew was the next morning, when Michael was found. We didn't know what had happened at first, but Kate had come down to the hotel lobby for breakfast and found it full of people. Police everywhere. Before she could call me, she overheard something that terrified her, and without speaking to me she left the island. She found a small hotel in Athens and called me from there. She begged me to keep her out of it, and she begged me to leave the island too."

"Why didn't you?"

"I hadn't met with the Curator. It was a genuine reason for my trip, Martin. I tried to persuade Kate to come back."

"But still you didn't contact the Curator," said Day quietly.

"What's this? Still don't believe me?"

"Mmm?"

"Alright, I did mean to speak to the Curator, but I also wanted to finish what we'd come here to do. I thought Kate would come back when she'd calmed down. I thought…" He let the sentence hang.

"You thought there was a burial site to be discovered."

"Yes."

"Where exactly is the place?"

"That's the problem. If Michael knew the location, he never told us. I've been all round the island since he died, but I haven't found anything. But you know what, Martin? I think he was probably right. It's there somewhere. Why else would he have been killed?"

Day noticed that Alex looked exhausted. He suggested more coffee and went to the kitchen to make it. Alex and Helen sat in silence for a while, Alex staring out to the valley with one hand over his mouth. Helen felt sorry for him.

"You all right, Alex?"

"I'm OK. Thanks."

"Can I ask something? If Michael was worried that his article might give away too much information about the whereabouts of the burial site, worried enough to withdraw the article from your edition, it must somehow reveal where the place is. Why was it so hard to find?"

Day, returning with the coffee, overheard.

"Excellent question," he murmured.

"I think Michael was right to deduce the presence of a burial site, but I don't think even he really knew where it was. The article doesn't give a location, but it would set minds working. Maybe nobody will ever find it."

"You may be right, Alex," said Day. "Naxos is a big island."

31

Alex declined lunch, saying he was tired and though he might try to get a rest. He looked as if everything had caught with him. He had an appointment with the police in the late aft oon, and Kate was coming back on a police launch that evening.

When he had left, Day and Helen ate a lunch of ft-overs. They didn't feel much like talking. Some of the things Al had said raised more questions than answers, but now was not th ight time to go through it again.

"What do you want to do with the rest of the day, elen?"

"I should probably get on with some work, but I n't really have the heart right now. Perhaps we should go and see   r friend Petros and I could take a look at the poetry?"

"Perfect. I'd like to get back to that mound of no , so that would suit me. May I at least take you for a relaxing eveni in Chora later? Fish dinner somewhere? I think it would do us bo good."

They called in briefly at Taverna Ta Votsala on the way to the Elias house. Day was still concerned about Maroula. Vasilios was out, but the customers were in the hands of an efficient local man who had joined the staff for the summer season, leaving Maroula time to sit briefly with Day and Helen. She insisted she felt better, and Day was reassured.

"Your Pater Giannis is a good man, Maroula. I liked him."

"He's a very good man. He grew up on the island, went away to train as a priest, and came back as soon as he'd finished his training. He's been here ever since. He was probably the same age as Maria Eleni's parents."

"What were they like? What kind of parents would leave a son behind for ever?"

Maroula thought about it. "They were very poor. They had a hard life. They struggled to survive, especially with three children to feed. And it must have been difficult to have such problems with the youngest boy."

"Do you mean he had mental difficulties?"

"He was wild. He was a difficult child."

"That's why they left him behind, is that what you mean? Awful. Does anybody know where the family went? Were there rumours?"

"Of course, in a small community there are always rumours. Nobody ever knew for sure."

***

At the Elias house the bright bougainvillea continued to dazzle in its rusty container by the door. Petros Tsifas opened the door promptly and beckoned them into the main room.

"Petro, this is my friend, Helen. Helen, this is Petro."

"It's very kind of you to allow me to look at Kyrie Elias's poetry," she said, shaking hands.

"It's a pleasure, I assure you. Nikos would be delighted and honoured."

Petros and Helen seemed to have taken an immediate liking to each other. The tall, poised, sixty-year-old Greek with e straight nose and piercing eyes made a striking contrast to the formidable English woman with only the beginnings of a summer tan. Their exaggerated courtesy could not conceal the warmth that was soon apparent between them. Petros proposed that Helen should follow him to the private sitting room where she could sit undisturbed at Nikos's old desk and spend as long as she liked looking at the poetry.

Day left them to it and resumed his usual place in the back room. He opened his laptop to the place where he had last been recording the locations on the island mentioned by Elias. He had no enthusiasm for the task. He stretched and checked the time and looked out of the window. He felt he had lost his impetus, the force which drove forward a good piece of research, and it would no lo.

He searched on the shelf for the most recent ring binders, and pulled down those covering 1998-2000. Surely a man so possessed as Elias became increasingly more focused, more driven, as the years went on. Day concentrated on the marginalia, the tiny details. Increasingly frustrated, he noted the smallest things that caught his attention. It was obvious that Elias wanted to keep his discoveries safe but sometimes evasions have a way of being noticeable, and when someone tries to conceal something the clue might lie in the smallest thing.

Nearly two hours later Day was ready to burst with boredom and despair. He had no idea what he was looking for. The word 'sanctuary' never appeared at all. All he had achieved was to note a few things that struck him as interesting, despite having no idea what they might mean. He went in search of Helen.

She was looking very content. Her laptop and dictionary were open, and she was surrounded by papers both hand-written and typed, spread out over the brown card folders in which she had found them. She looked up as he came in and threw himself into a chair.

"Hi Martin. Having a break? Some of these poems are beautiful. They remind me of the Greek poet Nikiforos Vrettakos. In fact, Nikos Elias has written one poem actually dedicated to Vrettakos. Some of the poems are really short – which is good for me, of course, trying to translate from the Greek – and most are about this island, its beauty, its light, its people. I'm making a lot of notes, as you suggested, especially of any specific places he refers to, but it's not that straightforward. A view of the sea , for instance, could be from anywhere, a mountain could be any of them, and so on. Anyway, I can tell you more later."

She looked at him properly. "Goodness, you look like you've had enough."

"I admit it's been a futile kind of afternoon."

"Oh dear, you do seem fed up. Look, I asked Petros if I could come back again, but he urged me to take the poetry home where I can study more easily. It's so trusting of him. I'll put everything safely together, and we can leave."

When they reached Filoti it was already the end of the afternoon and the shadows were starting to lengthen. They agreed to separate and rest for an hour, after which they would drive into Chora and enjoy a relaxing evening. Day couldn't sleep; he lay on his bed and thought over what Alex had told them and what he had seen in Elias's papers. Finally he put his questions aside, took a shower letting the water wash away the thoughts, and ironed a fresh shirt. He must do some more washing, he thought, or he would soon have nothing clean to wear.

***

Chora was pleasantly busy. Both tourists and locals were out and about, the tourists heading back from the beach or going out to the bars. The locals were still taking the evening stroll known as the volta. More than a walk, the volta was an occasion for dressing up, meeting friends and relatives, and being seen by your neighbours. It was a social occasion in itself, a highlight of the day. For the visitors it created an agreeable spectacle to enjoy over their cocktails.

Day and Helen took a volta of their own along the harbour's edge, where luxury yachts of all shapes and sizes were moored. Some were privately owned, while others offered fishing trips or tours of the local coastline and nearby islands. Several of these boats were even now returning from a tour and unloading their sunburned passengers, who would head for a shower and then out for their evening in Chora.

As they turned round to walk back along the wharf, Day's mind turned to food.

"What do you fancy to eat tonight?"

"I like your idea of seafood. How about you?"

"That sounds good to me. I'm not sure where we should go, I don't know the restaurants in Chora very well. How about we have a drink at Diogenes and see if they can recommend somewhere?"

"Excellent idea, Martin. You know, my head's still full of those poems. A drink is exactly what I need. Let's make it a celebration. The poetry is a wonderful discovery."

They took one of the tables with cushioned sofas at Diogenes bar. The waiter acknowledged Day from his visit the morning before with Alex. Day was impressed, asked his name and they chatted about fish restaurants in Chora. That done, Day wanted to hear if Helen had made any discoveries in the poetry which would help him in his current uphill task.

"Well, the poems seem to have been written over many years, although none of them are dated. Elias writes from the heart, and it's clear that he loved this island. There's a sadness in his work, and a beauty, and he has a magical facility with words which I can feel even in the Greek. So, what did I particularly want to tell you? Oh yes, he wrote a lot about a special church, a small church in the hills, which he would walk to along a stony footpath. It isn't named, unfortunately. He calls it 'my church'. I thought it could be a church called Agios Nikolaos, you know, Saint Nicholas because of Elias's name. Then he also talks a lot about peaks, mountains, hills. One poem I particularly noticed is called 'The Two Peaks', for instance."

"Nothing more specific? Naxos has many peaks. Could it be Mount Zeus?"

"I don't feel it's high mountains he's talking about, Martin, more hills or low peaks. These two particular peaks are a personal place to Elias. I'm afraid it could even be a metaphor, rather than a real hill. Whatever it is, it was very special to Elias."

"Oh dear," said Day. He wasn't comfortable with poetry, much less metaphor. There was no discouraging Helen.

"There's a particularly stunning poem called 'The ...atastrophe'. It's about the dreadful events in Smyrna in 1922, the ...res, the deaths, the forced exchange of populations between Gr...ce and Turkey. The poem is one of the longest and most complica...d, but alongside the historic story I feel there's also another one, a ...ersonal one. A personal crisis that Elias is exploring at the same t...e."

"When was this poem written?"

"As I said, there aren't any dates that I've found."

"Anything else so far?"

"One more thing stood out today. Remember you ...old me about a girl with a bracelet, and Petros telling you that it up...t Elias? I found a poem with the title 'The Bracelet'. It's about a ...mily heirloom handed from mother to daughter when the girl m...ries. It's meant to be worn on the girl's wedding day, but in the po...n it's stolen and the tradition is broken. The family are dogged by ba...luck ever after."

Day laughed, causing the woman at the next table t...ook at him. He was relieved to see Helen looking happier.

"I hate to laugh, Helen, but that all sounds very (...eek! The other poems are interesting, though. Good work! Right, ...dame, shall we go and dine? It's time we put all this to one side and ...d a really good plate of seafood and a chilled white wine."

32

Το Ναξιακό

The Naxian Newspaper

POLICE SEIZE ILLEGAL ANTIQUITIES HAUL

The Naxian received information this morning from the Naxos Police concerning the arrest yesterday of several men on charges connected with the illegal export of Helladic antiquities.

Inspectors Nomikos and Cristopoulos, jointly in charge of this operation, have not named the two men arrested on Naxos, but have confirmed that neither is a Greek national. Both men have been on Naxos for a period of about two weeks, during which time they have been under police surveillance in connection with a long-running investigation into illegal antiquities smuggling in the Cyclades.

It is believed that a horde of valuables dating from the Hellenistic Era, none of which originally came from the island of Naxos, were seized by police yesterday as the smugglers were preparing to transport the goods by boat from a temporary hiding place near a secluded bay on the southern coast of our island.

The articles were destined for nearby Heraklia, where it is known that the smugglers's boat is frequently moored, to be stored before being shipped to their final destinations. The boat's owner was taken into custody and an accomplice was arrested in Piraeus. Police are confident that these arrests will lead to the apprehension of further members of the smuggling organisation.

Today's arrests were made as a result of diligent police work over a considerable period of time, a police spokesman said, together with the testimony of valuable witnesses and the evidence given after his arrest by the captain of the transport vessel, who remains unnamed.

The police insist that these arrests are not connected to the recent murder of the respected American scholar, Dr Michael K. Moralis (author of *Mycenaean Incursions in the Cyclades*), at the Hotel Philippos in Chora.

The police expect to make further announcements in due course, which we will bring to our readers at the earliest opportunity.

33

"Martin? Alex here. Sorry it's early. Look, Kate and I would like to come up to Filoti this morning, would that be OK? It would be really good to see you."

"No problem. How about in an hour?"

"Thanks, Martin. There's something we want to tell you, something I know you'll be interested in."

"Oh, great. OK. We'll have the coffee ready for half past ten."

Alex and Kate Russell arrived in a hire car dead on half past ten. Coffee was soon ready on the balcony.

Kate Russell, whose appearance Day had only guessed at, was infinitely more interesting to look at than his imagination had suggested. She was probably in her early thirties but had the serious expression of someone older. She sat close to Alex, and Day decided that she and his friend looked a good match. Kate wore her hair tied back and delicate black-framed glasses that didn't conceal the beauty of her oval face and intelligent brown eyes. She was simply dressed in lightweight trousers and a pink blouse with the sleeves rolled up. A fine gold chain with a small pendant in the shape of a Cycladic figure was her only jewellery. She had a rare but appealing laugh.

Day and Helen made no secret of their curiosity about Kate's recent experiences, and she was ready to talk about them. She had arrived back on Naxos the previous evening. Reassured by a telephone conversation with the British Embassy in Athens, she had cooperated with the Athens Police, and had been brought back to Naxos by police launch.

On arrival she had spoken at length with Inspector Nomikos. Fortunately, he had understood why she had fled the island on the twentieth of May and hidden herself in Athens. In fact, when she told him what she had overheard and witnessed in the Hotel Philippos on the morning the murder was discovered, he had sat forward attentively in his chair.

Day was unable to prevent himself from hastening Kate's story along.

"What did you hear, Kate?"

"I came down that morning for breakfast to find the hotel full of police. Not only that, but it was a madhouse of staff, residents and press, and the lobby was thronged. I could tell something bad had happened, and Michael was nowhere to be seen. I went to the quietest end of reception to call his mobile, but then I noticed the man near to me talking into his phone. He had his back to me but I was close enough to hear what he was saying. He spoke in English with a French accent. He distinctly said, 'It's been dealt with, the American is no longer a problem'. He told the person on the other end to meet him at 8pm as planned, and to bring Panos. It occurred to me he might be one of the criminals Michael was afraid of, Emil Gautier. But what I overheard seemed clear - Michael had been killed. I got out of the lobby before the man noticed me. I went to my room and called Michael's mobile but there was no reply. So I packed, paid the bill and went to the ticket office at the Port. I didn't call Alex until I reached Piraeus."

"Why not? Surely he would have helped you?"

"I know, Martin, but he would have tried to make me stay. I admit, I was scared stiff. It was all I could do to keep everything together on the ferry. I called Alex from Athens, once I'd found a little tourist hotel to hide myself in."

"And Inspector Nomikos was OK with that?"

"Seemingly. He was charming. I made a statement, and was allowed to leave. I've been with Alex ever since. The police said they didn't think I needed protection, but I think that's because they have problems with manpower."

"Did you see this morning's *Naxian*? Alex?" Day asked.

"No. Why? Do they say something about Kate?"

"She isn't named, but the police have made some arrests, partly due to Kate's statement, I would think. The Frenchman and some others are in custody."

Kate grinned broadly for the first time.

"Thank goodness! So that might be why the police didn't think I needed protection."

"I expect you gave the police just enough information to be able to apply pressure on some of the men they suspected, and one or more gave up the others. However, the men have been charged with illegal antiquities smuggling, not in connection with your friend Michael. His murder remains unresolved at the moment."

"That's why we've come to see you. Kate and I think there's a link between Michael's death and the artefact racket, and not just because of what Kate overheard."

Day shuffled to find a comfortable spot in his chair. "Go on," he said.

"As I told you yesterday, this all began with an article written by Michael in which he outlined the possibility of an undiscovered burial site on Naxos that could be Mycenaean. It quotes various authorities and makes quite a good case, but I can't see anything showing where Michael thought the site was. I've brought the article on my laptop, Martin. I thought you'd like to see it."

"I would."

"When Michael first spoke to us he said there were two possible undiscovered sites on Naxos. We were surprised, because only one had been mentioned in his article. He said he hadn't included the other because it's now underwater off the coast. Anyway, Michael said he'd heard about an inscription on a church wall that referred to the second site, the one that he was keen to locate."

"How did he find that out?"

"He said he had a source locally. I thought he meant someone on Naxos, or perhaps in the Cyclades."

"OK. Go on."

"Alex and I agreed to come here with Michael to find the site and get it protected," said Kate, taking over the story. "Michael made it hard to refuse, he was so keen. So it was doubly cruel that, once we got here, Michael never once took us with him to look for it. He was going off by himself. We also began to wonder why he had the names of the supposed artefact traders. And the phone call I overheard, where he talked of a sanctuary, was very odd indeed." She turned to Helen. "You know, Helen, a sanctuary is unlikely to contain the kind of treasure which criminals want to steal. Whereas a burial site, where the dead were buried with valuable objects, that's a totally different matter. Michael always referred to a burial site."

Day nodded. The sanctuary thing had always puzzled him too.

"Did the police find Michael's mobile?" he asked. It was a detail he had been meaning to ask Nomikos but never remembered.

"No, it was missing from his room after the murder. I asked the Inspector," answered Kate.

"It's odd that the killer took the phone but left Michael's laptop," observed Day. "I suppose they panicked, or it was hidden and they didn't find it. Well, let's look at this one detail at a time. First, it's probably innocent enough that Michael knew the names of Gautier and Grogan, since Michael was helping the international police and US museums in their collaboration against the illegal trade. I made my own enquiries after Michael died, and I was told things about both men without going to too much trouble. It's just a matter of asking the right person the right question. Jim Grogan, the American collector, was in the market to buy a specific type of Mycenaean vase for his collection. Emil Gautier is a 'finder'. Michael may have jotted down their names together for that reason, not knowing they were on Naxos at the time. Alternatively, he may have suspected they were here, though we can only guess how. As for Gautier or Grogan, I don't for a moment think they were planning to extract valuables from the ground. I think Gautier may have been involved in a shipment being smuggled via Naxos, and Grogan, who sees himself as an adventurer-traveller-collector, decided to come and pick over the goods for himself."

"So you think Michael was honest?"

"I think we should assume so for the moment, Alex.   nfortunately we
may never know who he was calling from the hotel   out a sanctuary,
but the police may get something out of Gautier.   there anything
more you can tell us? What about the inscription   the church?"

"Absolutely no clue, sorry. It was just somethi   Michael once
mentioned."

"OK. Can I read the article now? Then we should t   ik of lunch…"

Day settled with Alex's laptop to read the article,   hich took him
about an hour. The others wandered to the cool o   he living room
and sat down to wait for Day to finish. By that ti   , everyone felt
much more relaxed. When they were ready to ea   hey put on the
grill, crisped up some flatbread and drizzled it wi   olive oil. Kate
cut some salad. Day looked preoccupied and kep   iis thoughts to
himself while they ate, and nobody disturbed hin   Helen watched
him discreetly. This is Martin at his best, she tho   ht. He loves it
when he has a difficult puzzle to solve.

When lunch had been cleared away, Alex risked   king what Day
made of the article.

"I've been looking for what Michael thought wo   lead someone
to the burial site. Like you, I saw nothing obvious   There's just the
reference to the old Naxos-Halki road, and a plac   iear some hills.
The problem is that road is very long and runs th   igh an area full
of hills. The reference talks of two adjacent summ   , a pointed one
and one lower. I guess you've searched along that   id, Alex?"

"Probably, they've all blurred into one now!"

"Let me think about this. I have an idea, but nothing substantial yet. I think I should go back to the Elias house this afternoon. This evening I'm having a drink in Chora with an old university friend, but I'll call you tomorrow morning if I come up with anything."

34

'He said he had a source locally.'

Those had been Alex's words, and they came back ⟩ Day in a flash of illumination as he drove to the Elias house so⟨ after Alex and Kate had left. Could Michael's source have been ⟨E⟩lias? Had Day been careless and failed to see something importa⟨nt⟩ in the papers? Perhaps there was some small reference which he ⟨ha⟩d failed to see. 'Only connect'. It was a quote from Day's favourite ⟨E⟩nglish novelist, E. M. Forster, and had become his mantra as a stud⟨en⟩t. In Day's line of work, the need to make connections was esse⟨nt⟩ial. Perhaps he was losing his edge.

Paralia Votsala was a welcome and familiar sight as he ⟨to⟩ok the downhill road towards the sea. A heat haze hung over the w⟨ate⟩r, clouding the usual clarity of the view to the horizon, turning a ⟨p⟩icture postcard vista into a mysterious luminosity of white and bl⟨ue⟩. It suggested a possible change in the weather. It was mid-afternoo⟨n⟩ the empty part of the day when Greeks take to their beds and visi⟨tor⟩s to the beach. No cars were parked outside the Elias house.

He let himself in quietly, assuming Petros to be resting. In the small room where Day worked, nothing had been disturbed. He spread his topographical map of Naxos on the floor ready to consult, and opened the binder for 1998. Now that he had a better idea what he was looking for, he was filled with excitement. He was searching for any reference to a submerged site off the coast, inscriptions on a church, or a place close to the Naxos-Halki road near two hills.

He had one other objective. If there was a connection between the murders of Moralis and Makris, as there must be because they had been killed with the same weapon, then there must be a connection between the two men. Therefore Day intended to look for any reference to Melanes, because the village and its environs seemed to connect them. Moralis, who was searching for his site along the nearby Naxos-Halki road, and Dimitris Makris, who had lived and died near there. If Michael was also connected to Elias, the clue might lie in these very papers.

Almost immediately, Day had some success. In the binder for 1998 he found a note that obliquely referred to an ancient site under the sea. It was expressed in archaeologist's shorthand.

1998 June
(Ref :1992 August) Rock fall. Underwater remains. Impossible to proceed.
Relying on Friday. Squeeze No. 92/8/AK.

'Underwater remains'. Just the thing! Day opened the binder for 1992 and searched for the report to which Elias referred. He found it quickly.

1992 August
Underwater remains off headland north of Akrotiri. Some interest, possibly Cycl. settlement. At low tide/from elevation some remains visible. Remains damaged both elements and man. Lge pediment, of later date? Foundations of possible mercantile area? Indication of substantial wall. Cliff damage, recent.

Day made sense of the shorthand without trouble. I told him that in August 1992 Elias had found the site of a possible Cycladic settlement beneath the sea. The remains could be seen at low tide or from the top of the headland, but were in a bad state due to the action of the tides and of people in the past, which was hardly surprising. Elias had also seen at least one item he thought belonged to a later period, the pediment of a classical building perhaps. The layout of some foundations had made him think that the area had been a place of commerce, something like a market, in ancient times. He had even spotted what he thought was part of a big wall. However, he had despaired of ever getting to the remains because of the difficult location.

Day picked up the large-scale topographical map of Naxos and searched round the coast, starting at Chora and working north. He was looking for a headland matching Elias's description. There it was, called Akrotiri. He could see a bay, a beach, a hotel and some houses. The coastline jutted out to the north of the modern village, and formed a headland. According to the map, the sea was relatively shallow in that area.

Day imagined Elias, the man in whose footsteps he was following, standing alone on the headland at Akrotiri, binoculars in hand, struggling to make out through the troubled surf of the wind-driven sea the outline of walls, the patterns of a possible settlement and possible fallen debris from buildings still held firm in the sea bed.

Day was sweating with excitement. He turned his attention back to Elias's note dated June 1998, and the cross reference to a specific piece of evidence called a squeeze. Elias had taken an impression of an inscription using archaeologists's 'squeeze paper'. This was like doing a brass rubbing but infinitely more sensitive, sometimes so sensitive that it was possible to identify the handwriting of the man who cut the letters. Day knew that Elias had a collection of these squeezes in the house. He hoped he was about to find one which showed the inscription on a church wall which Michael had believed led to a burial site.

Day made a mental note of the squeeze number and went quietly from his room to the library where, in a magnificent old cupboard clearly made for the purpose, Elias's collection of squeezes was kept. They were arranged by reference number and there was only one squeeze marked 92/8, meaning August 1992. He drew it carefully from its place, laid it on the adjacent table and opened it.

The impression of the ancient writing stood out on the paper, but Day was puzzled by what he saw. He understood the words, but not the significance. He took out his phone and photographed it. He wanted a second opinion, and he knew who to ask. He returned the precious squeeze to its storage place.

Back in his little study, Day opened the binder marked 1999 and thumbed through it. Beside most of the entries was written 'Friday'. Elias had occasionally written that he was relying on Friday. Day had only noticed these marginal references subliminally before, but they must be significant. Surely Elias worked on other days of the week? He checked from the beginning of the binder, and found them there too. And in 1998. And in 2000, the early months before Elias succumbed to his final illness.

Shelving the Friday puzzle for the time being, Day began to search for references to Melanes. He worked methodically, going back in date from 2000, checking every page written by Elias and even the photocopied articles. He was eventually rewarded by an entry from 1999, handwritten so badly it suggested Elias had been scribbling in a headlong rush.

1999 29th June Feast of Agioi Apostoloi. Girl, second time, not imagining the bracelet. What to do? P concerned, must keep him out of it.

This entry sounded more personal, more emotional, than Elias's other entries. It was what Day had been looking for. He would have missed it if he hadn't recently been reading through some books on Naxos that he'd found in his house when he moved in. The Feast of Agioi Apostoloi, or The Feast of the Apostles, was a three-day festival held annually in June in the village of Melanes. Melanes, there it was at last, and the girl with the bracelet was mentioned, the same note. This could be the connection Day needed.

He remembered Petros being confused by Elias's emotional reaction to some girl with a bracelet, and also that Helen mentioned that one of his poems was called 'The Bracelet'. Day sat back in his chair, both excited and confused. A girl wearing a bracelet is not, surely, something which should arouse strong feelings in a fifty-year-old gay historian. So what had really been going on? Why would Elias even notice a bracelet on a young girl's arm? The answer came to him softly, like the gentle movement of an evening breeze on your skin. He would notice if it was ancient.

Day turned the new idea over in his mind. The archaeologist, in the company of his unsuspecting partner, had attended the Feast of the Apostles, and on the arm of a young girl he had seen – what? – a Bronze Age armband perhaps? Day's mind recalled images of gold and silver jewellery recovered from the grave shafts of ancient Mycenae in the Peloponnese. It was the German archaeologist Heinrich Schliemann's terrific find, which he had claimed was the treasure of the heroes of Homer, including the famous gold mask he had called the 'Mask of Agamemnon'. Most people seeing such a bracelet on the arm of a local girl might assume it to be a cheap trinket. Not Nikos Elias.

What, then, might Elias have decided to do next? Perhaps he had believed that the girl had discovered the ancient site that he had been seeking for years, and had found the bracelet there. No, Day corrected himself, because he would have realised that if the girl had really discovered an ancient burial ground it would already be known all over the island. More likely the bracelet was the only object she had found, and she had decided to keep it and wear it herself. In that case, Elias would very much want to know where she had found it, or who had given it to her.

Day was pleased with his working assumptions. So, what else could he surmise? It was unlikely he would find anything in Elias's papers explaining what had happened next, and Elias had intended to keep Petros out of it so there was no hope there. Day tried a different approach.

If I were Elias, he thought, I would take immediate action of some sort. I wouldn't have been able to help myself. Soon after the festival I would have followed up my suspicions. The image of the bracelet would have burned a hole in my imagination. I would have gone back to Melanes and asked about the girl. But no, that would be too risky, it would attract unwanted attention. The locals knew Elias was an archaeologist, and if he had started asking about gold bracelets and locations it might start tongues wagging, and then everyone would be on their guard.

It was no good. Day gave up and returned to the papers. He studied the entries straight after the Feast of the Apostles. On almost every page he found the word 'Friday' in the margin somewhere. Day became exasperated, as much with himself as with Elias. Was the man mad? Did he have a religious belief that prevented him from working on any other day of the week?

Day leaned forward with his elbows on the table and his face in his hands. Inside the cup of his hands, inside his eyelids, it was dark. Inside his head, however, bright lights were shining. He laughed softly. Not for the first time he understood all those expressions like 'to see the light', 'a flash of illumination', and 'the light dawned'. He raised his head, and for a moment his sight was cloudy from the pressure of his palms. When it cleared, he reached for the map.

He heard footsteps outside the door.

"Petro, is that you?"

"Hi, Martin. Sorry, I didn't know you were here. Do yo need anything?"

"No, thanks. I'm just about to leave for the day. I'l ee you soon."

Once Petros's footsteps had faded, Day walked sof into the room that had been Elias's office. He quickly found what l needed, slipped it in his pocket and returned to his own room. H gathered up his map and closed down his computer. It was nearly x. He was now pressed for time and was annoyed with himself. He uld have to put all this on the back burner and drive straight to Cl ra for his drink with Paul. All the same, it had been an extremely pro ctive afternoon.

35

Helen spent the afternoon working on Elias's poetry. In the absence of a scanner, she had photographed all the poems and transferred the images to her computer. There were twenty-eight poems in all and many were short, only three being longer than a page. She was looking for references and images that would help Martin to understand Nikos Elias a little better, something that might offer a clue to show where Elias believed an ancient site to be hidden.

She translated steadily for two and a half hours without noticing the time. Suddenly exhausted, she closed her dictionary and went to make a cup of tea. Back on the balcony with the tea and her usual view, she cleared her mind of the poetry, the murder and the undiscovered site, and thought instead of the Makris family.

She could see a number of explanations for the disappearance of Maria Eleni. There was no proof of any of it, naturally. One idea in particular, desperately sad though it was, refused to be dispelled. She had shared it with Day, who had been sufficiently impressed to pass it on to Nomikos. It was that a DNA comparison should be made between Dimitris Makris and the woman in the shallow grave beneath him. The older body was the right age to be Maria Eleni Makris. Assuming, for the sake of argument, that the brother and sister had been buried in the same place, why not consider where that assumption might lead?

To start with, Maria Eleni could not have committed suicide or died by accident because she would have been decently buried, not left to lie in a shallow grave in a stone hut in the hills. Murder, then. In that case, why would the family not seek justice in the usual way? Answer: they either knew nothing about it or somebody stopped them.

Helen's imagination began to overheat. Maria Eleni could have had a relationship with a man which ended in tragedy. The man might have paid the Makris family to keep quiet and leave the island, saying that Maria Eleni had gone ahead. A secret burial would have been essential. It was just about feasible, and would explain how the family acquired money for their journey, but it was too fanciful, and Helen disapproved of fanciful things.

She had another idea. Dimitris himself, young and single and possibly hot-tempered, could have caused his sister's death. This version would explain why he was left behind when the family left Naxos, why the burial was kept secret and why Dimitris lived in isolation for so many years. It offered a clue why Dimitris' body was found in the stone hut where his sister lay. It wouldn't, of course, explain who had killed him.

Another of Helen's theories involved the idea of an undiscovered site. Did the Makris family find the site, sell off the treasure they found there, and thereby get the money to start a new life? Then something went wrong, they were discovered, the daughter died and was hidden in the stone hut, the family forced to flee. But if so, why leave the son behind? And again, who was the killer? No, it was all far too elaborate.

Helen struggled on trying to find an explanation in which she could believe. Had Dimitris, simple though he was, discovered the site himself and been killed by someone connected to the smuggling operation? No, she didn't like that idea, because the smugglers would know nothing of Maria Eleni's grave, so killing Dimitris in the hut would be too great a coincidence.

Helen washed her cup and returned to analysing the poems. A blustery wind had risen so she was pleased to be back inside the house. She was getting somewhere with the poems and beginning to enjoy herself. She started work on the poem called 'The Catastrophe'. As she had told Day, it was about the genocide at Smyrna in September 1922, and the mass migrations between Greece and Turkey which had such a terrible effect on subsequent generations. The tragic upheaval was still spoken of by the Greeks as the Catastrophe. Yet something about the poem itself struck an odd note. She found it surprising that Elias had used words such as *regret, sorrow, remorse, blame* alongside *cruelty, savagery, inhumanity, disaster, hardship, annihilation.* There had been precious little remorse shown at Smyrna. It was hard to put your finger on what was wrong, but it lay in the writer's choice of words. She sensed there was more to this poem than the events of 1922.

Finally, putting 'The Catastrophe' aside, she opened the translations she had made of 'The Church' and 'The Two Peaks'.

***

By the time Day returned from Chora she was once again on the balcony, this time with a book and a glass of wine. She was surprised to see him back.

"Hi, Martin, you're early."

"I went straight from the Elias house to Diogenes bar and waited for Paul for an hour. Not a hardship, of course, but no sign of him. No text, no Paul. I took a walk along the harbour to look for his boat, and there was no sign of that either. I suppose it could be moored somewhere else."

"Is he the unreliable type?"

"I don't know him well enough these days, but I don't think so. He was what you might call over-relaxed at university, but when you run a tour operation it must be vital to be reliable. Oh well, no problem, I'll go and get myself a drink and have a much better evening here with you."

He returned with a glass and settled himself on the balcony.

"I must see the police again tomorrow. There are things I discovered in Elias's papers today that I should share with them, and anyway want to get them to tell me more about the arrests, and the result of the DNA testing you suggested, if I can get it out of them."

"It's Saturday tomorrow."

"Good point, I've lost all track of time. I'll send Cristopoulos a text and perhaps he'll get back to me."

He sent the message using the number he had copied from Cristopoulos's card. Helen looked patiently at the mule and the blue beehives, sipping her drink.

"Are you going to tell me what you discovered?" she said.

"Of course. I remembered something Alex said about Michael having a local source. That would explain Michael's interest in Naxos. We know he's been researching his Naxos idea for some years, so it follows that he must have contacted his informant a long time ago. I wondered whether that might have been Elias."

"Brilliant, Martin. You could be right."

"Well, I searched among the documents for 1998 to 2000. I guessed any connection with Michael must have been in the very last years of Elias's life, otherwise Michael took an awfully long time working things out."

"Did you find anything?"

"Elias thought he had found two undiscovered sites on Naxos. The first was off a headland on the west coast not far from his own house. He had seen submerged shapes at low tide from the top of a headland, shapes which suggested that an ancient settlement lay under the water, not unlike the famous remains at Grotta. He gave up on this location, though, because it was submerged, and he wrote in his notes that he was going to focus on the other place."

"This must be the place he was looking for when he died?"

"I believe so. I then found a reference to an inscription. Elias seems to have thought this inscription related to the ancient site he was hoping to find. He took a squeeze of it, which I photographed on my phone. I'm going to show it to Aristos for his opinion."

"What on earth's a squeeze, Martin?"

"Not what it sounds like! It's a method of recording an ancient inscription. Archaeologists use squeeze paper to take an accurate impression of writing carved in stone. Think of brass rubbings from your childhood, but squeeze paper is much, much better. It can be pressed right into the smallest cracks made by the inscriber's tool. Epigraphists - the experts in inscriptions - have been able to identify specific 'handwriting', if you like, and even identify certain scribes from their characteristic chisel marks, all through the accuracy of the squeeze-paper method."

"And what does it say, this inscription?"

"It mentions Apollo, which strikes me as very oc␣ ␣it's the wrong period entirely. I want to hear what Aristos thinks.

"So do you think that Elias's ancient site is the same␣ ␣ne that Michael was looking for off the Naxos-Halki road?"

"Possibly," said Day thoughtfully. "I'll come to t␣ ␣t later. I found something else that seems to have led Elias closer t␣ ␣nding his site."

Day paused thoughtfully, much to the annoyance of␣ ␣is friend. Helen was not prepared to be kept waiting this time.

"Come on, Martin. Don't stop there!"

"Sorry. In 1999, Elias went to a traditional Naxian␣ ␣stival called the Feast of the Apostles. It's a three-day celebration th␣ ␣still takes place today. What's interesting is that it's held in the villa␣ ␣of Melanes."

"Melanes? The village near the stone hut?"

"Yes. Elias saw something at the festival which alarr␣ ␣d him. It seems trivial at first. He saw a girl wearing a bracelet. It up␣ ␣t him a lot, and he even wrote that he needed to keep Petros out o␣ ␣it."

"That reminds me of that poem you laughed abou␣ ␣the melodrama of a girl who loses a bracelet and the family hav␣ ␣generations of misfortune?"

"I thought of that at once when I found the refer␣ ␣ce to the girl in Elias's notes. Is that poem dated?"

"No, none of the poems are."

"Does it say anything helpful?"

"Not that struck me, but I'll check again tomorrow."

"Anyway, I might have formed a theory." Day took a long sip of his wine and a rather smug expression came on his face. "Elias wasn't somebody to notice what girls were wearing, as you know," he said. "A common bangle wouldn't have attracted his attention, never mind caused a strong reaction. But what if he'd recognised it as a piece of ancient jewellery….?"

"My God, Martin. You're right," said Helen. "He would want to know where she'd found it."

"Exactly. But I don't think Elias could risk showing any interest, being a local archaeologist. The entire local population would have started to speculate about what he'd discovered."

"So what did he do, do you think?"

"I have no idea, Helen. But I have two more important things to tell you. The first is why I must speak to the police. I'm afraid I stole Elias's old address book. I found the contact details of Dr Michael K. Moralis."

"So they knew each other. Elias was Michael's local source."

"It's a possibility, I think. I can't explain the long delay, but it's possible that Michael came to Naxos this month after working for many years on clues given him in 1999 by Nikos Elias. I think he believed he could now find the site, as he told Alex and Kate, but had no need or intention of taking Alex and Kate along with him."

"Does that leave a role for the smugglers in all this?"

"Mercifully, that's a problem for the police. I m; e another little breakthrough today that's far more exciting, Hele " Day sat back in the chair with an air of satisfaction and adopted theatrical tone straight out of one of his TV programmes.

"I shall call it - The Meaning of Friday!" he annou ed.

36

Andreas Nomikos nodded and waved Day to a chair in his office.

"I can give you twenty minutes, Mr Day. How can I help?"

"I'll be quick, Inspector. I made an interesting discovery yesterday which throws some light on why Moralis came to Naxos. Alex Harding-Jones told me that Michael mentioned having a source of information locally in connection with his search for an ancient site. I found Michael's name and US address in Elias's address book."

"So, let's assume they did contact each other, for the moment. When would that have been?"

"Before Elias died in 2000. I know, that's a long time ago. But let's assume that Michael wanted to ask Elias about the location of an ancient site. He was a mild-mannered academic, Inspector, entrenched in research and wholly absorbed by the Mycenaean era. He wasn't likely to be working with criminals, but he could have been searching for archaeological fame."

"So Michael Moralis wasn't an Indiana Jones," said Nomikos wryly. "How would you suggest he got himself murdered then?"

"I don't know. But I think the murder must be connected to Michael's search for an ancient site. Michael was already one of the foremost academic experts in the Mycenaean era now he wanted to make a real discovery. His name would be mentioned in the same breath as Arthur Evans and Howard Carter. I think Michael wanted that."

Nomikos nodded and shrugged in one elegant movement, keeping his shrewd blue eyes on Day. "Even if you're right, and Moralis contacted Elias over a decade ago, how does it get us further forward with discovering his killer?"

Nomikos had leaned back in his chair and was toying with a pen, in no apparent haste to conclude the interview. Day lost his patience.

"I'm just here to tell you what I found out, Inspector," he snapped.

"Fair enough, Mr Day," Nomikos conceded. "Thank you for that. It's possible Michael Moralis came to Naxos to follow up on information given him by Nikos Elias concerning an ancient site, but I need to find his killer. The antiquities smugglers consistently deny the murder. Gautier has been charged with the illegal artefact trading and we've arrested the Greek who was arguing with Grogan at the Taverna Ta Votsala, the same 'Panos' that Miss Russell overheard Gautier talking about in the hotel lobby. He was Gautier's strong man, but was nowhere near Chora when Moralis was killed. Grogan has been released: he had come to Naxos to put pressure on Gautier in connection with some personal deal. Gautier was furious and kept him at a distance. Unfortunately, Mr Day, nothing connects any of them to Moralis's death."

Day nodded. "How do you interpret the conversation in the hotel lobby which Kate Russell overheard? Gautier said, 'the American has been dealt with'. How can that not prove that Gautier was aware of Michael's death?"

"That's exactly why I'm certain that Gautier is somehow involved in the murder. He vigorously denies it, and appears to have an alibi for the time of death, but when asked about what he said into his phone he refuses to answer."

The firmness with which Nomikos replaced the pen on the desk suggested his frustration. Day decided to press his advantage before the policeman closed the interview.

"Did you receive my message concerning the two bodies in the hut?"

"I did, Mr Day, and the DNA comparison bears out your theory. They were siblings, there's no doubt. Those are the bodies of the sister and brother, Maria Eleni and Dimitris Makris."

Day nodded and looked firmly into the blue eyes of the Athenian policeman.

"Dimitris and Maria Eleni weren't the only Makris children. There was an older brother. Have you received DNA information for Michael Moralis?"

"It's a Greek surname, same initial as Makris. The older brother may have made good in America as a specialist in Greek history. As it happens, I asked for that check to be done myself, Mr Day. I'm expecting the results tomorrow."

The desk phone rang, and Nomikos spoke into the device briefly before bringing his full attention back to Day.

"Unfortunately, I have something to tell you now, Mr Day. It concerns the antiquities smugglers. We were sparing with the details we gave to the Press, and you must keep what I tell you between ourselves, as always. My reason for telling you is that you have a personal interest."

"What personal interest?"

"We've arrested five men. Here on Naxos we've arrested Gautier, Grogan and the Greek, Panos. We tracked the boat carrying the goods to Piraeus where it was apprehended and searched. Two arrests were made on the boat. They all implicated each other."

"Well done! What a coup!"

"The antiquities were shipped here from Patros via Piraeus. This was a well-managed operation using men with no knowledge of the freight they carried, leaving no easy trail for police to follow. The goods were repacked for onward shipment in various remote coves on the Cycladic islands. On Naxos this was at Kalados Bay, and there was another base on Herakleia. At Kalados they hid the shipment in an old house in the hills, using an old jeep that wouldn't attract attention. A small boat brought shipments discretely to Kalados and then on to Crete, from where we think they were collected by another group. Interpol has been trying to stop this racket for years."

"The news that concerns you, Mr Day, is that one of the men we apprehended in Piraeus was your friend, Paul Mett. It was his boat that transported the goods."

"Paul? No! That's incredible!"

Andreas Nomikos waited. Day's mind was flipping back twenty years to his days at Cambridge with Paul.

"And yet, Martin," said Nomikos eventually, "you say that in such a way I think you're not entirely surprised."

Day noted the use of his first name. Nomikos's large blue eyes were impassive, a policeman's gaze, but behind his words lay some sympathy and perspicacity. Day responded to it. He no longer had any sense that the inspector's time for him was rationed.

"Paul and I were meant to meet for a drink last night; he didn't show up. His boat wasn't in the harbour when I left the bar. He didn't answer his phone, and hasn't since. I suppose you know I've been calling him? Paul must have been already in Piraeus. Arrested even. Oh, that's awful news. Stupid bastard! What a waste!"

Nomikos nodded. "His tour business was the perfect cover for the smuggling. His boat came and went all the time round the Greek islands, never questioned. He wasn't a major player, just making good money on the side by selling the use of his boat. But he was fully aware of the cargo, so I'm afraid he's facing a serious charge."

He stood up, and Day also rose. They shook hands.

"I leave for Athens tomorrow. Thank you for your assistance and your, shall I say, creative participation. My official priority now is to ensure the outcome of the investigation into the illegal antiquities smuggling, at least as far as this series of arrests is concerned; it was my case from the start and I have to see it through. However, I'm mindful of the urgent need to resolve the murder of Dr Moralis, so I expect to return to Naxos in the near future. I may still get a confession to the murder from the men we have under arrest. Meanwhile, Inspector Cristopoulos and the local force will continue with the investigation in the normal way. So, perhaps we shall meet again."

"I hope so, Inspector," said Day, surprised that he not only meant it, but felt certain that this would not be the last time he stood opposite the charismatic inspector from Athens.

37

On leaving the police station, Day felt unpleasantly light-headed. He didn't know if he was stunned that the smugglers had been caught or by the news about Paul, but he wished he could sit quietly somewhere to think it through.

There was no time for that now. He and Helen had to buy a gift for Rania. He also needed something to eat. Leaving the car near the police station, he met Helen walking towards him. They agreed to call at a 'zacharoplastia', a confectionery shop, which was one of the delights of Greece as far as Helen was concerned, and the perfect place to buy beautifully crafted and expertly wrapped chocolates for Rania. Day agreed, with one reservation: lunch first, and then the purchase of the chocolate, or melted chocolate would be all that remained for Rania.

They went into the first decent place they saw - a taverna with outdoor seating under an invitingly shady canopy. They didn't want much to eat, but as they hadn't had breakfast, and the interview with Nomikos had exhausted Day, they ordered a large dish of stuffed tomatoes and red peppers which they ate with bread and a large bottle of cold water.

When they had finished, Day told Helen what Nomikos had told him about Paul.

"How do you feel now about him?" Helen asked. Day thought she was talking about Paul, but afterwards remained unsure.

"I'm processing it. I'm completely shocked, obviously. But now that I think about it, there were clues in Paul's behaviour even at college. There was always a bit of wildness, a lack of direction. Paul was never enthusiastic about any conventional career, like academia, teaching. He was by nature an opportunist and an independent spirit. Also, I should have realised that the cost of a boat was an extraordinary outlay for a freelance tour guide. There were little signs like that which I really should have picked up, I suppose. But still, he was my friend throughout our undergrad years. I'm really sad for him. That's his life done now. Prison, and then what will he do for a living? I just keep thinking it's such an awful waste."

"Yes, it's sad. You can't condone what he was doing, though. I suppose there's no doubt about it?"

"Innocent till proven guilty, but Nomikos seemed sure. It sounds like Paul made a confession. And now Nomikos is going back to Athens, he told me. He has to work on the smuggling case and leave the murders to Cristopoulos." A thought crossed Day's mind. "I wonder whether Michael's killer will actually get away with it."

"I detect a certain lack of confidence in the local police, Martin. But perhaps you're right."

They sat in thoughtful silence for a while. Helen was wondering whether to ask if Martin would leave the police to deal with it now, but she decided against it. She didn't want to risk encouraging him.

Day checked his phone and closed it again swiftly. "It's nearly two o'clock. Shall we make a move?"

They paid for lunch and walked to the zacharoplastia, where they ordered a large quantity of crystallised orange segments half-dipped in dark chocolate. The girl arranged a perfect quantity of them beautifully in the box, closed it, sealed it with a silver sticker, and wrapped it elaborately in two types of silver ribbon. With a final flourish of her scissors she declared herself satisfied with the job. She looked up to see her customers looking very impressed.

Back home in Filoti, chocolates in the fridge, Day and Helen went their separate ways for the rest of the afternoon. Helen lay on her back staring at the light from the window, which was wide open. She loved the fresh air of the valley, which was warm today and smelled of hay. She thought about what Day had told her, and about the blue-eyed and fair-haired police inspector who had clearly made an impression on him. Tomorrow their local police chief, Naxos's own Inspector Cristopoulos, would be in charge of his own police department again. Would he be relieved? Surely he would. Would he be able to resolve the three murders? She was less convinced.

Before she could reflect for very long on Martin's sadness about Paul, she fell asleep.

Day failed to get the sleep he needed that afternoon. He allowed himself an hour recalling all that he remembered from the old days about his friend Paul, then resolutely put his memories aside. He needed to decide how to ask Aristos Iraklidis for help. Despite it being his wife's birthday, Day had to speak to Aristos about the inscription this evening. Two heads were better than one, and Day wanted a second opinion. Would it lead to an ancient site somewhere on the island? Had it led Elias to an important discovery? Or had his search for archaeological celebrity been, from the start, just a sad wild goose chase?

38

The sixteen kilometre drive from Filoti to Agkidia, w ere the museum curator, Aristos Iraklidis, and his wife Rania owned beautiful white house, took them half an hour. This was one of Day favourite roads, passing through the small town of Halki and the t hill villages of Ano Potamia and Kato Potamia. After Kato Potami ley turned onto the old Naxos-Halki road, off which Michael Mo is had believed something of great antiquity waited to be discover l.

Agkidia, an old village, had recently become an e ansive area of luxury tourist accommodation because of its dist t views of the sea and Chora's old Kastro. It was a matter of an zement to Day that the Iraklidis house remained serenely aloof fi n the influx of summer visitors. Aristos and Rania had created an o s of restfulness and tradition.

The key to the house's serenity lay in its aspect. I effect it turned its back on the road, on the tourists and on the tant port. The front door faced the modern world, but the back o he house faced north-east, providing a shady sitting area and a g d view of the mountains. Here the couple spent most of their time beneath the vine-draped pergola. The hot plain that lay between the house and the sea were forgotten. The garden had a well and a water tank, which irrigated a garden of shrubs and flowers, a field of olive trees, and a small vineyard.

Day parked the Fiat beside two other dusty cars. There was nobody to be seen, but voices could be heard from somewhere behind the house. Ignoring the front door, Day waved Helen ahead of him up some stone steps that led to the rear garden. They passed a white cat lying asleep in the shadow of a sprawling caper bush; it took no notice of them.

Nobody was aware of their arrival immediately. Helen took in the hospitable scene under the pergola. A long wooden table was laid for eight. A magnificent round table made of marble, its edges carved with the Greek meander motif, was laden with plates and glasses. Comfortable chairs with white cushions surrounded the table in readiness for the guests. Everything was lit by dappled late-afternoon sunshine that fell between the leaves of the over-arching vine, and at the far end of the terrace a tall bougainvillea blazed in shocking pink.

An attractive woman saw them and broke away from her conversation with an elderly lady in a garden armchair.

"Martin, welcome!" she said, kissing him on both cheeks. "And Kyria Helen. I'm so pleased to meet you at last. Martin speaks about you so warmly. I'm Rania."

"Hello, Rania. Happy birthday! What a wonderful home you have. It's beautiful."

"Thank you. Come and meet my husband Aristos. Aristo mou, Martin and Helen have arrived."

The Curator made an immediate impact on Helen. He was a good-looking man with wavy white hair which was beginning to thin at the forehead, shining lights in his dark eyes and bushy eyebrows and moustache. He was smiling as if privately enjoying a clever remark overheard among children. His pleasure on seeing them was clearly genuine. Day produced their gift of chocolates, which was clearly a success. Rania took the box to the cool of the kitchen, and Aristos drew Helen towards the terrace. Day followed, grinning.

With a generous sweep of his arm Aristos introduced his family. "Martin and Helen, this is my mother, Anastasia. Mother, this is Martin Day and his friend Helen. Now, this is my wife's niece, Deppi. Short for Despina, of course. And this is her husband, ...ick Kiloziglou. And this is their son, Nestoras, our young great-nephew."

Everyone shook hands and, in that timeless way of new groups, began to form a number of separate conversations. Day was drawn to the old lady seated to one side. It was the first time he had met Aristos's mother. He knew Anastasia lived with Aristos and Rania, and had heard she was rather frail. She nodded at him, and he started to talk to her in his immaculate, old-fashioned version of Greek, liberally dotted with words from Ancient Greek learned when he was a schoolboy. The old woman's face creased into a map of wrinkles that seemed to be completely composed of smile lines. She was the model of an elderly Greek lady, he thought. Her silvery hair was drawn into a bun, and she wore a traditional black dress. Day guessed she was in her late eighties.

The person who did his best to avoid all conversation was the youngest family member, Nestoras, a serious little boy of about 9 or 10. He shook hands with them politely before running back into the sunny garden. He chased after an orange and white cat which had rashly shown itself, and disappeared. His parents laughed and let him go.

Soon they pulled the chairs away from the table and sat near Aristos's mother in her armchair. Day was not sure that Anastasia understood a word of English, which they were all using, but it did not seem to matter. She sat quietly smiling, nodding and content. Aristos arrived from the house with a bottle of white wine from the fridge, and poured out six glasses on the marble table.

"That's a magnificent table you have there, Aristo," said Helen, admiring the skill with which the rim and the single, massive plinth had been carved.

"Thank you, Helen. I bought it from a local marble artist by the name of Konstantinos Saris. I fell in love with it, but I also believe it's a good investment. He's already quite famous. Beautiful, isn't it?"

And so began an evening of Greek hospitality and relaxation. Day's mind wandered, revelling in the setting, savouring the wine, momentarily not involved in the conversation around him. He felt out of time, in a moment of significance, the kind that you remember years later. His senses felt agreeably heightened, and he knew he was smiling continuously. The wine was exciting to his palate and he felt joyful. His attention wandered to the leaves of an old olive tree, which were motionless. Some looked grey, some dark, some almost white as the sun's light played through them. His senses hummed with the fragrances from the kitchen, mingled with a fresh scent of unpolluted countryside, kept pure by sea and mountain.

He jumped out of his daydream and realised he was staring. Nestoras had returned, carrying the orange and white cat, which then scrambled from his grasp and ran away. The boy was standing by his mother's chair and leaned into her. She talked quietly to him, smiling, her arm round him. It was at this image of maternal tenderness that Day had been staring. He quickly turned to look at Helen.

Rania was inviting Helen for a look round the house, and they went inside together. Aristos excused himself to tend the barbecue on the other side of the house, and also left the group. Deppi, who had noticed Day staring at her and her son, gave him a smile.

"Nestoras is nine, and he'd much rather have someone of his own age to play with today. The poor cats are going to have to put up with a lot."

Nestoras, of course, picked this up. "But the cats like playing with me, Mama."

"Yes, Nestora mou. But cats like to sleep quietly when it's hot."

Day supported her by distracting the boy. "Your English is very good, Nestora."

"My Daddy speaks English all the time. Mummy is Greek, and Daddy is Australian."

Deppi explained. "We speak to Nestoras in both Greek and English at home. I'm originally from Syros, and Nick was born in Sydney, although his parents are from Thessaloniki."

"I see. I'm very impressed. Good for you, Nestora." His glance was on Deppi as he spoke. Her left hand rested fondly on her son's shoulder.

Day became aware that Nick had begun to show an interest in their conversation. "So, how did you two meet?" he asked him.

"I went to Australia to stay with relatives after I finished college," Deppi answered. "I didn't know what I wanted to do next. While I was in Sydney, I met Nick. I came home to Syros, and followed me."

Nick grinned, and now Day picked up his Australian accent. He couldn't believe he hadn't noticed it before.

"You see, I always wanted to live in Greece, Martin. Lots of people are drawn back to their roots, aren't they? I'd done my first degree in Thessaloniki, in architecture and restoration. After that, it was back home to Sydney for a graduate diploma in heritage conservation. That's when I met Deppi. In Greece I could be with her and also make a living - and where better than in Greece to be a heritage building restorer? So I found Deppi in Syros and set up a business - contracts were small at first, but every job was a pleasure. And here we are."

"So you live on Syros?"

"Yes. I can easily run the business from Syros because the ferry services run all year round, which is vital when I have projects on the mainland. We're close to Deppi's parents, and Nestoras likes the school."

Deppi interrupted excitedly. Day looked at her with unconcealed warmth.

"But we're planning to move."

"To Naxos?" Day said hopefully.

"Yes. We found a house we can't resist. It's a big old house near Plaka. It needs a lot of work, but it will be wonderful when it's done, and Nick can use the contractors from the business when they can be spared. It will be ready in a few months."

"We'll be almost neighbours."

"We will! Aristos told us you have a house here now. Filoti, isn't it? We'll be on Naxos before the autumn, so that Nestoras can start his new school, that's for definite. If the house isn't finished, which it might not be, we'll live on the yacht. Nestoras will love that."

"Yacht?" echoed Day foolishly.

"We have a plan, you see. In the winter we'll concentrate on the business. I do the administration and the accounts, Nick gets the new contracts, does the designs and runs the teams. But in the summer we'll leave the business in the hands of Nick's deputy during most of July and August. We'll never be far away if we're needed. Our plan is to take tourists on the yacht for whole days among the little islands and round the coves that can't be reached except from the sea."

"What a brilliant idea! I'm absolutely overcome with jealousy!" Day imagined this slender, dark-eyed woman and her husband under flapping sails navigating secret bays and swimming in shallow coves. My God, what a vision.

"We've started living on the yacht already when we come to see Rania and Aristos. Nestoras loves it. It's moored in Chora. You must come and have a drink with us, you and Helen."

"Absolutely."

"We've started to explore the waters round Naxos, planning our 'visitor experiences'. How's your navigating, Martin?"

Day bit back a remark about his poor seamanship. "Awful, I'm afraid. As are my knots. But I'm sure Helen would be a brilliant yachtswoman! She's the practical one."

"I like the way you commit your friend to the job when she isn't here!" Nick laughed. "We'll be happy if you just pretend to be tourists and tell us how we're doing. So, tell us about yourself, Martin. How do you plan to spend your time on Naxos? Aristos told me you want to spend the summers on the island, at least."

"Yes, I do. I'll probably be spending May to September here, doing my research and writing, which can be done as well here as in Athens, and I like it so much more on Naxos. I still have a small apartment in

Athens, if I need to be there. My agent in London is very good, he'll keep things ticking over for me, and if I need to go to London in the winter I usually stay with Helen, who has a place in Hampstead. If work dries up, of course, I'll be here full time living on beans and rice."

"I can't see that happening, Martin," said Deppi kindly, "I've watched some of your programmes. You're really good."

Her lovely smile was slightly teasing, and Day felt uncharacteristically embarrassed. "I don't know how long this freelance life will work for me," he said, "but so far, so good."

"Have you always been a freelancer?" Nick asked.

"No. After I graduated, I taught for a few years in a private school in London. I'm afraid I hated teaching. One good thing was that I met Helen there. She'd recently left Greece. Anyway, I resigned in 2010 and went to Athens for a few months, not sure what to do next. I had a piece of really good luck. Everyone in archaeology passes through Athens at one time or another, so it wasn't surprising that I met a guy from university who was making programmes for a UK history channel. I had some ideas, he supported me, we made programmes, and the books and articles followed. As I said, so far, so good."

Nick nodded, as one entrepreneur to another, and generously seconded his wife's approval. "Well, your reputation goes ahead of you, Martin. And it's a good one. Aristos speaks very highly of you too."

Day liked that; Aristos's good opinion was a thing of value. He looked at the Australian, and saw somebody whose life had followed a similar direction to his own, from the study of a subject about which he felt really passionate, to the move to a country close to his heart. They seemed to agree on Greece, and in general on what mattered most for quality of life.

"Talking of Aristos," Deppi said, "I'll go and see if he needs any help with the meat."

So saying, she got up and left the men together. Day watched her walk round the end of the terrace and disappear towards the barbecue. Nick was regarding him thoughtfully when Day looked back at him. Day quickly turned the talk to Nick's business.

"Do you have a restoration job ongoing at the moment, Nick? Apart from your own Plaka house, of course."

"Yes, I have two quite large contracts on the go. One is a private house in Athens, a gorgeous Neo-Classical building that will look superb when it's properly restored, and the other a very exciting job here on Naxos. The Naxos project is in the Kastro at Chora. I expect you know the Della Rocca-Barozzi House, where the summer music festival takes place? Fantastic Venetian construction, and very well restored some years ago, a great piece of work. There's always more to do, though, and the Archaeological Service found a bit more cash, so I have the honour of working on some of the older areas. There's quite a bit of pressure. We've got to finish before the end of next week, or at least make sure our work doesn't get in the way of the summer concert season."

"Do you specialise in Venetian buildings? Or do you have a favourite period?"

"Not especially. The Della Rocca-Barozzi building is a mixture of eras anyway, including even traditional island ceilings made of wattle over beam. There's seaweed and sand-mud insulation, beautiful old cedar wood doors, and secret locking mechanisms. I've brought my best team over from the mainland."

"I'd love to see what you're doing sometime, if I wouldn't be in the way. Oh, here comes Helen. It looks like she's come to call us to the table."

***

Imperceptibly the pure blue of the sky over the garden had faded to a delicate blush-grey, with a deep yellow haze radiating from the western horizon. It was what photographers call the golden hour, the time when the sunset throws the best colours over the landscape, before the richness of the light is lost and the cool colours of the so-called blue hour precede the night. When everyone was seated round the big table, Aristos rose to his feet, glass in hand, and prepared to make a toast. The rich light caught his raised glass.

"Thank you, all of you! Thank you for being here to help me celebrate the birthday of my lovely wife, Rania. We're both so pleased to see you round our table. It's a real pleasure to have both younger and older members of our family here today, and our dear English friends. I believe your glasses are full? May I propose a toast? To Rania!"

Rania smiled, flushed with the happiness of a person rarely in the spotlight. She lifted her hands in a gesture that included them all.

"Welcome to everyone. The food's ready, thanks to my wonderful niece, Despina. Without her it would be a very simple meal. Instead, we shall all have a real treat."

"You're the best cook around this table, Rania mou," laughed Deppi, softly. "You stay there, I'll bring the food out."

While Aristos placed a freshly opened bottle of white wine on the table, and introduced it with his usual enthusiasm, Deppi brought a succession of inviting appetisers from the kitchen - little platters of fish morsels, spicy dips and fresh bread, crispy fried vegetables, glistening black olives, tiny meatballs in a dusting of chopped herbs, squid pieces in lemon sauce, delicate mouthfuls of spinach and feta pie, soft red pepper slices, and charred pieces of grilled cheese.

Nestoras watched from the garden as they finished the plates of mezedes, or what his dad called starters. Deppi explained that he was entranced by the cats. He had discovered three of them. When asked how many cats they had, Aristos just shrugged and said the cats came and went. He would take them to the vet when they needed attention, and he got them all sterilised and innoculated, but they roamed where they liked and lived outside. The vet's bills weren't cheap, he pointed out, especially as the cats in the Cyclades were often born with a genetic problem affecting their eyes and noses. But they had the best food and care he could give them, poor things. Nestoras listened earnestly from a short distance away. Then he was off, following a small tabby cat. Nick laughed.

"He'll be back when you put the meat on the table. Can I smell lamb, Aristo?"

"You have a nose for lamb, Nick. Is it the Aussie in you, or the Greek? It is indeed lamb on the barbecue today. But first, will I tempt you to a taste of this rather special red wine? Helen, let me explain. We don't produce much commercial wine here on Naxos. As Martin knows, I'm very fond of the wine from our small family producers, and from other islands in this part of the Cyclades. But there is a commercially successful vineyard on Naxos which is a special favourite of mine, the 'Saint Anna' vineyard near Potamia, and this is their dry red wine from last year. I'd like to know what you think of it.'

Nick Kiloziglou raised his hand to accept a glass. "Before I taste that red, Aristo, can I ask the name of the white wine that we enjoyed earlier?"

"You liked that, did you, Nick? That was from a new wine-grower on Syros. You may know of it. The label is Ousyra. The winemaker is, in fact, from the UK, Martin, and he uses Greek grapes and method. I'm proud of that little discovery."

"I liked it very much," said Nick. "It's new to me, and very different. I'll have a look for it and get a stock for the boat. Especially if it will make you come and see us, Aristo!"

"I'll be there! So now, are we ready for the meat?"

While fresh bread was carried to the table by Nestoras, Aristos disappeared round the corner to fetch the lamb. He returned with a deep tin tray containing the fragrant meat, and put it on a deep stone shelf built into the house wall, where he pulled the meat apart with two forks and arranged it on a serving plate gorgeous enough to have been ancient. Everyone looked on and offered compliments to the cook. The fragrant 'Lamb on the Spit' was heady with garlic and fresh herbs.

Nestoras did a few jumps and had to be calmed down.

39

It was still very warm, and the Curator's guests were at their most relaxed. Deppi broke the spell.

"It's been so nice. But I'm afraid we should be going back to the boat soon. Nestoras will fall asleep in the car as it . It's been such a wonderful evening. Happy birthday, Aunt Rania. Will we see you when we're back in July? We could walk into the town and get an ice cream, and then get dinner somewhere. I'll be in touch. Perhaps Martin and Helen would like to join us?"

Everyone rose from their chairs and goodbyes were said. Aristos's mother took the opportunity to say goodnight and retire to her room. Nestoras was found in a cool corner of the house, drawing on a piece of paper he had found on Aristos's desk. Eventually the young family drove away towards the port, the light from the porch catching the dust rising from their tyres. Day stood looking wistfully after them as the taillights disappeared in a bend in the road.

The others had gone back into the house, except for Rania, who was standing beside him. She placed a hand gently on his arm.

"To which one have you lost your heart, Martin mou?" she asked kindly, a suggestion of indulgence in her voice. "Or is it that they make such a happy family picture?"

Day woke from his dream and gave a shrug. "How clever you are, Rania. You're quite right, I am feeling rather … wistful. And I don't know the answer to your question. Well, I probably do. I can't explain without telling you a little story." A small smile curled his mouth. "I'm an only child, brought up by a busy father. My mother died when I was ten. There was something about seeing Deppi with Nestoras. I know it sounds sentimental, Rania, but it was magical to see how loving they were together …"

Rania nodded. The wisdom of all Greek mothers seemed to lie behind her comment, which carried no suggestion of criticism. "You find a young mother very attractive. That's natural."

Day looked at her closely, but there was no disapproval, nor humour, in her face. She was simply giving a fact. Day felt a twinge of regret that Rania Iraklidis had seen the truth of his feelings before he had seen it himself.

"I'm afraid I'm in a world of my own sometimes," he muttered. "Now, may I give you a hand clearing the table?"

He offered Rania his arm, which she took and they walked round the house past the still warm barbecue and up the slope to the terrace. Day carried the plates and dishes into the kitchen, although Rania refused his offer to wash up. Aristos would help her later, she said, and Martin was still a guest. He must accept a small glass of tsipouro and sit with them for a while longer.

Day and Rania sat alone on the terrace with their little glasses of the traditional spirit, quietly chatting in the warm night. The drink was cool and spicy, and they sipped it slowly. They could just see Helen and Aristos at the end of the garden, where Aristos as pointing out his small vineyard by the light of a few bulbs hangi from the trees.

"I like your friend Helen very much, Martin. She's very open and warm person. When I showed her round the ho e, she told me about her ex-husband."

"She told you about him? She's clearly taken to you. e doesn't speak of him often these days."

"I understand now why she speaks Greek with sucl natural accent. She learned it when she was young and in love."

"I wish it had turned out better for her. It ended ve badly, I expect she told you."

"Not in detail, but I know she left him, left Greece nd returned to London, and that they never met again. He died a w years ago, is that right? And they never divorced?"

"No, there was no divorce. He was very religious, so was impossible for him to divorce. But for Zissis there were alwa other women, both after the marriage and sadly during it. I don't nk there's been anyone serious for her."

He could sense Rania looking at him in the darknes though he kept his eyes on Helen and Aristos in the garden. Rania oke tentatively, softly. "You and Helen never ... ?"

"Goodness, no. We are extremely good friends."

"As I thought. Forgive me for asking, Martin. Were re any children from Helen's marriage?"

"No. The marriage barely lasted long enough."

"Perhaps that's for the best, in the circumstances," said Rania. "She clearly loves Greece. And thanks to you, she can still come here quite often."

"Ah, she can go anywhere she likes. Her late husband left her very wealthy when he died. She gave up teaching immediately, and now she's doing what she should always have done, write books. It gives her freedom."

"Free and wealthy and talented. Quite an enviable situation, in the end," noted Rania.

They noticed that the lady in question was returning. It was about nine o'clock, and the warm Cycladic night was upon them. In terms of a Greek evening, it was early yet. Helen told Day that she was now extremely well informed about the cultivation of vines. Aristos went into the house and switched on some more wall lights that turned the terrace into a magical place. He returned carrying a bottle without a label.

"Forgive me if I don't join you in the tsipouro, my dear," said Aristos, "but I want Helen to taste this little wine. This bottle is from my own grapes, Helen. Of course I don't make the wine myself, but our friends who own a small vineyard kindly take my grapes and in exchange give me a few bottles. I like to think it contains at least a little of my fruit."

He pulled the cork from the already opened bottle and poured a little wine into a clean glass for Helen. It was a light red colour, and left bubbles on the side of the glass when Aristos held it to the light. He handed the glass to Helen and watched her reaction with pride.

With a smile of pleasure he turned to Martin. "Well, Professor Day, I believe you have an inscription to show me?"

"Indeed. I have a picture of it on my phone. I'm not sure you'll be able to read it in this light, though."

"Try me. We can always take it inside."

Day brought the image up on his phone and passed it to Aristos. The picture was quite bright in the gentle dusk of the terrace. Day tried to conceal his excitement. He knew what the inscription said, he also knew what it meant, that was not the hard part. The question was whether Aristos would interpret it in the same way as Day had begun to do.

"Mmm. It's a worn inscription, as you say, but its obvious what it says. Where did you say Elias found it?"

"In his notes he says that he found it on a church wall somewhere on Naxos."

Aristos handed back the mobile. "It says, as you clearly know yourself, 'Oros Choriou Ierou Apollonos'." He turned kindly to Helen. "It means 'the border of the sacred district of Apollo'. There's a border stone with the same inscription at Apollonas, near the kouros there. That whole hillside was sacred to Apollo, and the border was marked with stones such as these. The stone warned people that they were entering a sacred area." He turned back to Day with a puzzled expression. "I'm surprised you say it's on a church wall. From what you've already told me, I understand Elias wasn't referring to a church near Apollonas, was he?"

"No. Elias was looking some kilometres east of here in the Melanes area, and that whole expanse of hilly emptiness."

At the mention of Melanes, Helen shot Day a significant glance. Aristos was too absorbed in the puzzle to notice it but Day saw it from the corner of his eye.

"The inscription could be incorporated in a church in that area," Aristos went on. "In country places, where it was hard to bring building materials, people would naturally use whatever stones were lying around. This border stone could feasibly have been used in the building of a church, or as part of its boundary wall, or even been left leaning against a tree, I suppose. But there's no connection with Apollo in that area that I know of, which begs the question why the boundary stone was anywhere around there. You really have no idea which church Elias meant, Martin? There are about 200 churches on Naxos."

"I have an idea… Could we go inside, please?"

They moved inside, away from the biting insects and into the better light. Rania began making coffee. Aristos switched on his computer and entered his password. At Day's request he also brought out an old topographical map of the island. Then Day began his story.

"Rania, let me quickly tell you about Nikos Elias. For the last decade or so of his life, Elias held out the hope of making a significant archaeological discovery. He was looking at two sites on Naxos. One of these was off a headland near Akrotiri, north of Engares. He saw some remains at low tide when looking from the headland above the sea. However, despite being obsessed with this place for years, he eventually decided to give it up because it would be too difficult to excavate.

"His other obsession – and obsession isn't too strong a word, I think – concerned a different place altogether. I think our inscription on a church was connected to this second location. Unfortunately, Elias didn't say where he thought the site was, nor what he thought it might be. There are only some coded clues."

"What do you mean by 'coded', Martin?" interrupted Aristos. "You mean he deliberately tried to obscure his findings from anyone who might follow in his footsteps?"

"Exactly. Elias was an extremely secretive man, but occasionally he did drop his guard. He once saw a girl wearing a bracelet, at which he became very emotional. I think he recognised it as an ancient artefact, a Mycenaean gold armband. I think he began to search for a Bronze Age site near where he'd seen the girl. That was in Melanes in 1999. Do you know of any discoveries of ancient jewellery on Naxos like that, Aristo?"

"One or two things. Nothing of real significance."

Day was coming to the bit of his theory that most excited him, and for which he most needed Aristos's support. "I was completely in the dark about this until I noticed something very odd in Elias's papers," he continued. "Throughout his documents in the 1990s there's a single word written frequently in the margins, the word Friday. It occurs all the time, far too often, and its ridiculous to think it's the date of each entry. No other day or date is mentioned, only Friday."

Day stopped. It wasn't hesitation, it wasn't even one of his theatrical pauses. Something told him that Aristos was ahead of him, had already deduced what he himself had taken days to work out. Sure enough, Aristos was nodding.

"A church. You think he's referring to the church." It was not even a question. Rania and Helen still looked confused.

"I think so. You got there faster than I did, Aristos. Yes, the word Friday in the margins refers to a church dedicated to Agia Paraskevi, whose name literally means 'Saint Friday'. Perhaps Friday had even become his private name for the site. Anyway, I started looking on Google for churches called Agia Paraskevi, and of course there's more than one on this island, there are ten in fact, but now let me show you something on your map here ..."

They spread the topographical map on the table, and Day drew his finger from where they were in Agkidia, along the Naxos-Halki road about which Michael had been so certain, to Melanes. Just north of the kouros at Melanes was a small cross indicated a church. On the Curator's map it wasn't even named. Day stabbed his finger on the cross.

"The Church of Agia Paraskevi. I think this ties everything together. Michael Moralis was convinced that his so-called sanctuary site was near the Naxos-Halki road, which probably arose from an earlier conversation with Elias. Elias had found the inscription on one of the walls of the church and although he would have known that the Mycenaeans didn't worship Apollo, his notes reveal that he connected the inscription with the place he was looking for. More importantly, he deduced the site was near Melanes after seeing the girl with the bracelet there. The recurrence in Elias's documents of the word Friday is simply how Elias expressed his certainty that he was close to finding his precious site in the neighbourhood of the church with the inscription."

Day's enthusiasm caused great excitement round the table. In the face of his certainty, nobody could think of an objection. Then Helen took a closer look at the map.

"Isn't this church really close to the stone hut where we found poor Dimitris Makris?" she asked Day, giving him a look he didn't know how to interpret.

"You're right, Helen. I'm reliably informed by Google that the church lies less than fifteen minutes away from it by foot, and it would be only a two minute drive away. So, yes, it's very near the stone hut."

Day felt accused of something. He wondered if his pleasure at the discovery of the church and its connection with Friday had seemed insensitive to Helen. Aristos and Rania looked bewildered. Day had been true to his word to the police and kept most of the things he knew from them to himself, but now he felt something must be said. He chose his words carefully.

"We know of several connections now between ichael's murder and the two bodies in the hut near Melanes. Mich el and the local man were killed with the same weapon, and the dies in the hut were siblings. It's a long story! But I believe that if ve can find this ancient site it will help us to understand what's h pening. What's the matter, Aristo?"

The Curator was frowning.

"I agree with what you say, Martin, and I don't wa to be negative, but so far all you have is a church called Friday ar an inscription, which, if we can find it, only says that a certain plac vas once sacred to Apollo. There's no site. Or if there is, it's buried l neath a modern church where nobody will excavate it."

"I'm certain it exists, Aristo. Elias wrote some po y, and I have a feeling that he deliberately hid clues to the wherea outs of the site in them. Helen has been looking at them for me. W don't you take over, Helen?"

Day's excitement was infectious. Helen took her ph ie from her bag and started to bring up the poems.

"There are less than thirty poems, most short and any very good, but two poems stand out because they aren't very ood at all. I've come to agree with Martin that they were written wit he intention of leaving markers to the undiscovered site. For one th g, they're called 'The Church' and 'The Two Peaks', which straigh way suggested landmarks to me. This was before Martin told me out the Friday puzzle and the Church of Agia Paraskevi. I have my anslations here. I need your help with them, if you don't mind. It v uld be easier if we can see them on the bigger screen, Aristo?"

She sent the files to the Curator's computer. They tu ed to his screen and read together in silence.

The Church

Gaia, self-created from chaos, mother earth,
Creator of Heaven, first goddess of our imagination.

Mother Church, Madonna, God-bearer, Lady.

The line from mother earth was far from straight
Yet, that First Lady was the preparation,
The soil and earth from which grew Beloved Church.

Shield your eyes against the sun and greet the day
With clear eyesight, look up and raise your face.
Look to the East, whence came the Madonna,
Look east to Syros' rich icon of the Dormition
The Dormition of the Mother of God.

Reflect. The way is short but rocky,
The signs of guidance are few,
The Lady will prepare the way to the final resting place of the saved.

The Two Peaks

The siblings Castor and Pollux,
Dioscuri, sons of Leda,
Naxian Gemini,
Guardians of Helen.

One a mortal, the other a God.

Great Zeus, who loved his son,
Immortal Pollux, kept him half the year on Mount Olympus with the Gods,
The other half beneath the ground in the Elysian Fields.

Mankind on Earth, his nature half noble and half base,
His life half above, half below ground,
Finally leaves this earth to rest beneath the fields.

The Two Peaks, one soaring and one base,
Pollux and Castor, god and man,
One soaring and pointing to the Gods,
One lower and modest and mortal,
Beneath them the eternal Underworld.

Rania wrinkled her nose. "Are his other poems as heavy as this? The first one is so religious, and the second one practically incomprehensible."

"I agree," said Helen, "and no, the others are little poems celebrating the beauty of Naxos and personal subjects that are treated lightly. None of the others contain strong religious references or a heavy-handed use of classical myths. These are beyond one. If we can't see our way through the references, I don't think we can get to the underlying meaning."

"I'm no student of literature," said Aristos, "but they seem deliberately obscure. Shall we look at 'The Church' first? It seems slightly less difficult, a poem about the consolation of religion. Was Elias religious?"

Day answered confidently. "I'm pretty sure he wasn't. I've found nothing to suggest it and I've been through most of Elias's possessions. The only sign of Orthodox Christianity in the house is a small cross that Petros wears round his neck. I suppose given their relationship it's unlikely either of them were religious, although there's a question mark over Petros."

"In that case, let's try to unravel the poem. It starts with Gaia, the ancient Mother Earth figure in Greek mythology. Elias then connects Gaia directly with the Virgin Mary and the Greek Orthodox Church. In other words, he's linking antiquity and the modern church. I think we can assume that Elias was referring to the modern church where he found the inscription. That's already a good start. In the poem it says the line between Gaia and Mary is 'far from straight', perhaps meaning that the search isn't easy, but then I don't know what to make of the rest. The poem goes off crazily with the reference to the figure of Mary in El Greco's icon in the cathedral on Syros! What's that about? All I know about the icon is that El Greco painted Mary 'in dormition', in other words having fallen asleep in a state of peace."

"Perhaps the last line is referring to that," suggested Rania.

"Just a minute! There's something really wrong…"

"What, Aristo?"

"The poem says we have to look *east* to Syros. Syros isn't east of Naxos. Surely Elias wouldn't get that wrong?"

Helen was following Aristos's train of thought and took it a step further. "In that case, does the instruction to look east suggest he's giving us a different instruction? Telling us to look somewhere other than Syros? To the location of the site, perhaps?"

"If so, what else is he telling us?"

"Well, he talks of the earth and a 'final resting place', and of Mary lying peacefully asleep. All these suggest something on or under the ground. Could that be an underground site? A burial site possibly?"

"That doesn't explain about looking east to Syros," objected Aristos.

"Maybe he's telling us to look in an easterly direction," Day interrupted. "A deliberate mistake, perhaps, to wake us up to what he's trying to say?"

Suddenly into Helen's mind came snippets of Milton dredged up from her teaching days. She remembered telling the students to notice that whenever Milton placed a single word at the beginning of the next line, it was meant to carry special significance. She was suddenly sure that Elias was using the same technique.

"That single, emphatic word: 'Reflect!' That's an instruction, isn't it? Elias is telling us to use our brains. He tells us that the way is 'short and rocky' Maybe more than a metaphor for life, it may be quite literally true. The route we have to take is rocky, and not too far. And we must head east."

Aristos nodded as if only persuaded up to a point. Day had said nothing so far beyond the occasional word of encouragement. He preferred to keep quiet while the rest of them teased out the poem, heading in the same direction as his thoughts of the night before.

"East from where, though?" Aristos was saying. Helen sat back in her chair.

"From Mother Church. Martin's Church of St Paraskevi."

They were quiet round the table, and Day admired the conviction and excitement on Helen's face. He felt immensely proud of her. Now they were finding a way forward. He felt great relief, and realised how much he had been pinning his hopes on Aristos reaching the same conclusions as he had done. He had not thought that it would be Helen leading the way.

So, they were in agreement. The old historian, the secretive Nikos Elias, really had wanted to leave a message to ensure his work was not lost, his unsuccessful search was finally fulfilled. He may even have written this obscure poem, so unlike his other poetry, as a kind of legacy: *Start at the Church of Agia Paraskevi, look towards the east, follow a rocky way for a short distance, and there beneath the ground the ancient dead, in peace, in 'dormition'.*

"Well done, Helen," said Day warmly. "Now, what about the other strange poem, 'The Two Peaks'?"

"It's completely beyond me," said Helen with a touch of exasperation. "Rania, Martin tells me you're an expert on myths. Any ideas?"

"It's the legend of Castor and Pollux, Helen, but I can't see its relevance to all this." Rania pointed to the words of the poem on the screen as she named the characters. "Castor and Pollux are brothers. Leda is their mother but the brothers had different fathers.

Castor is mortal like his father, and Pollux is immortal, the son of Zeus. The legend tells how Castor is fatally wounded and Pollux asks Zeus to save his brother, make him immortal. Zeus changed both brothers into a constellation, Gemini the Twins. They were now both immortal but not in the way Pollux had wanted. As for this reference to Helen, it's the Helen we call Helen of Troy, who was their sister. Is Elias suggesting that the peaks are guarding something precious?"

Aristos had more to add to his wife's account. "Castor and Pollux were known as the Dioscuri, hence the reference there. I don't understand why Elias says 'Naxian Gemini', though. Nothing Naxian about the constellation that I'm aware of."

"Perhaps to make us realise that he's actually talking about a location on Naxos." suggested Helen. "Castor and Pollux are the two peaks, one of them has a connection to humans, and they are guarding something important and vulnerable."

"Zeus made a proviso when he saved Castor from death," Aristos continued. "This verse here refers to it. The brothers were allowed on Mount Olympus for six months of the year, but for the other six months they had to live in Hades, which must be the 'Elysian Fields' there in the poem. It's another suggestion of a place beneath the earth. Do you agree, Helen?"

"Could be. The next verse gives me the shivers. I think that Elias is referring to his own mortality. The verse beginning 'Mankind on Earth' could be autobiographical, do you see? Elias might have been talking about himself. Half a good man, half blame-worthy. And near the end of his life."

Day nodded reluctantly. Maybe Helen was right. A life spent 'half above, half below ground' was as true of Elias as of Castor and Pollux. Day marvelled that an Elias full of remorse and aware of his own mortality had still been full of a desire to are his greatest discovery.

"OK," he said, "but what about the last bit? The two :aks themselves. Other than being a reference to Castor and Pollux if course."

For a few moments nobody answered. Nikos Elias's ldle was almost tiresome to them at this point. Day knew they we : close. He was about to nudge his friends towards his way of thin ng when Helen made it unnecessary.

"It's another instruction, isn't it? If we look towards e east there will be two peaks, two differently shaped peaks, a taller e and a shorter one. The lower one is described as 'mortal', whicl night suggest a place where people used to live."

Aristos jumped on her words. "That's very good! A l beneath these peaks, an 'eternal underworld', which surely suggest he resting place of the dead. It's a burial site!" The Curator looke round at them with conviction and more excitement than Day cou remember him ever showing before.

One good look at the topographical map revealed at they needed to know. The contour lines due east of the little hurch of Agia Paraskevi near Melanes showed two hills. Aristos ope d Google Maps and located a satellite picture of the two peaks. On as pointed and steep, and below it stood a lower one with a round ummit.

Would it have been an attractive location for a Myce ean settlement? wondered Day, staring at the screen. Not on the face f it, he thought, but he knew there was only one thing he wanted t lo now.

"We need to go and see it, don't we? I want to walk lias's route and see for myself. Who wants to come?"

"It'll be rough walking, Martin, but I'll come. I'm free tomorrow if you are?" said Aristos at once.

"Excellent. You're up for it too, Helen? Do you think Nick would be interested? The more of us, the better."

"I'll call Nick," Aristos said. "I think it will appeal to him. Martin, I hope you realise there may be nothing there to see? Elias must have walked it many, many times."

"I know. But he was just one man. We'll be a team."

40

The search party assembled at ten the next mornii   in the car park
intended for visitors to the Melanes kouros. Nicl   had come with
Aristos, and Day and Helen were in the Fiat. Day   vas grateful for
having had some coffee before starting out. They   ight be in it for
the long haul. Everyone wore walking shoes, and   ristos and Day
each carried a stick, both as a hiking aid and for   aring away the
resident snake population. The morning was mil   and still, good
conditions for what they had in mind. Helen was th   est dressed for
the expedition, covered from head to toe against l   ing insects and
the Greek sun. She looked as if she was off to visi   Dr Livingstone
in the heart of Africa. Day was surprised by a sudd   surge of pride
for his old friend. As for himself, he realised that he   robably should
have covered up more. It promised to be hot.

They had decided to pass themselves off as a grouj   f hikers, which
was the reason for parking where they had rather tl   1 at the church.
Aristos had brought binoculars, and both Nick a   l Helen carried
cameras. These would enhance their tourist image   s well as being
useful for their real purpose: searching for signs of   1 ancient burial
site amidst the stony outcrops of Naxos.

Initially they followed Day along the empty Naxos-Halki road, the morning sun throwing their shadows ahead of them. At least the walking was easy here. To their left the arid fields fell away into the valley, while to the right the view was blocked by higher ground. Finally the road turned again and they saw the church, the first of their objectives. They crossed the empty road and walked towards it. Not one vehicle had so far passed them, and the church car park was empty.

The tiny Church of Agia Paraskevi was pretty and well maintained. It had the appearance of being well-loved. Spotless white paint covered its exterior walls. Its roof tiles and the caps on the boundary wall were painted a cheerful sky blue, and the twin flags of Greece and Naxos hung limply from flagpoles on either side of the building. There was no sound, neither of cars nor of voices; not even a bird disturbed the peace.

They approached the little church, their boots crunching on the grit path. Cables ran to one corner of the church roof, a sure sign that the church was generally in use. It seemed incredible luck that there was nobody around, especially as it was a Sunday. Aristos tried the blue-painted door, but it was locked. Day turned round to face the others.

"Shall we look for the inscription?"

He had failed to keep the doubt from his voice. The church was freshly painted, and there were no gravestones leaning against its walls, no pile of stone blocks nearby or in the scrubby land around. He had imagined, he had hoped for, some abandoned old headstones concealing among them an old piece of marble, or an inscription still visible on the church wall. He should have expected this delightful, tidy edifice, a well cared-for Cycladic church, one of hundreds like it. Anything that Elias might have seen a decade ago was probably long gone.

They spread out, although there was little enough ground to cover. Within minutes it was clear that nobody would find anything. Was it all over before it had begun? Frustration washed over Day. The Curator spoke for them all.

"There's no inscription here. The church has been restored since Elias's time, which after all is a decade ago. The whitewash is several layers deep. Any faint inscription will have been filled in. Or the inscribed stone could have been leaning against the church and has been cleared away. But you know, Martin, we don't need it now."

"What do you mean?"

"Well, look over there."

Aristos was standing on whitewashed paving to the side of the church with his back against the church wall. He was facing eastwards. The others turned to see what he was looking at. It was as if Elias's words were written on the landscape. A rocky outcrop stood absorbing the growing heat of the sun through its scrub-covered face. Day could see a small escarpment at one end, its open gash probably part of the marble workings in the area. To the right of the and facing the church directly were two perfect hills. The taller had a pointed peak. The lower, to the right of the pair, had a rounded summit.

Between these two hills and the Church of Agia Paraskevi lay an area of tough scrub, tall grass and rocks; there was no path through it and it looked a challenging hike. The land was beautiful in its way. Forming tight clumps of various heights, the scrub was every shade of green, grey and rust. Day regarded it with an archaeologist's eye. Every plant was dense and tough, its only means of survival in that landscape. Water was short here. He felt angry and cheated. This was no place to find a Mycenaean settlement. This was nothing but Cycladic wasteland.

Nick clearly felt differently.

"Come on. I'm not giving up now! Get a move on! It's not exactly the Outback, is it?"

It might as well have been, Day thought. If anyone had been watching the group of supposed hikers attempting to cross a landscape unblessed by walking paths, using only such tracks as had been made by sheep or goats, they would have thought them mad and been right. After an hour of beating their way with sticks and avoiding injured ankles among the rocks and hollows, they stopped to rest and drink from their water bottles. Helen wafted her hat in front of her face, which was pink with exertion.

"So what exactly should we be looking for? Can you give us some pointers?"

Day summoned the will to respond. His current negativity made his answer unhelpful.

"I can only tell you what I was hoping we'd find, given the possibility that Elias saw a girl wearing an ancient bracelet in the nearest village. A bracelet might have come from a small settlement, or possibly a burial area. What do you think, Aristo?"

"I was thinking along the same lines, Martin, but I'm not sure now. This area doesn't seem a good place for a settlement, much less one large enough to warrant the burial of an important family. At Komiaki, quite a long way north of here, a small settlement and a tomb were found. However, the valley near Komiaki was fertile and an ideal place to base a community. Looking round here, I can't see this area attracting settlers. But it's not impossible. There are two really isolated Mycenaean grave sites on Naxos, one near here at Apiranthos and the other over at Moutsouna…"

Nick, unable to take any more, got to his feet, bringing Aristos's conjectures to a close.

"Ok, so it isn't impossible," he said. "What exactly are the clues we should look for? What might suggest we've found something? Don't forget you're working with complete amateurs here."

Day, perched on the stone wall, was now thoroughly puerile with disappointment and feeling a strange antipathy to the eager Australian.

"I love your optimism, Nick," he said cuttingly.

Helen cut him off before he could say anything more offensive. "OK, now that we're here, let's see this through. Aristo, give us our instructions and coordinate the search party. Like Nick, I haven't come this far only to give up now."

***

Another hour and a half, and they had found nothing but rocks. The two outcrops, far from being peaks, looked much smaller once the party were near them. They hadn't seen a living creature and the very barrenness of the place was depressing. The four of them had split up to explore the area more efficiently. Helen could see the stocky figure of Nick scaling boulders, and the rangy figure of Day striding across gullies brandishing his stick. The Curator sat on a rock in a small patch of shade beneath the larger outcrop, apparently doing some thinking.

Helen had borrowed Aristos's stick and was searching a small area carefully, moving aside the vegetation. She was at the foot of the lower of the two hills not far from where Nick was exploring. She recognised Day's despair but still felt moderately optimistic. She remembered how Elias had referred to this place in his poem, calling it the more 'modest and mortal' of the two peaks. Mortality was suggestive of habitation as well as death, she thought, and might be the poet's code for an ancient site. Clearly her ex-husband Zissis had not deprived her of optimism after all.

Thanks to Aristos, they had some idea of what they were looking for. He had described, although without much hope, things that might give a clue to former human habitation. The trick was to notice anything that didn't belong in the landscape. No matter how small, anything that was shiny or a strange colour, anything that might have been worked by human hands, maybe sharpened, rounded or pierced, could be worth a second look. Any rock that seemed to have been shaped even roughly could be important: it might have a straight edge, a smoothed surface, regular scratch marks or indentations. And, of course, they were looking for pattern: large stones that might have been placed deliberately as part of a wall or building, though not, of course, the modern stone walls which were plentiful in these hills.

It was enough to get them searching. They had agreed to look round for an hour, after which they would re-assemble round the Curator and make a new plan.

When the hour had passed, Helen was the last to reach Aristos, picking her way carefully across the terrain. Day and Nick were bathed in sweat, reddened by the heat, filthy in pore and nail, and in Day's case visibly exasperated. Aristos got up politely and offered Helen his narrow perch in a thin slit of shade under the thorny remnant of a tree.

"Well, did anyone find anything?" she began.

"No," said Nick.

"Nothing," said Day, and wiped his forehead with a dusty, sunburned forearm. "You?"

Helen gave a small frown. "Well, maybe." She brought up her hand and opened it carefully, palm towards them. Two tiny objects stuck to her skin. One was a splinter of metal, like something from the floor of a mechanic's workshop, but richer in colour than an iron filing. The other was spherical and had a hole through it.

Aristos took the tiny pieces carefully from Helen hand, one at a time. He held the rounded object up to the light, and caressed the flake of metal gently in the palm of his hand.

"Well done indeed! You've done it, Helen. In my opinion, this is a flake of gold. Even after all this time in the ground you see how it still glows. And this, this is definitely a bead. It's been both smoothed and pierced. Do you remember where you found them?"

"Of course. I left my hat near the place so I could find it again."

They picked up their things and followed Helen to the place where her hat marked the spot, taking the most direct route across the rocky ground. As they got closer and the terrain became quite steep, they had to find a way round a large boulder of granite, steadying themselves on it with their free hands as they chose their footing. Day suddenly gave a cry.

"Aristo! Look!"

The Curator caught up with him as quickly as he could. Day's hand, which had been on the boulder, was now hanging in the air above it, index finger pointing down. He brought it back to his side when Aristos reached him. There, its chiselled lettering faint on the rough and dirty surface of the stone, was their inscription. Boldly it announced OROS CHORIOU IEROU APOLLONOS - Border of the Sacred Area of Apollo.

"So, Elias lied to Michael Moralis," Day murmured. "He misdirected Michael, saying the inscription was on a church wall, then left the poems as a series of directions to us, or someone like us. The only thing that Elias told Michael that had any truth in it was the Naxos-Halki road, which is very long. He made sure there was no danger of Michael finding the site. We, however, found his poetry, and here we are. Hello, Nikos!"

41

Day briefed the party before they began to search intensively around the spot where the bead and flake of gold had been found.

"Well, we found Elias's inscription, so we're probably standing now in the same place that he was. Let's see what he might have found. Remember, we're not looking for the entrance to the Great Pyramid. Local people have lived around here for three thousand years and not come across this site. It will seem insignificant to the passing glance. We're looking for more of these significant little objects, like beads, bits of precious metal and little seal stones (which are like little lozenges of metal with carving on them). Keep looking for the other things, the stones that have been shaped by man, rocks placed deliberately as a wall, that kind of thing. Remember, Elias may not have found the site, but there's no reason why we won't be able to spot things he missed; the weather could have revealed something since he was here. Right, spread out, and good luck.'

They moved off. Day watched them go and thought of Nikos Elias. Had he also been here? If so, what had he found? Were they fulfilling his life's ambition, or would they too fail to find anything? He pushed the thought away. They had found little of significance yet.

An hour later they came back together to compare notes. There was a determined look on Day's face. He opened his hand to reveal half a dozen tiny flakes of gold foil. Once he had found the first one, it had been easy to see more. He was deeply excited. He hoped he was right about where these tiny fragments might have come from. Gold foil had been used to line the inside surface of a type of burial chamber called a tholos tomb. The Mycenaeans built them for the burial of their most important citizens, their kings, their generals. The gold on the walls of the dark interior would catch the light from the entrance and the flames of the torches, glowing richly above the bodies that lay there amid their treasures. That image had always thrilled Day, ever since he had first heard of tholos tombs as a student. The tiny fragments in his hand made him dream that they might even now be close to one of the huge, domed, subterranean burial chambers of the Mycenaean elite.

Now who wants to be Howard Carter? he chided himself. He had just laughed aloud.

Helen had found three more pierced beads. They were faintly coloured despite the grime and weathering, which suggested a translucent material. Aristos, who had found nothing himself, said he thought they would turn out to be made of amber. She asked what they were going to do next. Nick grinned, beginning to turn away and move uphill.

"You could do worse than follow me!" he shouted over his shoulder.

Nick clambered to a piece of higher ground. At times they had to scramble on all fours. At the top, a stretch of crumbling dry-stone wall suggested they were in an abandoned modern-day field. Several old trees raised their battered superstructure above the level of

the scrub. Nick stopped at a place where the scru was dense, the
stunted trees were wizened and misshapen, the st e wall in ruins,
the grasses yellowed. Behind him a twisted fig tree d a dead thorn
bush blocked the way. When the others caught up, N ck's enthusiasm
became infectious.

"So? See what I mean? What do you think?"

Nick crouched by the dead thorn bush and pushe t aside with his
stick to reveal that it had been deliberately cut fr n its roots and
pushed into its current position. A few suckers fro the old fig tree
had been pulled through the dead thorn. Another y ir or so and the
camouflage would have been perfect, the secret beh d it secure. The
tangle of living and dead foliage was incontroverti y man-made.

Day gave the stuff a poke with his stick to scare vay any snakes,
then kneeled and reached through. Beyond the veg tation he could
feel two stone blocks, and pushed aside enough br iches to let him
put his head into the opening. The blocks were cut eanly along the
edge he could see, forming a kind of roof. Beneath hem was a hole
large enough for a small man to squeeze through; an tempt had been
made to back-fill the opening with small rocks. D stood away so
the others could see, holding back some of the th i with his stick.

"It looks like somebody's deliberately blocked off a gnificant hole."

"What's to say it isn't one of those natural subsi :nce holes that
farmers block up to stop goats falling into it?" ask Helen sensibly.

"It could be, but I don't think so. Look at those o upper stones
there, you see? They look like they were design l for a specific
purpose. They don't look like a farmer's wall. They' skilfully shaped
and placed together, quite deliberately. In fact, my ;uess would be
that they're the roof stones over an entrance."

As Day paused, Aristos finished his sentence for him without taking his eyes off the opening.

"An entrance to another Komiaki."

***

Day and Aristos took photographs and used the GPS on their phones to make sure they could find the spot again. It was time to return to the cars, get out of the midday sun. They needed to sit down in the cool and talk this through properly. Aristos suggested his house, as it was nearest, and the others agreed. The prospect of food, which was also promised, appealed to them all.

Day and Helen followed the others silently back to the car park, Day absorbed in his own thoughts. Occasionally he muttered how hot it was, as if to be sociable. Helen became impatient with him.

"I'm worried by how easily we found the gold flakes and the beads. They shouldn't have been outside the tomb just lying on the ground, should they? Don't you agree, Martin?"

"I do. Even though without them we may never have found the opening, it's bad news that we found them on the surface. I think it means that somebody has been inside and scraped about, tunnelling in like a dog, removing soil which contained these little fragments of gold and amber. Even worse, the little pieces would originally have been deep inside the tomb, so someone really has been inside. Oh God! The damage that's probably been done! Fragments discarded over the hillside like so much rubbish. And who knows what's been removed."

"So you think someone has been right inside? Not recently, surely? The fig had partially grown over the entrance."

"I agree, not recently, but if much time had passed since the gold flakes and beads were scattered about, they would have disappeared into the soil. Unfortunately for Elias, this isn't his work. Anyway, I don't think Elias would have been so clumsy. It seems he never found the tomb. The question is, who did?"

"And what exactly did they find inside?"

Day hoped his next assumption was correct. "With luck they didn't go very far beyond the opening itself. If this turns out to be a beehive tomb, the majority of it is far beneath the surface."

***

The dishevelled expedition party only began to recover once they were sitting on the cool terrace in Agkidia. It was the hottest part of the afternoon, and they felt every degree of it. They drank cold water and revived themselves with all manner of snacks brought by Rania from the kitchen. Helen wiped her brow and examined the smear of dust on her hand with distaste.

"What must those people in the car park have thought of us in this state? Only you looked respectable, Aristo."

"I did the least work," the Curator conceded. "The main thing is that nobody saw what we were really doing. We don't want the press to get wind of this, especially if the place is what we suspect it is."

"At least one person knows where it is - the person who blocked up the hole," Nick said grimly.

"You're right, Nick, but we do have one advantage over them, I think," said Day. "They don't know that we've found it. We have time to get the authorities to protect it. Let's look on the bright side - the opening could have been blocked up by a local who decided to keep quiet about it. Greeks know that if part of their property is found to have archaeological significance, it can be requisitioned by the state."

Aristos nodded, preoccupied. "Here's what I suggest, everyone. We have to follow proper procedure, and I know exactly who I'm going to call. Someone who will take me seriously when I talk about beads and gold and a bunch of amateurs! She's an old friend at the Archaeological Service, Aliki Xylouri. I'll get her to come over as soon as possible. And we must speak to the police. They must be told that the site needs protection. I'll call them tomorrow morning from the Museum. If I can get an appointment to see Inspector Cristopoulos tomorrow afternoon, would any of you like to be there? Nick, I know you'll be working.... Martin, would you come?"

"Of course. Just tell me when. Now, time we went home, I think, we badly need showers. Many thanks for the food, Rania."

"You're welcome, Martin. Can I ask you something before you go? What do you think now about a connection between this tomb site and the recent murders?"

"I honestly don't know. There are a few coincidences, such as the tomb site and the stone hut being near to each other., and Michael was looking for a site, possibly the tomb, before he was killed. But it's all circumstantial so far. I'm happy to leave it to the police. I just want this site, which was so important to Elias, to be properly excavated and some credit given to him."

42

Monday morning was a glorious day, reaching twenty-five degrees by ten o'clock. It was the heat that woke Helen, who felt heavy-limbed from the explorations of the previous day and heavy-headed from the red wine she had drunk with Day before bed. There was no movement of the lace curtains meant to deter flies from her open window. For a while she just lay there, listening. The house was quiet and only the occasional car or motorbike passed on the road.

In his room at the other side of the house, Day was staring moodily at the ceiling. He had found it hard to get to sleep despite the excellent red wine of the night before. He had been kept awake, not by excitement at their discovery, but by a dark disquiet. He had considered Rania's parting question and come up with answers he didn't like. So little did he like them that he decided to keep them to himself. There would be a time to share them with Helen, and with the world. He, like Elias, preferred to be secretive for now. At the moment he was filled with a powerful sadness that he had no desire to speak about.

His mobile told him it was past ten in the morning. The house was quiet. He swung his legs from the bed, switched on the iron that stood ready on the ironing board, and headed for the shower. The warm trickle of water was sufficient if not invigorating. Feeling better, he ran the hot iron over a fresh shirt and dressed quickly.

He and Helen arrived almost simultaneously in the main room. Helen was still in her dressing gown because her priority was coffee, which was soon scenting the kitchen. They sat with their cups on the balcony, watching as the only cloud in the sky left a shadow that hovered over the valley. When Helen went to take her shower, Day remained at the old table staring at the view. Its brightness contrasted unhappily with the dark nature of his thoughts. He had only a few hours till they were due to meet Aristos at the Police Station. Day needed to think clearly. He had a few facts, he had theories underpinned by some evidence, and he had pure hypothesis. He needed to decide which of these to share at the police station.

On the table, his phone vibrated. A text from Aristos confirming the appointment. *Meet at police station 1.30. Have talked to colleague in Athens. She arrives Thursday. We should take her to site together, OK? See you later. A. I.*

***

After a good brunch of such cheese, salad and bread that they still had in the house, Day and Helen set off for Chora. They drove along the country road to the town with the car windows open, relishing the wind in their faces. A sweet, dry smell of summer filled the Fiat. The sun fell fully on the driver's side for most of the way, and Day was glowing behind his sunglasses. They chatted occasionally along the way, of how warm July would be and how good it would be on Nick's boat, but said nothing of importance. Day had almost decided what he was going to tell the police, but he had no wish to talk about it yet. He had a sense that Helen understood.

In the square, Aristos greeted Helen with a warm hug, looking restored and determined. As they neared the police station, Helen told them she preferred not to come in and would see them afterwards in the nearby Café Seferis.

"But you must come in too, Helen," insisted Day. "You were there yesterday and found the first objects. Anyway, you need to hear everything so I can talk it over with you afterwards."

Helen conceded. She began to sense that Martin was planning something.

***

Once again they were shown into Inspector Cristopoulos's office, the man himself dwarfed by the big desk and peering assertively between two computer screens.

"Curator, Martin, Miss Aitchison – I understand you have news?" he enquired politely. "Curator, you look as if it's rather urgent."

"Yes, Inspector, it is indeed. I need to ask for your help. Do you know the tholos tomb at Komiaki? That is, Koronida village?"

"Of course."

"It's my belief that we've discovered another tomb like it, and I'm here to ask you officially to protect the place. This morning I telephoned the Archaeological Service and someone is arriving on Thursday. I hope she'll take immediate steps to enclose the area. Until then, it's completely vulnerable, and I need you to provide a guard."

Cristopoulos sat back in surprise. "That's astonishing news, Curator. Unfortunately, manpower is in short supply at the moment, as you may be aware. But tell me more."

"I think this may be a Bronze Age tholos or beehive tomb dating from about 1300 BCE. We found signs that someone has already been some way inside it. We have to assume that they may return at any time, which is why the place needs to be guarded."

"I see. Well, I think the Municipal District Council will want us to do so, so I shall arrange the guard you ask for. Where is the site exactly?"

"It's near the Church of Agia Paraskevi, the one near the visitor car park for the Melanes kouros. Do you know where I mean?"

"I know it."

"I suggest I take you to the spot myself, Inspector."

"We'll arrange that, Curator. Can you describe to me the size of the structure that requires guarding?"

"Ah, well, on the surface it's just a hole in the ground. Below ground it may well be over thirty feet deep and nearly as wide. We don't know whether the hole leads into the roof or the entrance tunnel."

"A hole in the ground..." murmured Cristopoulos.

"The hole is in a corner of what was probably someone's field," Day continued. "An attempt has been made to close it with stones. Someone has also concealed the entrance with vegetation. We found some tiny fragments of gold and amber on the ground nearby, which suggests someone has managed to get some way inside. The tomb itself must be some distance further into the hill, hopefully undamaged."

"The hole could be dangerous if anyone managed to get inside," added Helen. This seemed to convince the policeman.

"I see. Well, Curator, I'll arrange for some men to accompany us to the place and for a guard to be posted. I take it you'll be contacting the Municipal Council yourself?"

"I can do, by all means. Thank you."

Cristopoulos turned back to Day. "I have some news which you'll find interesting, Martin. If you will permit the digression, Curator?"

He smiled his rare and rather paternal smile, which temporarily gave the impression that he could be contradicted.

"I've received the pathology reports now. You were right, Martin. Michael K. Moralis of New York was the sibling of Dimitris and Maria Eleni Makris. He was the elder brother, Michalis."

Helen felt her skin tingle, even though the news confirmed her original theory. "So, all three Makris siblings are dead," she said.

"Unfortunately, yes. One who died before the family left for America, one who never left the island, and one who recently returned."

"What else did the report say, Inspector?" Day asked.

"Dimitris Makris had been dead about a week when you found him. He was killed in the hut, a single stab in the back as he was bending over. He was placed on his back, almost 'laid out'. He didn't bleed extensively. His nails were torn and there was soil beneath them from the hut floor, but no DNA that might match his killer. There was no evidence at all that might identify whoever killed him.

"As for Maria Eleni's body, the results aren't as helpful. She died at least seven years ago, and was about 20 when she died. She was killed by a blow to the head. She was lying on her back and her hands were crossed over her chest in the same way as her brother."

Day sighed. "I suppose Gautier and his friends haven't admitted to killing Michael?"

"No. Thanks to an excellent lawyer, Gautier has said very little. Grogan, of course, is being attended by a lawyer from the States, so we won't get anything from him either. Forgive my cynicism. The other men we've arrested are frankly not the big players. They all deny any knowledge of Moralis."

"Perhaps it's time to look elsewhere for Michael Moralis's killer, Inspector." Helen tried to keep the impatience from her voice. "There may be a link between Michael and the antiquities smugglers, but there absolutely is one between the murdered siblings. Michael and Dimitris were killed with the same knife. Both from behind, I believe? Dimitris and Maria Eleni were both laid out after death, and as close to each other as possible. Doesn't it suggest a single killer, somebody who knew the family? Somebody who links all three victims?"

"What you say makes sense, Miss Aitchison, but let's remember that Moralis had Gautier and Grogan's names in his computer, and they are all in the antiquities business in their way. My superiors want me to continue with that line of enquiry for a little longer, I think."

"Have you questioned Petros yet?" This was from Day, who had been wondering why the police had not talked to Petros after searching the Elias house.

"We had a short chat, Martin. He has no knowledge of the victims or suspects in the case."

Day knew the moment had come.

"Look, Michael was clearly not the man I thought. I've revised my ideas and I'd like your opinion, if you can give me the time."

The room fell quiet. To Day it was as if the police station was in suspended animation. Cristopoulos sat back in his chair and laid his glasses on the desk. He wore the expression of a man who felt he had been here before.

"Go ahead, Martin," he said.

43

Day shifted his chair so he could see everyone. He particularly wanted to watch Helen. He was glad he had already planned what he was going to say. He warmed to his subject now, as he might on a broadcast.

"I think I know what Michael was really doing here on Naxos. We know he invited Alex Harding-Jones and Kate Russell to come with him to look for the tomb, and yet Michael kept them at arm's length from the start. I believe Michael had two reasons for coming to Naxos. But first, let's consider his genuine hunt for an undiscovered site that he was convinced was here, somewhere off the long Naxos-Halki road.

"I found Michael's name in Nikos Elias's old address book, so I think his local source was Elias. I'm guessing that Michael called Elias and asked for information about a Mycenaean site he had guessed was on the island. Elias was looking for the same site, it had been his life's work. He must have wanted to protect his research and give nothing away. He probably gave Michael the name of the Naxos-Halki road, hoping to get rid of him, and perhaps a few other pieces of misinformation too. We'll never know what was said between Elias and Michael. I'm pretty sure that Elias didn't guess that Michael was one of the Moralis family. Why would he? The man he was dealing with was a well-known American historian from a university in New York.

"That historian, though, was still Michalis Makris underneath. Like many people who live far from the land of their birth, Michael may always have intended to come back. His desire to locate the Bronze Age site was connected with this nostalgia but it wasn't the whole story, I think. I read the article that Michael submitted to Alex and Kate for publication. It's well written, but certainly doesn't give away the location of the site, not even a good hint. Michael withdrew his article from the edition, saying it was to prevent others from finding the site, but this can't have been the real reason since the article gave nothing away.

"My guess is that Michael decided he wanted something else. Sure, he wanted to visit Naxos and find the site, with Alex and Kate as witnesses. But he had a secret motive, which was to find his brother, Dimitris.

"So, the three of them arrived on Naxos and settled into their accommodation. Michael must have been annoyed when he found that Kate had booked into the same hotel as him. Kate and Alex had begun to have doubts about Michael, so Kate had booked into the Hotel Philippos to keep an eye on him. However, Michael always gave her the slip, taking the hire car and going off alone. Michael wanted peace and quiet to find his brother.

"Dimitris, as we know, had gone wandering off some time before. It must have been difficult for Michael to track his brother down, especially as he had to be discreet to prevent rumours that might reveal his true identity."

"Why did he need to hide his real identity, Martin?" interrupted Helen.

"I think he wanted to keep it from Petros Tsifas. Rumours travel fast in small island communities. Michael must have known that Elias was dead, but he didn't want Petros to know he was here. I'll tell you why in a minute. Here I need to make a couple of assumptions, which subsequent events will have to prove or disprove.

"First assumption, slash guess: While Michael was searching for Dimitris and for the location of the tomb, he came to the attention of Emil Gautier. They may not have met, but they certainly became aware of each other. Michael knew that Gautier was involved in antiquities trading through working on the Met Museum's task group. Gautier had observed Michael's persistent search of the island and saw it as a threat to his smuggling operation. Whatever happened, they were both now on each other's radar. Michael wrote the names of both Gautier and Grogan on his laptop despite clearing almost everything else from it. Gautier, I believe, took measures to ensure that Michael didn't compromise his operation.

"Second assumption, slash guess: The girl whom Elias saw at a festival in Melanes in 1999 with a gold bracelet on her arm was Maria Eleni Makris. Elias recognised the bracelet as being Bronze Age, and guessed it had been taken from the site he'd been looking for all his life."

Cristopoulos could restrain himself no longer from determining the quality of the evidence.

"Can you prove these assumptions, Martin?"

"Not yet. Most of the people in question are dead. We'd need a confession. Gautier, Grogan, or Petros Tsifas."

"Why Petros?" Helen had to ask. She watched Day's mouth tighten.

"We know Petros was at the festival when Elias saw the bracelet. It was noted in Elias's papers. We also know that Petros knew Gautier in Paris when he was young. Petros probably knows a great deal more about this than he wants us to believe."

"Petros Tsifas must be brought in for questioning at once."

"With respect, Inspector, I have a better idea," said Day, following his plan. "It's now mid-afternoon. There's time for your colleagues in Athens to put a couple of questions to Gautier now, providing you with important information before you question Petros Tsifas."

"And what might those questions be, Martin?"

"Gautier claims not to know Moralis, right? Tell him you know differently. Get him to admit to thinking that Moralis was a threat to the smuggling operation. Tell Gautier that he isn't suspected of Moralis's murder, but maybe leave a small doubt in his mind. Then ask him for everything he knows about Petros Tsifas. Remind him you know they were arrested together in Paris twenty-five years ago. Did he know Petros lived on Naxos? Watch him try to pin all the blame on Petros, just as he did in Paris. I told you, we need confessions, and this is the best way to start getting them."

As Cristopoulos appeared to consider this, Aristos chose the moment to press his own agenda.

"Inspector, time is moving on. May I remind you that we need to secure the site?"

"Of course, Curator. If you would all be so good as to excuse me now, I have some arrangements to make. Shall we say, Curator, we meet in front of this building at four o'clock to go to the site? I'll take you in my vehicle, and arrange for you to be brought back as soon as we've seen the location."

"Thank you, Inspector."

The session with Cristopoulos was clearly over. Day, Helen and Aristos left the police station and squinted in the bright sunlight of the square. Aristos decided to return to his office in the Museum for a while, so Day and Helen began to walk towards the sea. Day wondered how long it would take her.

"So, Aristos and the police are going to be busy at the site this afternoon, and meanwhile the Athens Police are going to ask those questions of Gautier. What are we meant to do, Martin?"

"I suppose we're meant to become ordinary members of the public again, my dear Helen."

"That doesn't sound like the Martin I know."

They walked on, talking about everything that had happened. At the end of the bay, standing on the sand which, later in the evening, would be full of tables, chairs and people watching the sunset, Helen asked the question Day had known she would ask.

"Why did you make Inspector Cristopoulos delay speaking to Petros? Are you going to tell me now?"

44

Day had known she would see through him. She saw to the heart of matters. If she approved the course of action he wanted to take, he wouldn't hesitate. However, at the moment he certainly was hesitating.

"What did you make of what I said about Petros back there?"

"You carefully didn't say how you thought Petros was involved," she replied, staring out to sea without seeing it. "You implied that the police should have questioned him already, and then you told them not to question him. I can see that he might be the only person alive with knowledge of Elias's discovery of the tomb. Is that why he's important?"

"I didn't say that Elias did discover it."

"OK. All the same, Petros knew Elias better than anybody, and he knew what happened when Elias saw the gold bracelet on Maria Eleni's arm. I suppose he also knows how close Elias came to finding the site."

"I agree."

"Do you think Petros knew that Michael was Michalis Makris, and that he had returned to Naxos?"

"I have a theory about that, but it's all based on guesswork. I think someone else told Petros that Michalis Makris was here, and it filled him with panic."

"Why would it?"

"The past. I think Petros's life is dominated by the past, especially the years he shared with Nikos. I think he knows a lot more than he's saying. I also think he's involved in these deaths. I put the police off for a few hours for a specific reason. I want to speak to Petros myself, alone. What do you think of that? Am I being stupid?"

Obviously she wanted to say yes, but Helen waited before answering. She rested her eyes on the line where the sea met the sky. It was faintly turquoise, a mere idea on the surface of the water. Apart from the faint line, the afternoon sun whitened the sea and the sky with its power, bleaching their colours in an aura of illusion.

She wanted to tell Martin not to even consider taking such a risk. Did he mean that he thought Petros was a murderer? He should leave it to the police. He should definitely not risk confronting the man alone. She had always respected Martin's brain, despite his occasional intuitive leaps in the dark, but was this in any way sensible? What if Petros turned violent? It was a crazy idea.

At some point, however, Helen realised that the decision would not be hers.

"Why do you want to do this, Martin? You know it's a job for the police."

"I've been trying to avoid admitting it to myself, but it's for my own sake. I like Petros and I want to ask him some questions and understand what has happened here. On the other hand, if I'm right and he's done a series of terrible things, it may be impossible to understand."

"If that's the case, there will be nothing you can do for him and it's a serious risk to you. Why put yourself in the way of danger, if you really think Petros capable of killing?"

"I want to give him the chance to tell his story to a friend."

"Oh, my God, Martin! That's madness! I thought you had a strong sense of self-preservation."

"You're right, and I do. I'm still going to talk to him alone. Now." Day had already turned away and begun to walk back to where they had left the Fiat.

"Can I dissuade you?" she said to his back, following him.

"I asked you because I wanted to see if you could. I take all your reservations, and add my own. But I still need to do this." Day was several steps ahead of her. She put her hand on his arm to stop him.

"In that case, you must take some precautions," she said. He was listening, at least. "This is what we'll do…"

Helen's plan required time to put into place. They walked briskly back to the car, and drove towards the Elias house, but not with the intention of calling there. Not yet.

45

Pater Giannis walked solemnly into the taverna and Vasilios rose to greet him with hand outstretched. Day and Helen stood too, greeted the priest, and they sat down together. Day made the story as concise as he could and outlined his request, not omitting a warning that some danger was involved. Giannis raised his brows at this and lowered his chin, as if looking at Day over the rim of non-existent spectacles. He reminded Day that he was a broad-minded man, and his first thought was for Petros, who still had religious beliefs and was entitled to the help of the church.

The sun was lowering itself towards the sea when Day and the priest set out from the Taverna Ta Votsala to walk along the beach road to the Elias house. They were watched by Vasilios and Helen for most of the way. The priest asked how Day planned to conduct the meeting with Petros, and how he thought Petros would react.

"I've decided not to plan this too much, Gianni. I think he and I have a decent enough understanding for an offer of help from me to be accepted. If I'm wrong, things could be difficult. Hopefully with you there it's unlikely. I'd like you to be a silent presence initially, taking over when you see fit. We need to establish the facts, after which I think he may turn to you."

"I'm happy to be guided by you, Martin, as long as possible. I don't know the facts as you do. Petros and I have known each other a long time, but he's shared nothing of this with me."

Day could think of nothing more to say. They completed their walk in silence, and it was Day who knocked on the door of the Nikos Elias Museum.

The door was opened so promptly that Day suspected Petros had watched their approach. He opened the door fully and took a step back; his strained face and the absence of his customary smile and greeting made Day's stomach lurch. Pater Giannis spoke gently.

"May we come in, Petro?"

Petros nodded and stepped further back, opening the door to its maximum and leaving it open. He walked ahead of them into his house without a word. He led them into the main room, where the walls were hung with photographs taken while Elias was alive, pictures of the island and one or two of Elias himself. Cupboards and shelves displayed items Elias had collected. In the middle was a large traditional wooden table with six heavy chairs. The three men seated themselves.

Pater Giannis took a chair at the far end of the table, leaving Day to sit opposite Petros. Day broke the silence.

"Petro, I think we need to have a conversation together, a rather difficult one, which is why the priest and I have come alone this evening, to see you while we have time and privacy to go through everything that has happened. Do you agree?"

"Certainly."

"So, you can guess what we've worked out? I think I know what's happened, and believe me, Petro, I want to help. Giannis too."

Day realised with surprise that he had said no more than the truth. He did want to help. He wanted to understand, and then possibly to help.

Day had not expected to see Petros's eyes well with unshed tears. With a sudden movement, Petros pushed himself away from the table with both hands as if to stand up and run away. Day froze in his seat, still holding Petros's eyes with his. Petros remained in his chair.

"What have you worked out, Martin?"

"I think the recent murders on the island are connected, and also that there is a great deal of history behind the deaths. I want you to tell me the whole story. I give you my word that I won't interrupt unless I have to, nor will Giannis. You can start at the beginning and tell us everything."

Petros appeared to bite back an abrupt response. "Where is the beginning, Martin? How long ago is that?"

"If you ask Gianni that question, we could be here all night!" Day said, trying to lighten the mood. "But begin wherever you want. Just one thing – we're not the police. Tell Giannis and me the bits you won't tell the police. The reasons behind the actions. You know, Petro, it's all over now, and we're here to offer you our support."

Petros Tsifas relaxed back in his seat, still gazing at Day.

"I didn't suspect when I met you that we would ever have such a conversation, Martin. I only hoped that you would be the person to whom I could leave Nikos's legacy. I don't have the skills, the connections, the cleverness; but you do, I saw that at once. It's all I want, you know."

As he had promised not to interrupt, Day just nodded.

"I came across Emil Gautier in a café in Chora. It was very early this month. He was drinking a coffee, looking out at the pavement. He waved to me and beckoned me over. He seemed surprised to see me. I realised later that he had probably planned the whole thing and just made it look accidental. I knew he came to Naxos from time to time, probably for something on the wrong side of the law. I knew Emil in Paris when I was young. Did you know that? Do you know he got me into trouble? Well, I was very young and naïve, but I had enough sense to put distance between us as soon as I could. I came here to Naxos. That's when I met Niko. We got together almost immediately ..."

Petros allowed his eyes to settle on the portrait of Elias on the wall facing him, somewhere above Day's head. His hand went to the small cross at his throat.

"I sat down with Emil and ordered a coffee. That was my first mistake. After a while he talked about an American who had recently arrived on the island. He said this man was driving round hunting for an undiscovered sanctuary, and Emil was worried he was getting too close to some of his business interests. Emil was clever, kept it light. I fell for it because Emil had deliberately mentioned the undiscovered site. I asked him for more details. Emil said the man was a historian from America. Where exactly was he looking? I asked. The answer scared me, it was not far from our site. Niko's site. I was sure this American would find it and take the credit. Emil saw how anxious I was. He offered me money to keep a close eye on the American for him. I agreed, but for my own reasons. I needed to protect the site. I went to the American's hotel a few times and eventually I saw him. A stocky man in middle age with a beard, wearing American clothes. I started following him."

Petros stopped talking, perhaps thinking how things would have worked out differently if Gautier had never used him. Day felt he needed a prompt.

"This was Michael Moralis, then? How did Gautier know that Moralis was on Naxos and the reason for his being here? How did he know in the first place?"

Petros shrugged sadly. "Emil has ears everywhere. He knows things. I didn't ask him."

"So, did Moralis find the entrance to the tomb? Yes, Petro, I know about the tomb. I found it yesterday with the help of some friends. I know where it is, and I think I know what it is. But don't worry – I found it because of Nikos, the clues he left for me to work it out. It's Nikos's discovery. We'll talk about that later. Meanwhile I'd like you to tell me if Moralis ever found it?"

"I don't think so."

"When, in that case, did you realise that Moralis was a real threat to you?"

Petros Tsifas got up suddenly from the table and paced the room. The priest and Day exchanged glances, but there seemed no immediate threat of violence, nor did Petros seem about to run. He had begun to wear a distanced look, as if he were looking into the past.

"Moralis? I didn't recognise him, Martin. I guess you know who he really was? Young Michalis Makris had changed a great deal in America – he'd aged, done well, put on weight, bought smart clothes, changed his accent, even his walk. I didn't recognise him at all. I followed him when he searched the Melanes area, but he didn't find the tomb. It turned out that the site was only one of the things he wanted to find. He was mostly searching for his younger brother, Dimitris.

"Dimitris hadn't been seen for some time. Do you remember, Pater? Up till about March this year I'd taken food to him at his old family house in the hills beyond Melanes, like Niko and I had done every week since the family left the island without him. Then one day he wasn't there. I thought maybe he'd gone crazy at last and wandered off. Anyway, it seems his brother managed to find him, on Friday 17th May to be exact. Nothing would have happened if Michalis hadn't found Dimitris."

Petros went to stand at the window behind Giannis's back, looking out at the sea. The priest managed to resist the urge to turn and watch him. Day had a clear view, and saw Petros's hand surreptitiously wipe his face. He seemed unable to continue. Day decided to prompt him again.

"I was wondering, Petro, whether Michalis might have made contact with you? I thought he might have done, might have remembered you from his childhood. Possibly even asked you if you could help him find his brother."

"No. No, he wouldn't have done that."

Day let that go. He felt sure now that the whole story would come out without him directing it. He was willing to wait.

"It was the younger brother who found me," Petros went on at last. "Dimitris came to see me that same day. He was in this room. He said he'd just been with his brother for the first time in twenty years. He was very emotional. In fact, he was on the edge of hysteria. He said he'd been talking for hours with Michalis, and after Michalis had left he'd decided to come and have it out with me. He was really beside himself. He wasn't making sense. He kept saying he'd been talking with his brother, and I thought he was raving. Then the penny dropped. I realised he really had been with his brother, and that he meant the man I knew as Michael Moralis.

"Dimitris was in his early teens when Michalis left Naxos, and although he knew something bad had happened to his sister, he couldn't remember anything. Shock, I suppose. Now Michalis had come back and driven Dimitris half mad, pushed him over the edge. Dimitris remembered everything now, or thought he did."

Petros turned to face Day. "Dimitris was screaming and shouting, Martin, saying that his big brother had told him everything. He knew that Niko had killed his sister, Maria Eleni, and forced his family to leave Naxos."

46

Day said nothing. Petros Tsifas's encounter with Dimitris Makris had led to horrific events about which he must now talk. To talk, in this case, would be to re-live. Petros remained at the window. He was only a dark silhouette against the orange glow of the sun, which was setting inexorably, just like every other evening, right outside the front of the house.

"Dimitris was completely wrong, of course," said Petros in a clear voice. "He claimed Nikos had wanted a relationship with his sister and killed her when she refused. Dimitris demanded to know where his sister had been buried. He cried a lot. He said he wanted to hold her in his arms. He broke down completely.

"Martin, Gianni, you know about Niko and I. We were happy together. There's no way Dimitris was right, Niko had no interest in women, and anyone but poor Dimitris would have seen it. I was so angry, Gianni. Niko would never hurt anyone. He was the gentlest of men. And the Makris brothers were going to blacken his name, his reputation. Everything he was, everything he achieved, obliterated by scandal and lies. I tried to calm Dimitris down but nothing worked. He wouldn't listen. This was the same young man who had accepted the food and gifts that Niko and I had been bringing to him for twenty years, accepted them with a smile. Now, so changed and full of hatred."

Day nodded, and gestured to Petros to return to his chair. Reluctantly, Petros did so.

"Why did you really look after young Dimitris for all those years?" Day said. "Tell me truthfully. You know why he was mentally disturbed. You know why he stayed on Naxos when his family left. You even know why the family left."

"Martin, give me time. I can't talk about that yet. I'm sorry. Just let me tell this my own way."

"OK. Go on."

"I told Dimitris that I knew where his sister was buried, but that Nikos hadn't killed her. Then I said I'd take him to his sister's grave. I'd take him right that minute, I said. It quietened him down completely. He began to cry. We both did."

And it was then that the tears fell finally onto Petros's cheeks. Pater Giannis leaned in towards him. Petros carried on with his story but his face remained white.

"I drove him to the kouros car park. It was dusk, but we could see our way to the hut. It was pitch dark inside, so I turned on the torch I'd brought. Dimitris hadn't said a word since we left the house. I told him his sister was buried beneath the earth floor where he was standing. He fell on his knees and began to scrabble at the earth. He made no noise, he just dug with his bare hands.

"He didn't notice when I brought the knife out of my jacket. It was one of those hunting knives that close up into the handle, and he didn't even hear when I clicked it open. It was Niko's old digging knife, I've carried it with me since he died."

Petros gave a small smile towards Day. "Don't worry, Martin, I don't have it any more."

"I didn't plan to kill him, I was like an automaton. I had no thought. It was an awful place, he was so wretched, I had to stop him scrabbling at the ground, I had to stop it all. I don't really remember any more. You know what happened.

"Afterwards Dimitris's face was calm, the grief and the pain were gone. I turned him onto his back and laid him out, closed his eyes, crossed his hands. There wasn't much blood. It was going to flow straight down now, to his sister.

"I drove back here and had a shower, hid my stained clothes outside under the rocks. I'd become a murderer. I'd killed an innocent boy, because that's all Dimitris really was, and yet, even so it wasn't safe. I couldn't leave it there. Michalis Makris would know within twenty-four hours, he would know something had happened. So, what was I to do?"

Outside the house, the sun had slipped into the sea. The quality of light had changed to blue, and the room had become dim. None of the men suggested the electric light.

"What did you do, Petro?" encouraged Day.

"I phoned the hotel where Michalis was staying and left a message for him. I left my name, said I'd heard that he – that is, Michael Moralis – was on Naxos, and that I remembered that he and Niko had been in touch many years ago. I said if he needed any help from Nikos's papers he could call me."

Day couldn't stop himself. Suddenly he knew what had happened next.

"He called you back, didn't he?"

"Yes, that same evening he called me from his mobile. He said he was looking for some undiscovered sanctuary. I pretended to understand and said I thought there was an annotated map among Niko's papers which might help him. He suggested I bring the map round to him at the hotel. We could have a drink, he said, and maybe I could even bring him any more papers I could find that were relevant. He sounded very friendly. I didn't know what to make of that – this was the man who had told Dimitris that very morning that Niko had murdered their sister. I believe he wanted everything I could give him on the tomb's location, and his personal revenge could come afterwards. I felt his obsession about the tomb even in the short while we talked."

Day could imagine the scene in the hotel lobby. Moralis had armed himself with an ouzo, just as the receptionist had said. He had called the number Petros had left him, pretending, as Michael Moralis, barely to remember that Elias had had a partner. He spoke as an American scholar speaking to the custodian of Elias's research. It was an astonishing performance, Day thought. So driven was Moralis that he had invited the partner of the man he believed responsible for his sister's death to meet him for a drink.

"I have no idea how I got through the next day until I was due to meet Michalis. This time I knew what I was going to do, you see. I didn't think there was anything else I could do. That's the truth, Martin."

Day nodded. He found it oppressively hot in the darkened room, and was aware that there might be danger in darkness.

"We need to put on the lights, Petro."

"No, please don't. I can't go on if you do."

"Wait a moment."

Day put on the light in the next room and returned to his seat, leaving the door ajar. Just enough light came in to make out the faces round the table. He encouraged Petros Tsifas to continue.

"Michalis opened the door of his hotel room to me like I was an old friend. I played the part. He didn't offer me a drink after all, he just wanted to see the map. I gave him a map on which I'd drawn a few interesting marks, meaningless things. I took it with me when I left. I took his mobile too, because it had my number on it. I threw them in the sea, with the knife. But that came later. Michalis and I talked about Niko. Michalis claimed to admire Niko and be grateful to him, and said he would make sure he was given full credit when he published his findings. There was a gleam in his eye. There was probably a gleam in mine, but he didn't notice. This was the man who had lied about Niko. And now he wanted to steal his life's work.

"I was in the hotel room with Michalis for nearly an hour. We told lies to each other like professionals. All the time I knew what he was really thinking, and what he planned to do, and what I had to do. It took me a long time, because …"

Now Petros was unable to continue. The tears which had ceased for a while were now clearly on his cheeks again, only his stubble preventing them from falling from his face. His voice was broken.

"Because I didn't want to do it. I decided not to. I didn't have the courage."

Gianni spoke before he could stop himself. "Courage, Petro?"

"Yes. All I felt was weariness. Desire to give in. Willingness to lose the whole battle."

Day couldn't wait patiently any longer. "What changed?"

"I can't remember. Something he said, some laugh, some gesture. I remember it all like you remember a bad illness or a high fever – you know it happened but your mind is misty. I left him poring over the map on the coffee table. I excused myself and went to the bathroom. I flicked open the knife as I flushed the toilet, went back to him and did it. Before I could think again and change my mind.

"I did my best to cover my traces in the hotel room, like wiping things I'd touched. I left the hotel, as I came, without being noticed. It wasn't difficult. It was a Saturday, there were lots of people coming and going. When I got back here I rang Emil. I told him what had happened with Moralis. He didn't seem surprised. He said I was to get on the first available ferry and leave the island. There's a late boat, as you know, on a Saturday. I was on it. I texted Vasilios saying I'd been called away on some family business and the museum would be shut for a few days. He looks after the place when I'm away."

Pater Giannis chose this moment to break his silence. With a glance at Day, who nodded, he spoke to the man who now sat with his head in his hands.

"Petro, my son, it's time to make confession now, not to us but to our Lord."

Petros Tsifas nodded as he raised his head and wiped his face with both hands. Day, judging there was no risk to the priest, went to the kitchen to call Helen.

47

Day returned to the main room after having told Helen that Giannis and he were safe and that Petros had admitted the murders of Michael and Dimitris. Helen, still with Vasilios in the taverna, told him there was no sign yet of the police.

Day hesitated outside the room where he had left Petros with Giannis. He didn't know what to do, and he didn't have any time to work it out. He didn't want the police to arrest Petros Tsifas; more than anything he wanted to prevent it. He didn't understand himself, always the taker of the moral high ground and a resolute law-abiding citizen. What had come over him? Yet now he wanted to be able to prevent the inevitable capture, trial and imprisonment of this troubled Greek who had been unable to withstand the double pressures of the strong-willed Emil Gautier and his desire to protect the man he had loved. Day strained his ears for sounds of sirens, but there were none.

He cursed inwardly and made himself re-enter the room.

Petros and the priest had resumed their places at the table. Giannis said that Petros had something more to tell Day.

"I'm ready to answer the question you asked earlier, Martin. I think it will make more sense to you now. I've told Pater Giannis. I think it's clearer in my mind."

"When you're ready, Petro."

"Niko and I knew the Makris family in the way everybody knows everybody around here. One day we went to a festival in Melanes. Niko saw the girl there, Maria Eleni Makris, she was about eighteen, a wild young creature. Niko noticed the gold armband she wore as a bracelet. He knew at once what it was. He'd glimpsed her wearing it before, so briefly that he hadn't been sure, but now he knew for certain it was Mycenaean jewellery. The girl wore it like a cheap bangle. Nico was so excited he could hardly control himself – this could mean there really was an undiscovered Bronze Age site in the area. Then he realised that, to have the armband, somebody had broken into the place and taken it, and anger overcame his excitement. It was all I could do to stop him speaking to the girl at the festival.

"In the end I couldn't stop him. This undiscovered Mycenaean site had been all Niko had thought about for years. We went together to see the Makris family. They denied it at first, but then it all came out. They'd been moving their mule to graze on a piece of land that wasn't theirs, and when they drove in the stake for the tether they found the hole. It was overgrown, they said, but was clearly a hole that led downwards, and the air inside was oddly cold. Niko could hardly speak, knowing what this might mean. The father and older brother said they had shifted some rocks and got some way inside, where they'd found three objects. They never found a space that opened out, no tomb of any kind, just those three objects piled together. Niko told me later that the objects could have been found years earlier and hidden near the entrance, but nobody had ever returned for them.

"Niko was upset by what the family told him. When he'd listened to their story, he put on a stern voice and suggested the Makris family had done something very wrong, but with luck they could be saved from the consequences. He demanded to see the objects. When he held them, he didn't speak. Then he made the Makrises a proposal. He would give them a great deal of money, named a considerable sum, enough for them to leave the island and settle in America. He told them they would be able to avoid the consequences of their actions as long as they left very soon and left the three objects behind.

"Maria Eleni burst into tears at this last part, snatched her armband and ran out of the house. Young Dimitris ran after her. The parents and Michalis remained and agreed to Niko's suggestion. It was the escape ticket they had always dreamed of, they didn't need persuading.

"Over the next days, Niko cashed in some savings and gave a large amount of money to the family. But tragedy had already happened. Maria Eleni wasn't a very clever girl, any more than Dimitris was quite right in the head, although before the accident Dimitris was just a bit simple. He told us what happened. Crying and running from her younger brother, Maria Eleni fell and knocked her head against a rock. You've seen the terrain around here, it needs care, and Maria Eleni was in tears and running headlong. I found the two of them some hours later. Dimitris was in shock. Maria Eleni was dead. Dimitris never recovered his senses. He went into denial, forgot what had happened, blanked it all. The family, of course, were distraught. Nobody knew what to do. The parents were afraid Dimitris would blurt out everything, ruin their chances of a new life, so a funeral was out of the question. It was the father who decided on the lie that became the story they left behind – that Maria Eleni had taken the ferry already and gone ahead of them to visit relatives. I was given the job of burying Maria Eleni's body in the shepherd's hut. The family didn't even want to be there.

"Soon afterwards, the parents and Michalis left Naxos taking very little with them. Dimitris, however, refused to go. He was clearly out of his wits, although remembering nothing of the terrible accident. Niko promised the family that we would take care of the teenager until he was well enough to follow them, so they left without him. We all thought it was temporary, but Dimitris never agreed to leave the island.

"Niko and I did look after him. It was our duty. After Niko died, I continued.

"After the family were gone, Niko found the entrance to the tomb from their description. This may surprise you, but we didn't try to go further inside than the Makrises had. Niko wanted to leave it undisturbed. He was going to take the right course of action and get the Greek Archaeological Service involved. But his health declined very rapidly. He didn't do anything about the tomb because he hoped he'd get better and be able to take part in the excavation. The cancer swept him away like a rip tide. He died within two months."

There were no tears now. Petros had cried for Nikos until there were no more tears to cry. His eyes were glazed. Day thought again that Petros was looking backwards into the past.

"And the three objects?" he said. "The police didn't find them when they searched the house…"

"This may surprise you, Martin, but soon after we found the entrance hole to the tomb, Nico and I returned and, with some ceremony, we put the objects back into the hole, as far inside as we could reach and covered up the entrance again. Niko wanted them found by the excavation."

"But they're not there now, are they?"

"No. How clever of you. When you first wrote to me, a few months ago, you asked if you could come here, see Niko's things, and maybe do some work on his life and discoveries. I was certain you were going to be the one to take over Niko's legacy. I couldn't do it myself. I was just its guardian for a short time, and I don't have long to go. My health isn't good. I went and got the objects back from the entrance hole, to give them to you at the right moment."

"You mean, you retrieved them from the tomb, and brought them here?"

"Yes. It was difficult, I'm too big. Niko was a much smaller man than me, and he'd put them as far inside as he could. I had to dig like a dog to find them inside the hole. It had been falling in for nearly twenty years too. Once I had them, I filled up the hole again and tried to conceal it with rocks and branches."

"I noticed that."

"I'd like to give them to you now, Martin. The police will surely be here soon, and you must have them."

"The objects are here? But how did the police search miss them?"

"This is an old house. Smuggling isn't a new thing on these islands, Martin, Emil didn't invent it. Houses like this were built with places to hide both contraband and people."

Day remembered a saying he'd once heard. 'Smuggling and Greece are like bread and olive oil.' Then his strange desire that Petros should somehow be saved from punishment returned with a violence he didn't expect. "You didn't think to hide there yourself, Petro? Tonight?"

"Of course, but I didn't want to. I know what to expect, Martin, and I'm prepared for it. I did what I did. So, how do we do this? The objects are outside. Do you trust me to leave the room?"

"Giannis and I will come with you, Petro."

"Of course. This way."

They picked up torches as they passed through the kitchen at the back of the house. It was small wonder the police search had failed to find the hiding place. In the cliffs some distance behind the house was a natural fissure. Day shone his torch into the opening. Folds in the rock made it hard to see, but the tunnel turned sharply inland and there was just enough room for a man to crawl inside. The area didn't seem to be part of the Elias property, and Day doubted it had occurred to the police to extend their search that far.

"You only need to reach in your arm, Martin. You'll feel a canvas bag on the right, in a niche."

Day did as he was told, while Petros stood waiting with Giannis. The sound of several vehicles on the road beyond the bay and the glow of headlights told them that the police would soon arrive. Petros made no move. Nor did Day, though he considered it.

Day brought a strong canvas holdall from the niche and shone his light into it. All he saw was plastic bubble-wrap. He re-closed the bag. Their torches were both directed at the ground, so he couldn't see the faces of the other two men.

"Let's get back to the house. We should be ready for Inspector Cristopoulos," said the priest.

Petros nodded and turned to look directly at Day.

"Martin, will you take care of them? Will you make sure? Can I leave Niko to you now?"

48

Day and Giannis walked back to Taverna Ta Votsala after the police had left with Petros Tsifas. Day was desperate for a drink. Giannis excused himself, saying he would like to talk to Day in the next few days if possible, to which Day agreed. Vasilios and Maroula were busy serving their customers. When they were finally left alone, Day turned to Helen gratefully. He owed it to her to tell her everything that had happened.

"Thank you for suggesting Giannis be there this evening. I was able to talk to Petros, and Giannis's support was perfect. Petros didn't offer any violence. Sadly my guess was right - he killed the Makris brothers, for reasons that seemed to him insurmountable, but he killed to protect Nikos Elias. Giannis and I were no threat to him. Quite the opposite. Look, I'm happy to tell you everything, but I really need a drink. Can we go home?"

"Of course. Let's get some food from Maroula and go now."

Helen drove, with Day slumped in the passenger seat. He was suddenly unable to function. He felt exhausted and incredibly sad. Nothing of the excitement remained, none of the challenge to resolve the mysteries that had absorbed him for the past few weeks. The triumph of finding the tomb, the resolution of the Makris family deaths, the appalling news about Paul, all muddled in a blanket of depression. Petros's last words wouldn't stop repeating themselves inside his head, and the vision of his quiet weeping in the dim room would haunt Day for a long time to come.

They said nothing in the car. Helen focused on the dark road and its treacherous bends, driving slowly as if her passenger were a sleeping baby that she didn't want to wake. Day's silence, though not in itself unusual, was this time an uneasy one. She herself was so relieved at the safe outcome of the evening that she felt more than usually upbeat. The possibility that the night could have ended quite differently was a shadow knocking on her optimism and wagging its finger.

The village lights of Engares, then Melanes, the Potamias and Halki, punctuated the unlit mountain road as she drove to Filoti. It was a relief to reach home. Day woke from the silent place where he had been seeing and thinking nothing. He unlocked the door, switched on lights, and opened the balcony shutters. He slumped into a chair beneath the single lightbulb on the balcony and pulled round him a sweater he found on the table. Helen brought two glasses and a bottle of wine, and placed them in front of him. Day didn't move, so she poured the wine for them both. Then he moved. He drank steadily until half his glass was empty. Then he looked at her and smiled.

She put the oven on low and put Maroula's food, in its foil containers, inside before rejoining Day on the balcony.

"How are you feeling?"

"Worn out. Worn down. Sad. Incredibly sad, for Petros, for the Makris family, for Michael... even for Paul."

"I do require every detail, Martin, but not tonight. It can wait, unless you need to unload it. Why don't we drink this bottle, eat something, and get some sleep? Tomorrow you must speak to Cristopoulos. Perhaps tomorrow night you can tell me what happened."

"You do make such sensible suggestions."

***

At some point in the late evening when he was feeling almost visionary, but before the point when he became maudlin, Day excused himself and went to his room. He sat out on his room's tiny balcony for another hour, speculating on the events of the evening, events which Helen as yet knew little about, which had culminated in the arrest of the otherwise rather likeable Petros Tsifas.

When nothing moved in Filoti and only the occasional barking of dogs broke the silence, Day came indoors, closed the shutters and switched on the bedside lamp. For a moment he sat on the end of the bed and looked at the canvas bag next to him.

He had heard that even the most experienced field archaeologist could be overcome by wonder upon seeing an ancient artefact emerge from an excavation. The objects were usually in pieces, needing skilled expertise to reveal the beauty of the original. Occasionally, he had heard, their craftsmanship was immediately and breathtakingly apparent.

In this case, however, a mere hack of the broadcasting industry ('Professor' or no) was about to hold in his hands just such an object. An object which – apart from an occasional outing with a mule-owner or an obsessed historian – had been buried for several thousand years. It was a moment to savour, and perhaps excusable that at this point Day was more than a little drunk.

Today he had confronted a friend who had killed twice and had been given a bag of extraordinarily precious artefacts. He had – with the connivance of a man of the church – carried away these artefacts, albeit for their safekeeping. Such an extraordinary day merited a glorious conclusion of some kind. He was not so drunk that he did not realise the enormity of the moment. He considered calling Helen, but felt too emotional. He would make it up to her tomorrow.

He pulled the canvas bag towards him, opened it and brought out the bubble-wrapped objects, three individually enfolded items. They felt barely heavier than the plastic wrapping. Delicately he began to unravel them from the material that protected and hid them. He was careful not to touch them with his fingers, only to allow them the light of day on the soft bed of their opened plastic cocoons. Finally, all three were in front of him.

In the poorest condition of the three Mycenaean objects was a small jar with two handles, a stirrup jar, often used for containing aromatic oils. The stirrup jar was about eight inches tall and decorated with brown lines in an abstract pattern. The fact it was in two pieces didn't spoil his wonder. The pieces rested together in sweet alignment as if awaiting restoration. The belly of the jar was so perfectly rounded as to be sensual. The pair of delicately curved handles that framed the neck of the jar begged to be held, though Day resisted.

The second item was an unbroken terracotta figurine about five inches tall. Day knew what it was. It was a Bronze Age female figure in the shape of the Greek letter T and called a Taf Figurine. A strange, wide headdress formed the top-bar of the T, and the whole figurine was painted with decorative wavy lines which subtly suggested the female shape. The object, which was three-dimensional and would fit beautifully into the hand, seemed both delicate and solid.

Finally, there was the infamous bracelet, last worn by Maria Eleni Makris. Dully glowing, it was a simple shape in pure, old gold. Roughly three thousand years old, the story of this piece of jewellery in the last two decades alone was one of drama and death. In some ways, this was not inconsistent with its purpose in the tomb.

49

At the museum, Day asked at the reception desk for a word with the Curator and the man phoned through to Aristos. Turning from the desk to look at the entrance foyer, Day recalled the last time he was here, listening to Paul Metts address his tour group on the subject of Cycladic figurines. It seemed a very long time ago.

"The Curator is in his office. He'd like you to go up, Mr Day."

"Thanks."

Day took the wide, shallow old stone steps two at a time. He felt much better this morning, but the spring in his step was deliberate rather than spontaneous.

"Good morning, Martin. This is early for you."

"You're right there, Aristos. Everything's a bit mad at the moment. I need to ask a favour. Please would you put these things in your safe? I'd really rather not be the one to lose them."

Aristos glanced at the canvas bag which his friend had unceremoniously placed on his desk.

"What's that? What do you have there?"

"Inside this bag are three Mycenaean objects found near Melanes. You can have the whole story, of course. There's a bracelet, a stirrup jar and a Taf figurine."

"Show me!"

Day carefully unwrapped the finds again. They stared at them on Aristos's desk without speaking.

"That bracelet, Martin. Is it the one Elias saw on the girl's arm?"

"I believe so."

"And the other objects?"

"All three come from the tomb we found on Sunday. The Makris family discovered them many years ago. I've had them with me since last night, and while I know I did the right thing to hold onto them, I'll be glad when they're not my responsibility."

"Of course. I'll put them away now. I have time for a coffee, you can tell me everything."

"I'm afraid I'm expected by Inspector Cristopoulos, but afterwards we could get a coffee perhaps?"

"Call me when you get free. I mean, after you've spoken to the police. They're not about to arrest you, are they?"

"Very funny. See you later, Aristo. And thanks."

***

Cristopoulos was standing at the front desk of the police station as if he had been waiting for Day. He looked less weary than usual, even perky.

"Martin! Good morning! Come through, please."

"Good morning, Inspector. I came as soon as I could."

"You've chosen a good time, Martin. Petros Tsifas has told us a great deal already about what happened last night, and indeed about the events of the past few weeks. He's making a confession now. I'm satisfied we've got the person responsible for the murders. His story is detailed and conclusive. All the same, I'd like to hear about your part in last night."

"Of course, Inspector."

Here we go, Day thought.

He settled himself meekly in the customary chair facing Cristopoulos across his massive desk. One of the computer screens had been moved to one side to accommodate the pile of extra paperwork which it appeared the Inspector had been studying before Day's arrival. Cristopoulos picked up his biro and flicked the button on and off a few times before he spoke.

"It would appear, Martin, that yesterday in this office you deliberately side-tracked the police investigation in order to give yourself time to visit the prime suspect by yourself. True?"

"Ah. Well, that's how it turned out, Inspector. I hope the line of questioning which I suggested was useful to you ..."

Cristopoulos held up his hand to prevent Day saying anything more. "Don't make it any worse. The only reason you're not in more serious trouble, Martin, is that your suggestions bore fruit. More on that later. Tell me what you did after leaving here yesterday afternoon."

"I did some thinking. That kind of thing's been known to get me into trouble before, Inspector. I thought a great deal about what we'd discussed, and what I knew of Petros Tsifas."

"Go on."

"Yes, so in short I decided to go and see him. I had a fairly good idea that he might have killed Dimitris and Michaelis Makris, so I spoke to Pater Giannis and asked him to come with me. He agreed. Together we asked Petros to talk to us. He knew that this was his only chance to explain himself to us before being arrested. He isn't a vicious man, Inspector; we felt in no danger."

"It was extremely risky and I can't condone it, Martin. Either of you could have been hurt and Tsifas could have escaped."

"I know. I apologise."

"Thankfully that didn't happen and Tsifas didn't resist arrest. It could have turned out very differently."

Day grimaced. "Those were more or less my friend Helen's exact words, Inspector."

"Perhaps you should listen to her in future, Martin. However ..."

Inspector Cristopoulos thrust down the biro where it lay for the rest of the interview, nestling in the crease of a document. He crossed his arms and sat back in the chair, a picture of resignation tinged in equal measure with admiration and exasperation.

"Go on, then. From the beginning please," he sighed.

Day's professional ability to make a narrative both clear and riveting became clear in the monologue that he gave the policeman. From his first discussion with the Papas to the final safekeeping of the artefacts, his description was thorough and accurate. He crafted it for police ears, omitting Petros's relationship with Elias, the alarm that Giannis and himself had occasionally felt during the evening, and Day's own impulse to allow Petros to escape.

"Giannis and I decided that the right thing to do with the artefacts was for me to keep them until this morning. I've just given them into the safe-keeping of the Curator, Kyrie Iraklidis."

"Yes, I agree that was the best course of action. Tsifas told us he gave you the objects."

"Has Petros been cooperative?"

"Yes, fully cooperative, and he's shown a great deal of remorse. I was concerned that he might harm himself, so I had a watch kept on him during the night. I sent for a doctor to examine him this morning."

"A doctor?"

"Yes. I wanted an opinion on his state of mind, and also in the night he seemed to be taken ill. I suspect he had a minor heart attack. The doctor has confirmed heart weakness, pending tests."

Day felt a stab of pity that brought back his conflicted feelings towards Petros. He had done his best to bury them since the previous night, but clearly they had not gone away. He pushed them to one side and changed the subject to the career criminals for whom he felt no sympathy.

"What did you get out of Gautier?"

"He admitted that he deliberately sought out Tsifas with the intention of using him. He knew Tsifas lived on the island, and that when he needed a puppet he knew where to find one, as he put it. He knew how to manipulate Tsifas from their Paris days, and he regarded him as some kind of sleeping asset. Well, he needed Tsifas now. Moralis had been asking questions about unoccupied houses near the village of Moni, near Melanes, and Gautier's local spies passed this on to him. Moralis was probably looking for his missing brother, but Gautier didn't know who Moralis really was. He thought he might be on the trail of the smuggling operation, and one empty house near Moni in particular was being used by the traffickers. Gautier needed to get rid of Moralis, so he manipulated Tsifas. We can't prove that Gautier wanted Moralis dead, and now it seems Tsifas had his own reasons for killing him. Let's just say that Gautier wasn't unhappy when he got a call from Tsifas in a panic, saying he'd just killed Moralis."

"What did Gautier do then?"

"He told Tsifas 'as a friend' to get the next ferry off the island and lie low on the mainland for a while. Tsifas did this. Next day, Gautier arrived at the Hotel Philippos to find out for himself if Moralis was dead, and that's where Kate Russell saw him. The call she overheard him making was to one of his group, probably the Greek called Panos, reassuring him that the American had been 'taken care of', in the old American euphemism. Miss Russell was right to be alarmed, she had heard correctly."

"Has this Panos guy been arrested too?"

"Yes. Your friend Paul Metts led us to him. In fact, Metts has been very helpful, which will put him in a better position when it comes to court. He's explained the set-up as much as he knew it. Gautier was one of the top men in the wider smuggling operation. As for Jim Grogan, according to Metts he was a real fly in the ointment to Gautier. He turned up unannounced and definitely unwelcome, to put pressure on Gautier regarding some personal deal they had between them regarding the object Grogan was currently determined to acquire. Grogan didn't trust Gautier an inch. Grogan has a history of being very hands-on with the acquisition of his collection, and his presence on the island is in character. Gautier made him take the room at Taverna Ta Votsala, as far away as possible from his operation and in an isolated location, and told him to stay there. That's rather like telling a goat not to cross the road. The burly Greek called Panos, who was seen in an argument with Grogan at the Taverna Ta Votsala, was ordered to keep an eye on him. And the choice of Taverna Ta Votsala was no accident, because Panos could keep an eye on Tsifas at the same time."

"Couldn't Gautier have just got Grogan to leave Naxos?"

"Metts says a lot of money hung on the Grogan deal. Grogan has money to burn. He was a valuable customer to Gautier, if a difficult one."

"Are you going to be able to prosecute Grogan?"

"I'm not sure about that, Martin. His lawyer is first class, and Grogan's been around a long time. He's a wily one. We're satisfied he knew nothing of the murders."

Day nicked his head in an involuntary movement of disgust. The Inspector looked at him unblinkingly.

"At least, Martin, I've been able to tell Alex Harding-Jones and Kate Russell that they're free to leave the island at any time, or indeed to remain and enjoy their visit properly if they wish. I'm satisfied they had nothing to do with the criminal events of recent weeks."

"That's good news."

"The International Antiquities Trade Task Force, based in the US, has been clearing a few things up with our people in Athens. Apparently, Michael Moralis belonged to a group called the US Museums and Art Fraud Alliance, a group working with Interpol to try to stop illegal antiquities theft. Before leaving for Naxos, Moralis was told about Grogan and Gautier, and knew they were in the Cyclades. Alex Harding-Jones was already known to Moralis, but it looks as if Moralis might have suspected him of being in league with the traffickers. That explains the three names on Moralis's laptop to my satisfaction. We will never be sure."

"I see. Poor Alex. I doubted him too at one stage."

"Ah. What else? Do you remember the man you saw near the Melanes kouros just before you found the body of Dimitris Makris? We located him. A tourist. Austrian."

Day laughed, the first laugh he could remember for a while. It seemed that Cristopoulos had a sense of humour. "Oh. I'd forgotten him," Day said.

"So, I believe your part in this investigation to be at an end, Martin. I have to say that, although at best unconventional, your contribution has been both interesting and fruitful. May I offer you my personal appreciation, and my sincere hope that you now resume your life as a writer and broadcaster?"

There it was again, the dry wit.

"And leave police work to the police? Absolutely! I shall get out of your hair, Inspector. And I'm grateful to you, too, for allowing me so many courtesies and liberties."

"Indeed," said Cristopoulos heavily.

They rose and shook hands. As they did so, Cristopoulos slipped an envelope into Day's other hand, no word said. Day glanced at it. It was marked 'Personal' in elegant handwriting, but was unsealed. He nodded to the policeman, and left the room.

50

Day walked straight to join Aristos at Katerina's taverna. Katerina ensured they had a quiet table, enabling Day to bring his friend up to date. Aristos listened calmly and without a great deal of comment. He appeared to be someone for whom the bizarre aspects of human behaviour no longer held any surprises. Only one thing provoked a reaction from him.

"I'm amazed that anyone would dream of returning artefacts to the site from which they had stolen them," he said.

"Yes, it can't have happened often, can it?"

"It comes down to Elias's character, I think. From everything you've told me, I picture him as one of Tolkien's hobbits. There he was, secretly working on his own, squirrelling things away, hiding his treasures. Or – what was his name? – Gollum, obsessed with his Precious."

"You're not far wrong, Aristo. Obsession is right. Little wonder Elias's work hasn't been more widely appreciated – he made sure nobody came close."

"Not the ethics of our profession, is it?"

"No. Talking of which, what time does your colleague from Athens arrive on Thursday?"

"She'll be here just after eleven. I'll meet her and take her for coffee, and perhaps you can join us? Or would you rather meet us at the site?"

"No, I'll join you for coffee. Where?"

"Here, at Katerina's."

***

Back in Filoti, Day found Helen working on a painting. It was the first time she had tried any painting since arriving on Naxos. Her canvas was covered in different colours, which she explained was simply the under-painting and she was finding her way round a portrait.

"Who's the subject?"

"Petros," she said." Don't ask me why, it's a face I want to paint, that's all."

"I'm amazed you can remember it without a photograph."

She gave him a cold look, which he ignored and went to fetch them both a glass of cold water from the bottle in the fridge. Throwing himself into a chair near her, he took a long drink and reflected on the morning.

"I left the artefacts with Aristos before going to the police station. I'm relieved they're off my hands."

"I'm glad you showed them to me this morning. I won't ever forget the feeling of cupping that figurine in my hand, even in the plastic wrapping. Knowing how old it is, and how few people have held it since it was buried…"

"It's an incredible feeling, isn't it?"

"What happened at the police station? Was Cristopoulos angry with you for seeing Petros alone?"

"He did make his feelings clear, and obviously he felt I'd manipulated him."

"He's right! You did."

"But as it turned out, they got quite a lot out of Gautier at that latest interrogation. Paul's been helpful, too. Poor Paul, what a mess he's made. I'll tell you everything Cristopoulos told me over dinner. After I left Cristopoulos I took Aristos for a coffee to bring him up to date. He was very curious once he saw the artefacts, of course. He said Elias reminded him of a hobbit, or Gollum, secretly busying himself in pursuit of his great objective."

Helen smiled. The image was a good one. "Neat idea. Is that how you think of Elias, Martin?"

"I'm not sure yet. I'm not sure we know where Elias's involvement in all this begins and ends. I'm not going to give up on Elias, though. I want to see it through. What impression have you got of him, Helen?

"Well, I only know him from the poetry and hearsay, but there's much to admire."

Day reached into the pocket of his jacket and brought out the envelope.

"Petros is apparently not well. The Inspector sent for a doctor for him this morning. Possible heart attack. However, just as I was leaving Cristopoulos handed me this letter from him. I'm sure it's not procedure, but Cristopoulos doesn't seem to be a stickler for the rules. Thank goodness."

"Is that really a letter from Petros? Have you read it?"

"Yes. As I'm sure the police have too. Go ahead, read it yourself."

Helen took the single sheet of paper, torn from a desk pad, out of the open envelope. The handwriting was regular and elegant.

Dear Martin,

Thank you. I know how bravely and kindly you have acted towards me, choosing to treat me with humanity and generosity despite the terrible things I've done. I'm grateful you gave me the chance to explain myself a little.

I loved Nikos. He had a historian's mind and the trusting heart of a child. I found my true place here with him. When he died I lost my way, but clung on to my determination to keep him with me, to make sure he was not forgotten, that his achievements were known, that his reputation wasn't tarnished. It seemed I was about to fail, and it was hard for me to deal with. I lost sight of Niko himself, his basic goodness, and somehow of the beauty of Greece.

I'm not concerned for myself now, but I can't help but be filled with despair at my failure to protect Niko's legacy. Not for my sake, but for his, and for what he achieved. I entreat you, Martin, to please consider completing what you've begun and writing the story of Niko's working life. If you can bring yourself to do this, you will have made something good come from a great deal of ill.

I would like to put in writing here that I, whose it is to give, officially give you everything in the Elias estate, including the house, with permission to publish as you see fit, without condition. As for the poetry, Helen is very welcome to have it.

Again, from my heart, thank you.

Petros.

Helen handed the letter back to Day sadly. She began to mix a dark red on her palette and make small marks with her brush on the portrait.

"He doesn't apologise. I wish he had put that in writing to you, Martin."

"Perhaps it's too late for apologies, or he doesn't have the words," said Day. "Does it seem out of place to you that he talks of the 'beauty of Greece' in that way? It sounds strange to me. As if he's glorifying what he did."

"Not really. It strikes an odd note to us Brits, but in the context of Greece, of Elias and Petros, of the Makris family, no, it doesn't seem out of place. You know what I've been thinking? I liked Aristos's comparison with a hobbit, but I'm not reminded of Tolkien. I'm reminded of Greek Tragedy. The awful inevitability of disaster in all this, the years it's been in the playing out, the good intentions ruined, the noble characters brought down by obsession, pride, love…"

"Hang on a bit, you're not an English teacher any more!"

"Oh shut up, Martin."

For a few moments Helen added marks thoughtfully to the portrait. Day, for once, was the one staring at the valley. He was thinking of

Petros, and his own struggle against wanting to save Petros from the punishment he had brought down on himself. Helen's next question was strangely in tune with Day's thoughts.

"So, will you do it? Complete the Elias biography as Petros asks?"

"Oh, I think so. Will you translate the poetry?"

"Yes."

51

Day could not remember having such a sound sleep as he did that afternoon. Three solid hours had passed before he opened his eyes. He could hear a shower, meaning Helen was up and about, and then he heard her leave the bathroom. He lay on the bed a little longer, then got up and stood at the window. Late afternoon, maybe early evening. He didn't need to check the time. He made his own way to the shower, and afterwards put on his last remaining clean shirt. It was a particularly English-looking one, a crisp blue stripe on a white background, and yet very un-Greek. He gave a small smile at his reflection, not knowing quite why he felt rather insecure.

In the main room, Helen was at the table looking through papers. Day suddenly knew he was starving, and said so.

"I don't remember eating properly in days!" he mused.

"It's still early, Martin. Shall we have a drink before we go to Thanasis's?"

"But of course! Would you like wine or gin?"

"A small G&T, I think."

Day made the drinks and they took their usual chairs on the balcony. The shepherd and his dogs were returning down the track having moved the flock for the night. Waves of gentle warmth reached the balcony, wafted by a barely perceptible breeze. Helen relaxed into her chair happily.

"This is becoming a rather pleasant evening routine."

"Cheers," said Day before taking his first swallow. "We've run out of lemon, I'm afraid. Must go shopping."

"Time for that tomorrow. Then on Thursday you're meeting Aristos and the lady from the Greek Archaeological Service, aren't you, and going on to the site? That will take most of the day."

"I'm looking forward to meeting her. Aliki Xylouri. Wonderful name."

"I'd like to spend tomorrow working here. A break for the supermarket would be good. I must do some washing too. Then probably more work on Thursday."

"So the novel's going well?"

"I'm working on Elias's poetry."

"How's the portrait of Petros coming on?"

"Slowly. Shall we set off for dinner?"

"Yes. I could eat an entire goat!"

***

Tuesday, early in the evening, was clearly the right time to arrive at Thanasis's taverna. They were the only customers, and the entire family came to welcome them, including Thanasis's wife, whom he introduced as Koula. Day and Helen seemed to have endeared themselves to her for their appreciation of her souvlaki. She smiled constantly. They were ushered to what the family regarded as the best table, the one kept for name-day celebrations and local dignitaries. It seemed to be identical to the others, but an honour had definitely been conferred.

"You are our best customers. Welcome! As you can see, we are free to give you our complete attention this evening! Sit, sit!" beamed Thanasis.

Vangelis brought menus, the bread basket with cutlery, the glasses and the cold water, and poured the water for them with a flourish of hospitality.

"What would you like to drink? Red wine?"

"Yes, please. And what does Kyria Koula recommend this evening?"

Koula herself answered from across the room. She spoke in Greek as her English seemed confined to Good Morning and Good Night, but she had heard and understood the question. Vangelis provided a commentary in English after her every sentence.

"Pastitsio, my own recipe. It is the best you will eat… I use lean veal, I mince it very fine, and I add sweet red wine, little pieces of prune, Italian parmesan and our best local Mizithra cheese."

"My mother's pastitsio is the best in Naxos."

"Then we need a portion of that, please. And to start with, do I see here chickpea fritters, with your own caper and garlic dip?" Day was referring to the menu, for a change.

"My mother's Skordalia with Kaparia is amazing!"

Everyone laughed, and the family went off to prepare the order.

"What exactly is this divine treat we have in store, Martin?"

"Ah. I think they're spicy little fritters made of chickpeas, with a dipping sauce which is a variation on the traditional garlic dip, skordalia. Skordalia isn't usually a favourite of mine, but here they've made it with the addition of capers. Capers are a speciality of Sifnos, you don't find them so much here on Naxos. I thought we should try it."

"I approve. And let's plan a few days on Sifnos later in the summer. They have really good ceramic shops there, I've read. After we've gone back to that nice woman with the pottery shop in Apollonas, of course."

"I'm up for all that. And why don't we go swimming soon? The sea must be starting to warm up."

When Thanasis brought their red wine, mellow and soft from the local supplier, it was time for Day to tell Helen everything she'd missed. She still hadn't heard in detail about the evening when Day and Giannis had confronted Petros. Day had told her a small amount over the phone that evening, and enough since then for her to piece together the basic facts, but now she demanded every detail, the emotions in the room, the discovery of the three objects hidden by Petros. She listened without interruption till he'd finished.

"So perhaps none of this would have happened if Gautier hadn't enticed Petros into following Michael Moralis."

"Quite possibly. Gautier has much to answer for. And if Michalis hadn't found his brother Dimitris sleeping rough in Mona and driven him into a frenzy with his lies about what happened to their sister,

Dimitris wouldn't have gone to Petros. What happened to both brothers afterwards was more or less inevitable."

"Michalis must have been letting off years of pent-up emotion. He probably never thought Dimitris would go and accuse Petros. He wasn't to know how unstable his brother had become."

"It was a turning point in both their lives when their sister died. Maybe they both lost control of their emotions when they found each other again."

"I still think it's a modern Greek tragedy," mused Helen. "Don't you, Martin?"

"Not sure. Do you see Petros as the tragic hero? Or the brothers? Or Elias?"

"I do feel Petros is, in a way, a flawed hero. Perhaps Michael too. Two months ago Michael had a wife and a scholarly reputation in New York. In the space of so little time, everything changed so much, everything was lost …"

At this point the chickpea fritters and delicious caper and garlic dip arrived to interrupt them. Day lost all interest in Greek tragic heroes.

"My God, this is eye-wateringly good. The woman's a magician."

"You've invented a new adjective, Martin. You're right, though, the flavours are amazing."

"Why does anyone eat at home, when you can't make anything as good as this?"

"Martin, have you noticed us eating at home much?"

"Mmm. Which reminds me, we owe Aristos and Rania."

"Yes. We'll get them over next week," she agreed, taking a second spoonful of the dip. "You can cook."

Vangelis brought the plate of pastitsio and raised an eyebrow as he lifted the empty wine jug with a sorrowful face. Day nodded.

Helen still had some questions that required answers. "Did you never feel Petros might be violent or make a run for it? Especially when he knew that you'd realised what he'd done?"

"There were a couple of times when he made a sudden movement or got up from the table quickly, I did get a lurch in my stomach. I think Giannis felt it too, but nothing happened. Later, when the room became almost too dark to see him, the whole thing did start to feel surreal, and it was stiflingly hot in there. Petros was dealing with big emotions, but I don't think he ever considered lashing out or running."

"How did you find the artefacts?"

"Petros showed us where he'd put them. The objects were in a hiding place in the rocks which used to be a place for contraband in days gone by." Day turned his attention back to the food. "Wow, this smells good. Can I serve you with some pastitsio, Madame?"

"By all means."

They focused on their dinner. Koula's Pastitsio, a twist on the traditional dish of minced meat, onions and tomatoes with pasta, cheese and cream, topped with a thick layer of béchamel sauce, was a luxury version. Day pronounced it the best he'd tasted.

They sat back in their chairs to savour the wine and finally relax. Day completed his account of the night before, and summed up his meeting with Cristopoulos.

"I'm sorry to hear Petros may have had a heart attack. The rest of his life is going to be very difficult. Maybe he'll be sent to a secure hospital rather than to prison."

"I don't know about that, Helen. I don't know what happens in Greece. But it's good that Cristopoulos was willing to have him medically examined."

"How old do you think Petros is?"

"About 60, I'd guess."

"Poor guy. Perhaps I shouldn't say that after what he did."

"He'd be the first to blame himself. There lies the difference between him and Gautier. One of the differences…"

Just as Day was considering telling Helen how he had contemplated helping Petros to escape arrest, he felt his mobile vibrate in his pocket. A text.

"It's a message from Alex. Did I tell you that he and Kate have been completely cleared by the police? Alex is inviting us to dinner at Agia Anna on Friday night. At a taverna on the beach."

"Wonderful! One of my favourite places!"

"That's a yes, then, is it?"

***

They chatted for a long time, under no pressure from the taverna, enjoying the sense of closure which filled the evening unobtrusively, like the distant humming of bees in summer. It was like when the 50mph winds that can ravage the Cyclades for days on end suddenly die down, and the innocent blue skies return, bringing with them a blessed quiet. Thanasis brought them a plate of fresh oranges, peeled and cut and easy to eat with a fork, and a glass each of tsipouro, the local distilled spirit, not particularly cold so the delicate flavour could still be tasted.

"Do you remember I mentioned a strange poem by Elias called 'The Catastrophe', Martin?" said Helen, having sipped her tsipouro.

"Dimly," he said, taking a second sip of his.

"It's about the genocide in 1922 in Smyrna, but there's a kind of subtext which I couldn't understand, something personal. He writes of the historical events in a way which isn't completely straightforward. I think I know why."

Day tried to look encouraging.

"It may be a bit of a leap, but I think Elias was actually writing about the catastrophe of Maria Eleni's death and the emigration of the Makris family. The Greeks of Smyrna were forced to leave their homes in Asia Minor and resettle on the Greek mainland. The Makris family found themselves in the USA. Do you see where I'm going with this?"

Poetry was not Day's strongest point, and he could only repeat himself.

"Dimly."

"It doesn't matter that the poem doesn't set you on fire, Martin. This is just another example of our secretive friend Elias using poetry to express his emotions. He must have seen Maria Eleni's death as his fault, I think."

"Have you considered that Petros might not have been telling us the truth when he said her death was an accident?" said Day, giving voice to something he had been pondering for some time.

"You don't think she was murdered too? Do you think Petros is covering for Elias?"

"That would be in character, wouldn't it? I don't think we'll ever know. If Elias had something to do with Maria Eleni's fatal blow to the head, Petros would probably take the blame himself or make up an excuse to preserve Elias's reputation. But it could have happened accidentally, just as Petros described."

"We must leave it, then. Either way, Elias was right – it was a catastrophe."

52

Katerina's taverna was busy; it appeared it was a popular venue for locals and tourists alike. Katerina's husband, Cristos, was in charge that morning, while Katerina herself could be heard in the kitchen supervising lunch. Cristos was a big man in his forties with an extensive belly and a wide smile to match. He waved Day to a table as if they were old friends. Realising he had arrived before the others, Day explained he was expecting the Curator and another friend any minute. Cristos's smile widened still further.

"Ah, the Curator," he grinned. "We are honoured to have you with us, Kyrie. Shall I bring you a menu?"

"Just a frappé for me, thank you."

"With pleasure."

Cristos left Day checking his mobile phone. It was nearly half past eleven, and still no sign of Aristos and his friend from the Archaeological Service. Perhaps the ferry had been late. Just as Day reached the end of his messages and placed the phone on the table, his coffee arrived. Day suspected Cristos's particular attentiveness was only due to the mention of the Curator, who seemed to be universally revered in Chora.

Before Day could raise the coffee to his lips he saw Aristos arriving, gesturing to the woman with him to enter first. They were smiling like people who loved each other's company. Day stood up to greet them. Cristos came over to fuss and offer menus, and for a few moments there was convivial chaos round the table. Aristos and Cristos collided in their attempt to pull out a chair for the woman, who laughed. It was an attractive, no-nonsense sort of laugh, Day thought.

"Aliki Xylouri," she said, holding out her hand. "You must be Martin."

"Martin Day. Lovely to meet you, Dr Xylouri."

"Aliki, please. Aristos has told me all about you."

"Ah. It's always interesting to hear that, it covers so many possibilities!"

"You don't need to worry at all, Martin. So, I understand you've been having some adventures together?"

"Yes, we have indeed."

Aristos ordered coffee for himself and Aliki from the attentive Cristos, which diverted the woman's attention from Day and gave him a moment to look at her. In one sense she was a typical Greek woman of her generation and education – confident, well-dressed, well-groomed. In another way, hard to put your finger on, she was far from typical. Her face and her hands vied for your attention. She had a mass of shoulder-length, grey hair partially restrained by the sunglasses that perched like a black hairband on her head. Wisps of heavy fringe escaped this control, giving her a slightly wild look. Her nose was long and straight in a beautiful oval face with high cheekbones. She had the air of someone who for many years had been presenting herself tastefully and attractively, no expense spared. Her large gold earrings were probably 24 carat, as were the heavy rings on her manicured fingers. She looked in her early sixties and as powerful a personality now as she had ever been throughout a long and interesting career. Day had looked up Dr Aliki Xylouri on the web, and knew she was one of Greece's foremost living Mycenaean experts.

It was sadly obvious, Day reflected, that both Aristos and himself were eating out of her hand.

As they waited for the remaining coffees to arrive, Aristos turned back to Martin.

"Sorry we were a little late, Martin, but you know what it's like when you try to walk and talk at the same time. Aliki and I haven't seen each other for about four years. My fault, I should go to Athens more often, there are lectures I should attend and friends I've neglected. None more important than Aliki."

Aristos gave a small bow of the head to his companion. She smiled and waved a well-manicured hand. Day noticed the gold bracelet on the wrist that she raised. It was not Mycenaean, but it was a bit of class.

"We're old friends, Aristo mou, we just pick up where we last left off."

"That's true. Now, Martin, I think you should pretend that I haven't told Aliki anything at all about our discovery, and tell her the whole story."

"The whole story?" said Day. It seemed he was always being asked to start at the beginning.

"Yes, well most of it. It's important she knows about the connection with Nikos Elias and Michael Moralis especially."

"OK. Ah, here's your coffee."

Once the coffee was in front of Aristos and Aliki, Day began his narrative.

"This story – the story of the tomb which you'll see later – starts more than twenty years ago. A local historian and archaeologist called Nikos Elias suspected the existence of a major Mycenaean site in the central hills of Naxos as long ago as the 1980s, but he was a secretive man, which means that nobody else in the field was aware of his work. He progressed slowly because he was working alone. I can't stress too much how introverted and possessive Elias was about this research of his. Despite an enormous amount of good, well-documented work on other matters, Elias made only the most encoded notes on the subject of this site. Therefore, when he was contacted in the 1990s by an American scholar asking about a Bronze Age site on Naxos, he certainly didn't want to share any good clues.

"The scholar who contacted him from New York was Dr Michael Moralis. You've probably heard of him, Aliki? Michael was an acquaintance of mine. Michael probably said that he'd discovered the existence of a site while carrying out some academic research. Elias must have been filled with horror – someone else was on the trail of his secret site, his life's work. I believe that Elias gave Michael a couple of false clues to deliberately mislead him, to prevent him from finding the place before Elias himself. Michael, however, was on the right trail already. He thought the site was somewhere near a main country road called the Naxos-Halki road, and he was right. Elias seems to have confirmed this to Michael, but threw in a false clue about some inscription on a church wall. There was an inscription, but it's not where Elias said it was.

"Elias kept searching and probably forgot all about Michael. He discovered that a local family had found the site and had removed three ancient objects from inside it. The objects were Mycenaean.

The next thing he did seems incredible. He actually put the artefacts *back* inside the opening, intending to unearth them himself when the site was excavated.

"Meanwhile, Michael Moralis continued his research, and as you probably know he wrote an important book on the Mycenaeans in the Cyclades. He recently wrote an article for a British edition of essays on the Mycenaeans in the Aegean, which my friend Alexander Harding-Jones from the British Museum and his former student Katherine Russell of the University of Warwick are currently compiling. About a month ago Michael retracted his article, refusing to allow it to be published. Alex and Kate spoke to him, and the outcome was that the three of them decided to visit Naxos this month to look for the site together. That was Michael's idea.

Aliki interrupted Day with a graceful extension of her fingers.

"Sorry to interrupt, Martin. Am I right in thinking that up to this point there's been no involvement with any official archaeological association?"

"That's correct. In fairness, nobody but Elias knew the location or nature of the site."

"Please, go on."

"Once on Naxos, Michael started to spend a lot of time driving round the island by himself, leaving Alex and Kate unsure what he was up to; the plan to look for the site together seemed to have been discarded. I should say that Nikos Elias is no longer with us. He died in November 2000, never having shared his ideas.

"Michael didn't find the tomb, I'm sure of that. As Aristos might have told you already, Michael was murdered in his hotel room last month. I'm happy to tell you about it, but shall we keep to the story of the tomb for now?"

"As you prefer."

"I began to work on Nikos Elias for a possible biography. I'd already set this up with the custodian of the Elias museum before arriving on Naxos in April. Although Elias didn't discuss the site in his notes, he did leave some clues. These clues pointed to a certain small church and the landscape near it, such that Aristos and I, with the help of two friends, managed to locate the probable entrance to the tomb."

"Good work, Martin. Now if I may I'd like to hear about the three artefacts you found."

"Aristos has them at the Museum, you can see them later yourself. There's a gold armband, a stirrup jar (it's broken, but the sherds are in good condition), and a female figurine in Taf form."

"Mmm. Aristos told me you've found no evidence of wholesale looting, at least as far as could be seen. These objects, how do you think they came to be so close to the opening to the tomb when they were found by the local family?"

"That remains a mystery, Aliki."

Aliki replaced her coffee cup on the table and sat back.

"We may never know, of course. Thank you, Martin. I can tell there's much more to this story but that's a helpful start. You might be interested in something that I found by chance while I was researching a different Aegean site altogether. It's a reference to a settlement in central Naxos; historians have always assumed it describes Komiaki. I suspect it may refer to your site instead. It means that while Komiaki was, as some scholars think, ruled by an early king of Naxos, the tomb that you've discovered could be that of a rival ruler. I think we're talking about two different settlements, two different tombs. There are indications that this third settlement was built far from *both* the coastal settlement at Grotta *and* the inland one at Komiaki, because people wanted to be safe not only from the usual pirate threat but also from hostile groups of their own people."

"Three rival factions, on such a small island? That would be extraordinary, wouldn't it?"

"It's certainly intriguing. Of course, it's only a theory. It does suggest there might be a chance of finding a settlement near your tomb. Have you finished your coffees? Shall we go and see the place now?"

She was clearly excited. Her eyes flashed and she gesticulated lavishly as she talked. Aristos paid for the coffees and they walked to the square. A strong breeze had got up in true Cycladic style, blowing Aliki's hair about her face as they walked. They left Chora in two cars and followed the road to Melanes in convoy, losing the coastal wind as they wound their way up into the central hills. At the car park for the Church of Agia Paraskevi they parked next to two police vehicles, both matted with dust. An officer approached them, shook hands, and pointed to where his colleagues were sitting in the shade of a bent tree next to an area cordoned off with red and white tape. Far away across the expanse of scrubland between the church and the peaks, the local police had so far not attracted too much attention.

Day noticed for the first time that Aliki Xylouri was now wearing sensible shoes and thick trousers, well-worn and practical. She placed a rugged cotton hat on her head, and extracted a top-of-the-range iPhone from her bag. It was a toy of the kind Day could only dream of, incorporating several cameras, enabling the owner to take 3D images. She smiled at them, turned, and bent into the trail, setting a brisk pace for them to follow.

53

"You look awful!" said Helen when Day emerged from his room the next morning. He had slept heavily after the expedition with Aliki Xylouri the day before, and was flushed and groggy.

"One of Zeus's thunderbolts must have struck me in the night," he groaned and threw himself in an armchair. "Before I forget, Aristos just sent a message. We're all invited to Deppi and Nick's boat tomorrow. We should get there for lunch, about twelve. And we're to take swimming gear and towels. Hats, sun screen for you, that kind of thing. Absolutely no gifts, he says."

"Why is the sunscreen just for me, Martin Day?"

"You know I don't bother with it."

"Well, you should. I think you've got a bit of sunstroke."

"I'm just getting old. And I need a frappé."

They took the Fiat, as Day felt too delicate to walk, and headed into the village, which was full of visitors because the bus had just arrived from Chora. At Café Ta Xromata, which was at one end of the long village street, Day and Helen were relieved to find their favourite table still available. They sat there in the morning sun, Helen on a yellow sofa and Day on a lime green one, and in the fullness of time somebody came for their order. Helen asked for a slice of bougatsa, an amazing custard-filled filo pastry specialty, sprinkled with cinnamon.

"How are you getting on with the novel?" Day remembered to ask, watching her enjoy the pastry.

"I haven't thought about it for a while. I'm more interested in Elias's poetry."

"So, your Greek's coming back to you, is it?"

"It seems to be all in there somewhere. I just needed a reason to bring it out again. When are you going to get back to your research into Elias?"

"Soon, next week probably. The first thing will be to speak to the Tourist Board people and close the house to visitors. And somehow I have to get the key to the place. Probably see a lawyer about my rights to the material. It can all wait till next week."

"The legal part will be complicated, I expect. Right, I have a suggestion. Let's go back to Melanes and get all this out of our system for good. Let's go and see the kouros that we never reached that day we found Dimitris's body. Maybe it will lay some ghosts for us. OK? I'll leave some money for coffee."

***

They parked in the same spot as they had on that memorable day when Helen had been drawn to the stone hut. It was all rather too fresh in their minds, but that was, in a way, the whole point. Helen led the way up the path that led to the kouros, seeing in her mind's eye the Austrian tourist walking down towards them. Inevitably they stopped when they reached the little trail to the stone hut and stood to gaze at it. Red and white tape had been wrapped round it like a box of chocolates. Apart from that, it looked as abandoned as it had before. Day touched Helen's arm lightly, and they turned away and headed uphill.

It was too early for other visitors and they saw no one. Day was surprised to feel excitement, experiencing his usual enthusiasm for antiquity. This kouros had been carved to a greater extent than the two others, the ones at Flerio and Apollonas. Then, like them, it had been abandoned for ever in the quarry. Day remembered seeing it some years before and was pleased to be visiting it again.

There was no ceremony, no corner to turn. They reached the top of the steps and the kouros lay in front of them on the rock-strewn hillside, all but unprotected in the long yellow grass. The markings of a stonemason's tools were visible on the head, where you could make out braided hair. The feet were broken from the legs, which may have been why the statue had been left unfinished, never to stand proudly in a temple on the mainland.

Helen leaned against a convenient rock and opened her camera. She wondered why she felt nothing. Day was clearly quite emotional as he stared at this gigantic piece of antiquity. For her, the kouros was not particularly exciting. This enormous piece of marble, dark with age, seemed barely more meaningful than the ground from which it came. It lay, alone and unwanted, staring upwards.

Then she understood. She had not succeeded after all in dealing with Dimitris Makris, and this attempt to put it behind her had been too optimistic. Both man and statue lay on their backs, staring emptily upwards, no future ahead of them. Coming here had been a mistake after all.

"I'm heading back down, Martin. I'll wait at the car if you're not done."

Day nodded and followed her. They returned to the car, walking separately, wrapped in their own thoughts.

***

She felt better when they had left Melanes behind and reached home. The view of the valley and the gently rolling hills opposite were comforting to Helen, sitting with Day on the balcony with lunch and cups of tea. She picked at a plate of grilled pitta drizzled with oil, and little chunks of crumbled mizithra cheese. She had no real appetite but hoped that eating would improve her mood. Day seemed to be in fine spirits. Clearly the visit to the kouros had helped him considerably. He declared he would pass up a siesta that afternoon and read his book, an account of travelling in the Middle East by an intrepid and liberated English lady adventurer.

"You seem to have recovered remarkably from your exhaustion, Martin."

"Yes, I'm feeling much better," he said, feeling rather guilty. "The trip this morning did me good. Like a turning point. When we were walking up those steps to it, we were still in the awful last few weeks where everything and everybody was looking backwards - Elias, Petros, the Makris clan, and we too. Standing by the old kouros, the last of the trio, was like putting a full stop to it all. I'm sorry, I know it wasn't so good for you. We must just get on, get busy. I'm full of plans for the future now, I'm looking ahead. The work, the summer, normality again. We'll make some fun trips in the coming weeks, go to the lovely places around here like Sifnos and Syros. And see friends, like meeting Alex and Kate tonight. And then tomorrow we've got lunch with Deppi and Nick. Normality - and better than normality, real pleasure. I'm sure you'll feel better soon."

"You really like Nick and Deppi, don't you?"

"Yes. Don't you?"

"Of course. Do I need to keep an eye on you, Martin Day?"

Day was startled but then gave a wry smile. "You know me too well. But no, you don't need to stand guard, I'm not that kind of guy."

"Good. I'm going to have a rest. See you later for our trip to Agia Anna."

She took her plate and cup to the kitchen and he heard the door of her room close. Day didn't immediately pick up his book. Helen had known him a long time. He ought to listen to her, both to what she said and what she didn't need to say.

***

The Taverna Xenia at Agia Anna could be called a touristy restaurant, but in Helen's opinion it had the best sunset view on Naxos. Tables were laid on the terrace in front of the taverna and also on the strip of beach between the restaurant and the sea. Now that it was dusk, the staff were taking away the beach parasols, which they rented out during the day, and replacing them with more restaurant tables. Many were tables for two, for the ultimate romantic sunset dinner.

Alex and Kate were already at the taverna, sitting at a table for four at the edge of the terrace with an uninterrupted view of the beach and the sea. The sun was already low and powerfully orange. Just as the waiter arrived with their drinks, the sun began to lose its perfect rotundity, to become flat-bottomed, to slide below the horizon. People were gathering at the edge of the sea, some with cameras, others simply gazing out. Very soon they would be only dark silhouettes, black figures against the golden sky. As the last of the sun slipped into the water and darkness covered the sea, the people on the beach would applaud. This happened every night. It never failed to seem magical to Helen.

Alex persuaded Day to join him in a Mythos beer to quench their thirst, while the women made a start on the wine. The waiter had been a little peremptory, but he was a busy man and all diners were the same to the busy restaurant staff in Agia Anna. The personal treatment was not what people came here for. They came for the view, the sunset, the atmosphere and the fish. It was more than good enough.

At Alex's suggestion they decided to order the food to share, and Day was volunteered to choose it. He ordered a whole grilled fish, small plates of shrimps and fried squid, and some mussels. Chips were naturally part of the order. Day was so happy that he announced that dinner would be his treat.

While Day was still studying the menu and the other pair were admiring the colours of the sunset that were now infusing the sky above the vanishing sun, Helen took a moment to look discreetly at Kate and Alex. Understandably they appeared a great deal more relaxed than she had seen them before. This was how they normally looked, before coming to Naxos with Michael Moralis. Alex occasionally covered Kate's hand with his on the table. She wore a lightweight summer dress in a delicate material and her natural glow replaced makeup or jewellery. She looked younger this evening. Alex, on the other hand, was at the age when men fill out and begin to look more serious. He, at least, was looking his age, probably about 45, Helen thought. Only five or six years older than Martin, Alex was built like a businessman while Day still had something of the student, or dilettante, about him. It was clear that the two men had a reliable friendship, one which had been strengthened by recent events rather than damaged by them.

The last of the sun vanished beneath the horizon, the people at the shoreline clapped, and Alex raised his beer in a little toast.

"I'm very glad you could meet us tonight, both of you. We owe you a great deal. I'm certainly not letting you pay for this meal, Martin. This is absolutely on me, and the least I can do."

"That's very kind," Day conceded graciously. "I hope you're staying around so we can repay the favour one evening?"

Kate shook her head sadly, looking into Alex's face. "Unfortunately we're leaving on Monday. Term starts soon for me, the examination term. Joy of joys. Alex can be a bit flexible at the British Museum, but it's not so easy for me at the university. So we want you to come and see us when you're in London, as soon as possible."

"Delighted," grinned Day. "We can go back to that little place in King's Cross, Alex …"

"Why not? I guess you'll be in Greece most of the year, though, Martin?"

"I don't have any plans yet. I'll probably need to spend some time in London during the winter. I'll try to twist the arm of a good friend of mine who lives in Hampstead to put me up …"

Helen grinned. "You don't usually have to apply much pressure, I seem to recall. And if we're going to a little place in King's Cross, I certainly can't refuse, can I?"

"Brilliant. So, what will happen about the edition of articles on the Mycenaeans in the Cyclades?" asked Day. "I hope it will go ahead?"

"For sure it will. We won't have Michael's article, of course, but it will be a good volume. As for the site that Michael was describing in his article, I think it's for you, Martin, to tell that story in your work on Nikos Elias."

"Don't worry, I intend to. Elias will be given credit for his part in finding the tomb, though I'll have to tread carefully, given all that's happened."

Kate put down her glass as the waiter arrived with their first dishes. "Martin, can you explain to us what really happened to poor Michael?"

"I think so. It has to stay between the four of us, the trial … anyway, it's confidential. Shall we save it for after we've eaten? This fish looks amazing!"

***

They finished their meal and sat with the last of the wine. Day began to tell the story of Michalis Makris, from the moment his sister wore a Mycenaean bracelet and was spotted by an archaeologist who knew exactly what it was. He told them about a poor man called Dimitris whose mind had been affected by the violent death of his sister and her unexplained secret burial, and finally he told them how Michalis, no longer the scholar Michael Moralis but a driven and damaged former islander, and met his death as a result of having become a threat to Petros Tsifas.

Kate pulled a scarf round her shoulders as if she felt cold. "So Michael was looking for his brother when he went off alone," she said. "It's always astonishing to be made to realise how little you know anyone, and how ignorant you are of other people's lives."

Nodding, Day continued. He told them about Emil Gautier's role in Michael's death, and the truth behind what had Kate overheard in the lobby of the Philippos Hotel.

"I'm afraid I don't believe Michael managed to find the burial site after all," he said. "I'm sorry, he got quite close, working it all out from the States. I wish there was some way we could leave some tribute to him, some recognition of how close he came. He was a very good scholar. His past was so difficult. His life was quite tragic in many ways."

"I'll contact his colleagues at CUNY when I'm back in London," said Alex, "and tell them about Michael's final piece of research. Perhaps his last paper could actually be published. They'll be doing a retrospective, and they should be aware of his achievements. And I'll write to his wife."

There was little more to be said about Michael Moralis, and nothing needed to be said about Kate and Alex, as their every gesture confirmed their attachment to each other. Their obvious happiness was infectious, the last touch to what Day felt to be the healing warmth of that night. Only one small cloud remained for him. He knew he could never share with any of his friends that he had briefly wanted very much that Petros should escape arrest, and some fragment of Day's own regret and guilt would always linger inexplicably somewhere in his memory.

They finished the wine and talked until long after it was growing quiet among the tavernas. Only a delicate reflection of the lights from the houses along the beach silvered the gently tumbling waves.

Suddenly Day realised they had reached the end. He was sorry to see Kate and Alex prepare to leave, and realised that the evening had been a great solace to him. Now, both for himself and Helen, what lay ahead was a period of reflection, readjustment and recalibration. Lawyers and agents would have to be contacted, an aspect of his work he disliked. Then he remembered Deppi and the invitation to lunch the following day. Smiling, he stood to say goodbye, gave Kate a hug and shook hands with Alex, having considered hugging him too.

"See you in a few months," he promised them. Alex laughed and embraced him unselfconsciously. 'Thanks, Martin," he murmured.

Day watched them begin the short walk to their hotel through the still buzzing lanes of Agia Anna. They held hands as soon as they left the taverna. Kate turned and gave a last wave before they rounded a corner and were gone.

"We'd better go home too, Martin," said Helen. "Come on. I'll drive."

Day left some extra change on the table for the waiter, and they walked slowly to the car park and climbed into the Fiat. Leaving the coast behind them, Helen drove Day very carefully back to Filoti. As they left Chora, she saw his head gently tilt to rest on the door. He was fast asleep.

Made in the USA
Middletown, DE
19 September 2022